W9-BZC-441

VOLTRON FORCE
TWIN TROUBLE

STORY BY
BRIAN SMITH

COVER AND INTERIOR ART BY
HORACIO DOMINGUES

ADDITIONAL PENCILS BY
PEDRO PABLO PEREZ VALIENTE

ADDITIONAL INKS BY
GUILLERMO PEREZ

ADDITIONAL COLORS BY
ALEJANDRO SANCHEZ

Voltron Force vol. 3: Twin Trouble
Story by Brian Smith
Cover and interior art by Horacio Domingues
Additional pencils by Pedro Pablo Perez Valiente
Additional inks by Guillermo Perez
Additional colors by Alejandro Sanchez

Cover Art/Horacio Domingues
Graphics and Cover Design/Sam Elzway
Editor/Traci N. Todd

Special thanks to Scott Shillet for always being awesome.

Voltron Force ™ & © World Events Productions.
Under license to Classic Media.

The stories, characters and incidents mentioned in this publication are entirely fictional.

Printed in the U.S.A.

Published by VIZ Media, LLC
P.O. Box 77010
San Francisco, CA 94107

10 9 8 7 6 5 4 3 2 1
First printing, October 2012

PARENTAL ADVISORY
VOLTRON FORCE VOL. 3: TWIN
TROUBLE is rated A and is suitable
for readers of all ages.
ratings.viz.com

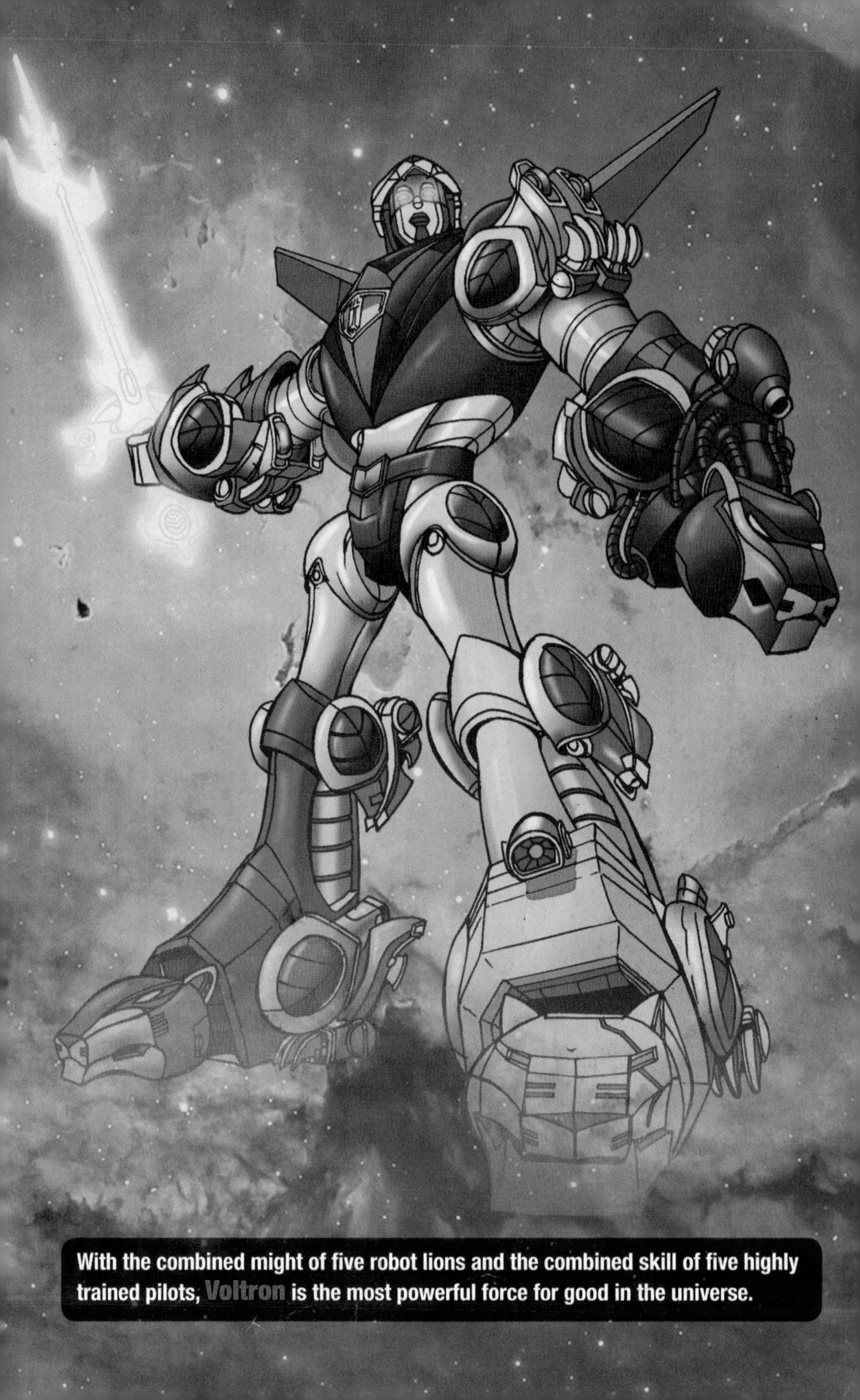

With the combined might of five robot lions and the combined skill of five highly trained pilots, Voltron is the most powerful force for good in the universe.

VOLTRON FORCE PILOTS AND CADETS

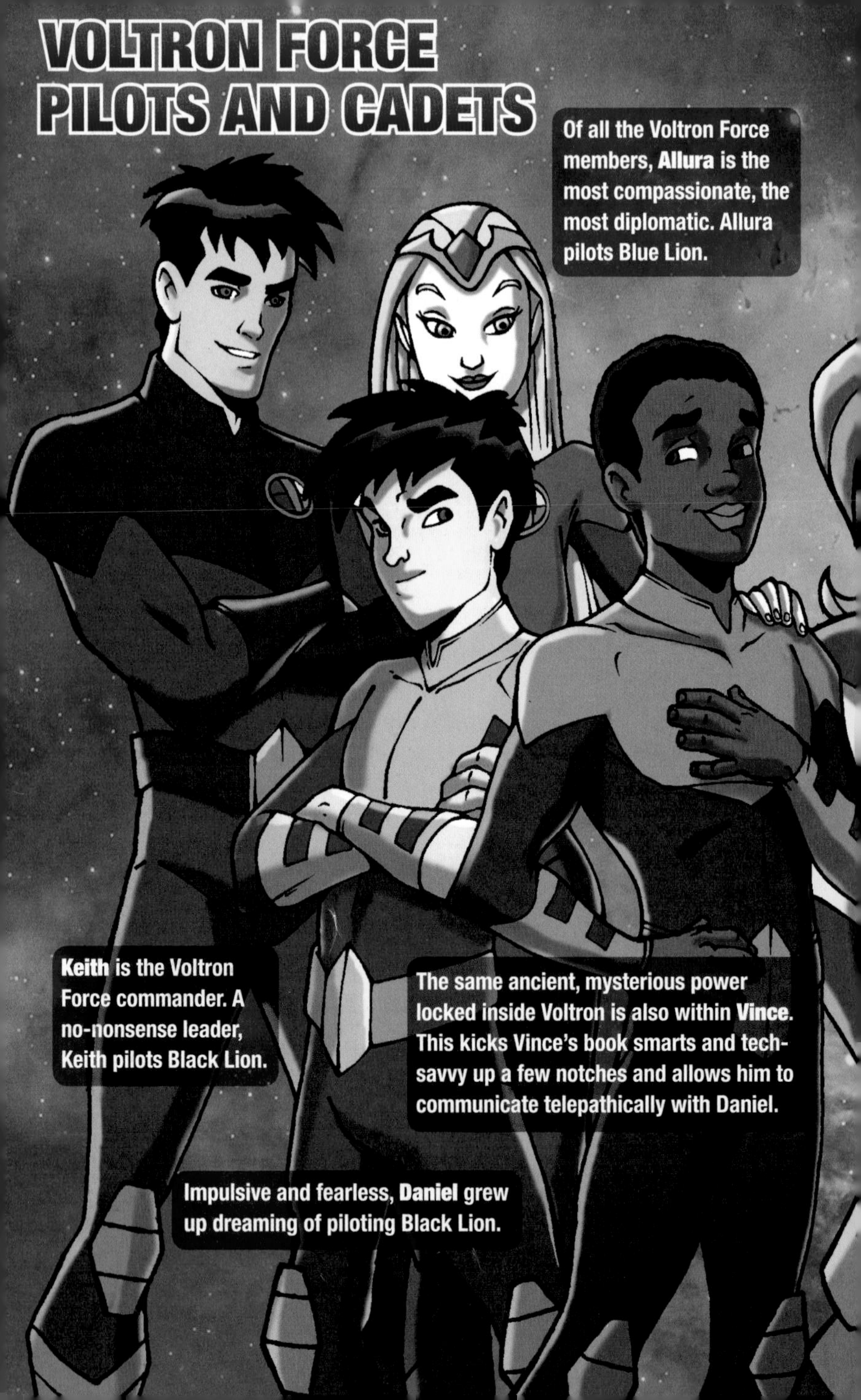

Of all the Voltron Force members, **Allura** is the most compassionate, the most diplomatic. Allura pilots Blue Lion.

Keith is the Voltron Force commander. A no-nonsense leader, Keith pilots Black Lion.

The same ancient, mysterious power locked inside Voltron is also within **Vince**. This kicks Vince's book smarts and tech-savvy up a few notches and allows him to communicate telepathically with Daniel.

Impulsive and fearless, **Daniel** grew up dreaming of piloting Black Lion.

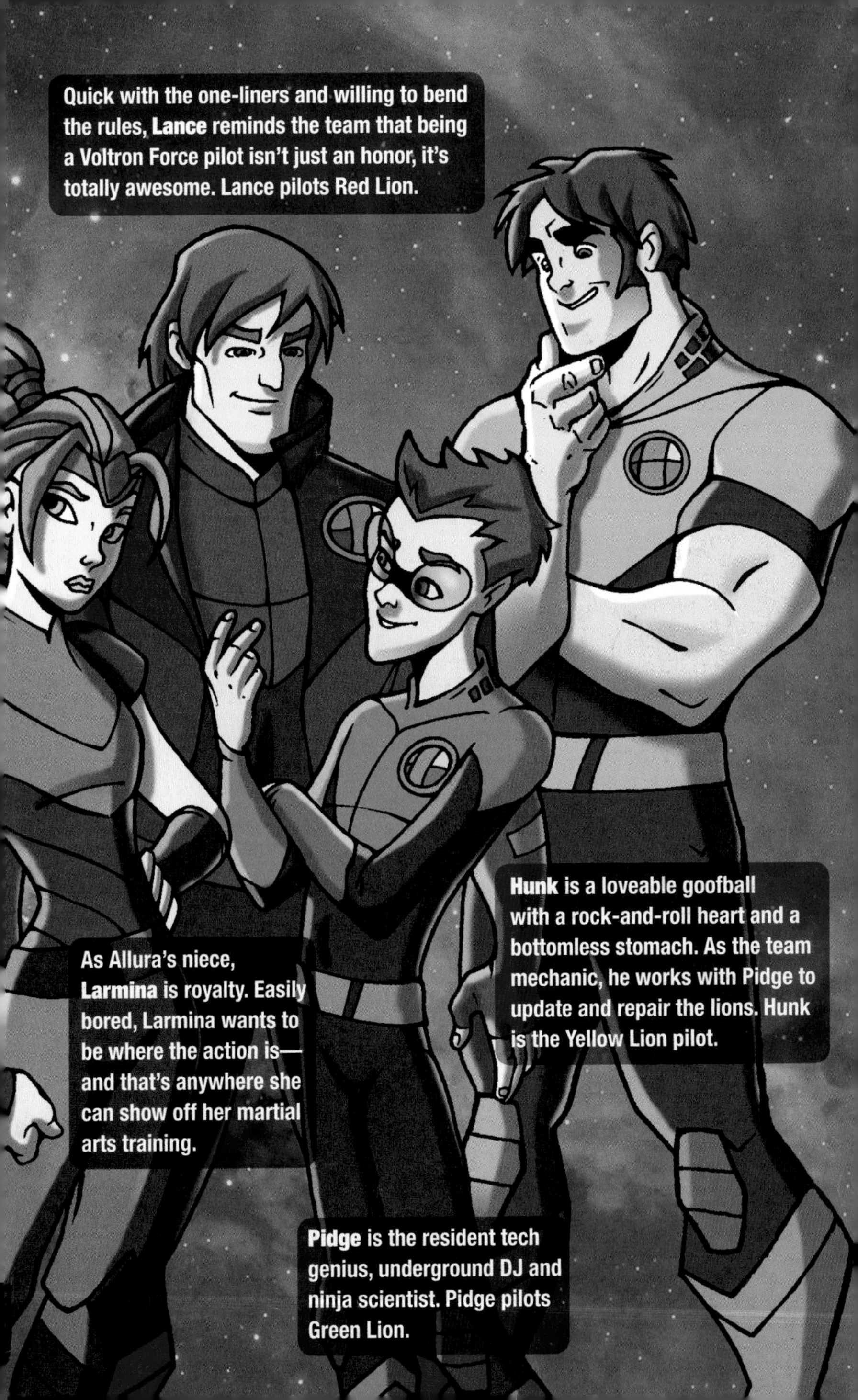
Quick with the one-liners and willing to bend the rules, **Lance** reminds the team that being a Voltron Force pilot isn't just an honor, it's totally awesome. Lance pilots Red Lion.
Hunk is a loveable goofball with a rock-and-roll heart and a bottomless stomach. As the team mechanic, he works with Pidge to update and repair the lions. Hunk is the Yellow Lion pilot.
As Allura's niece, **Larmina** is royalty. Easily bored, Larmina wants to be where the action is—and that's anywhere she can show off her martial arts training.
Pidge is the resident tech genius, underground DJ and ninja scientist. Pidge pilots Green Lion.

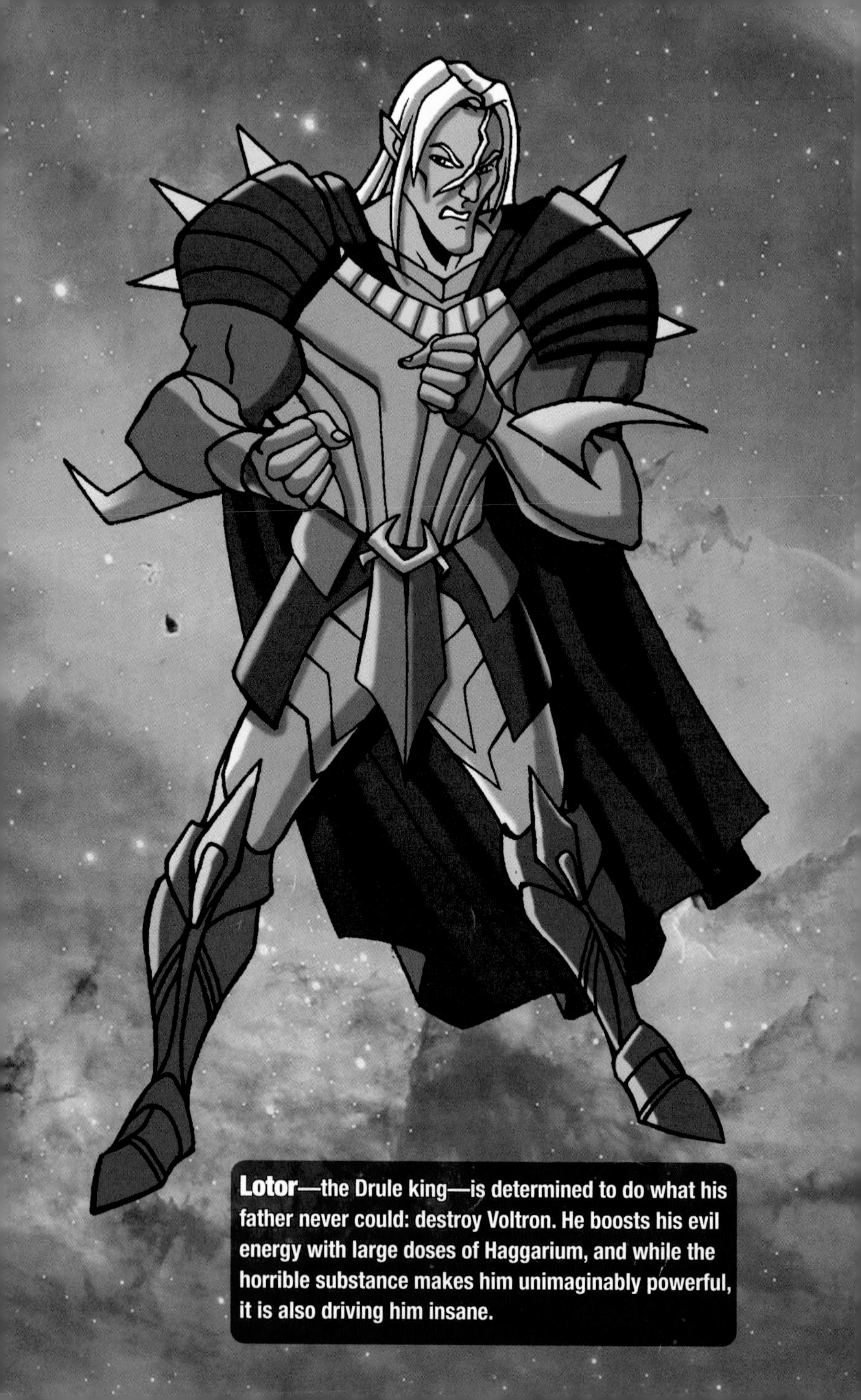

Lotor—the Drule king—is determined to do what his father never could: destroy Voltron. He boosts his evil energy with large doses of Haggarium, and while the horrible substance makes him unimaginably powerful, it is also driving him insane.

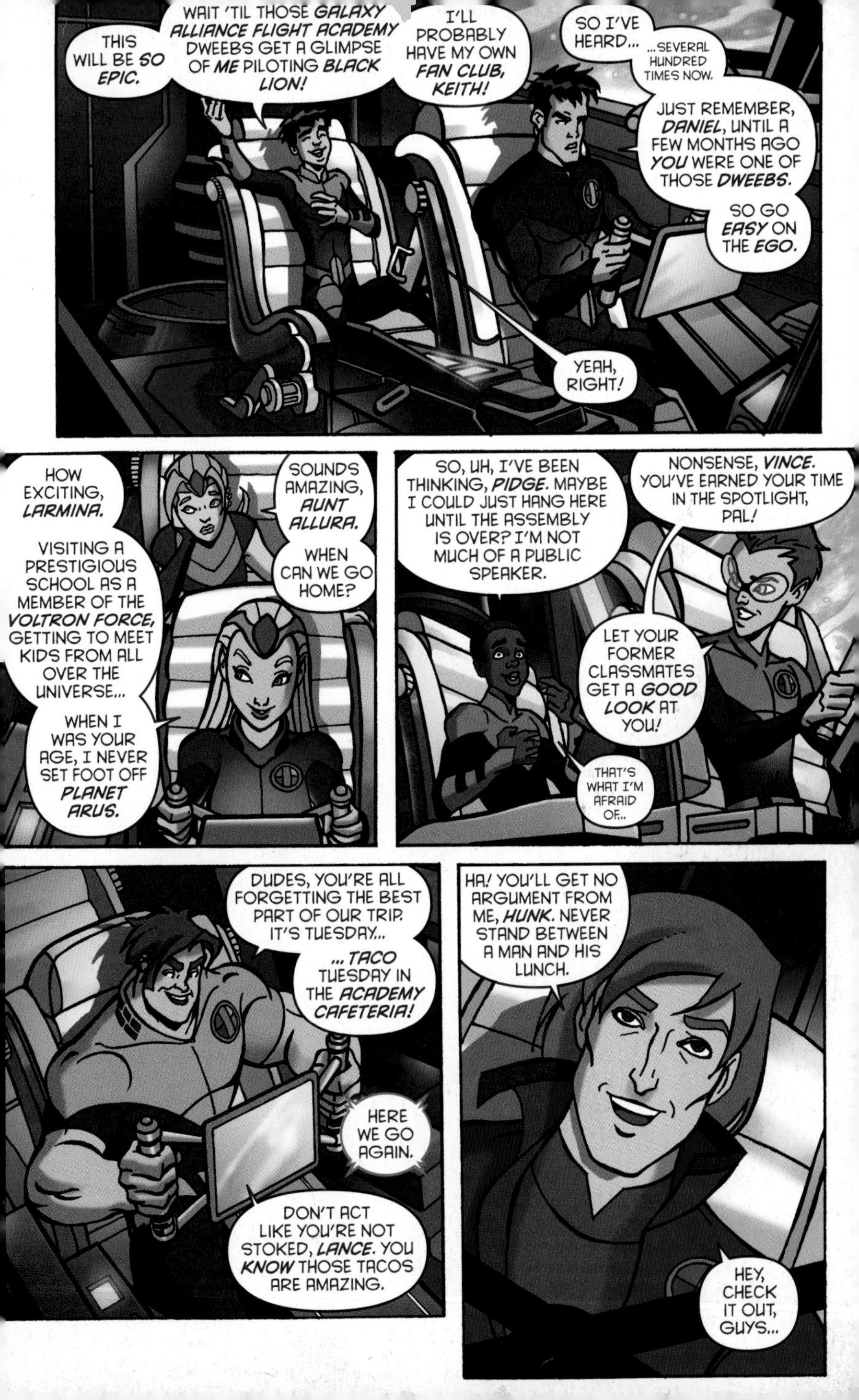
THIS WILL BE SO EPIC.
WAIT 'TIL THOSE GALAXY ALLIANCE FLIGHT ACADEMY DWEEBS GET A GLIMPSE OF ME PILOTING BLACK LION!
I'LL PROBABLY HAVE MY OWN FAN CLUB, KEITH!
SO I'VE HEARD...
...SEVERAL HUNDRED TIMES NOW.
JUST REMEMBER, DANIEL, UNTIL A FEW MONTHS AGO YOU WERE ONE OF THOSE DWEEBS.
SO GO EASY ON THE EGO.
YEAH, RIGHT!
HOW EXCITING, LARMINA.
VISITING A PRESTIGIOUS SCHOOL AS A MEMBER OF THE VOLTRON FORCE, GETTING TO MEET KIDS FROM ALL OVER THE UNIVERSE...
WHEN I WAS YOUR AGE, I NEVER SET FOOT OFF PLANET ARUS.
SOUNDS AMAZING, AUNT ALLURA.
WHEN CAN WE GO HOME?
SO, UH, I'VE BEEN THINKING, PIDGE. MAYBE I COULD JUST HANG HERE UNTIL THE ASSEMBLY IS OVER? I'M NOT MUCH OF A PUBLIC SPEAKER.
NONSENSE, VINCE. YOU'VE EARNED YOUR TIME IN THE SPOTLIGHT, PAL!
LET YOUR FORMER CLASSMATES GET A GOOD LOOK AT YOU!
THAT'S WHAT I'M AFRAID OF...
DUDES, YOU'RE ALL FORGETTING THE BEST PART OF OUR TRIP. IT'S TUESDAY...
...TACO TUESDAY IN THE ACADEMY CAFETERIA!
HERE WE GO AGAIN.
DON'T ACT LIKE YOU'RE NOT STOKED, LANCE. YOU KNOW THOSE TACOS ARE AMAZING.
HA! YOU'LL GET NO ARGUMENT FROM ME, HUNK. NEVER STAND BETWEEN A MAN AND HIS LUNCH.
HEY, CHECK IT OUT, GUYS...

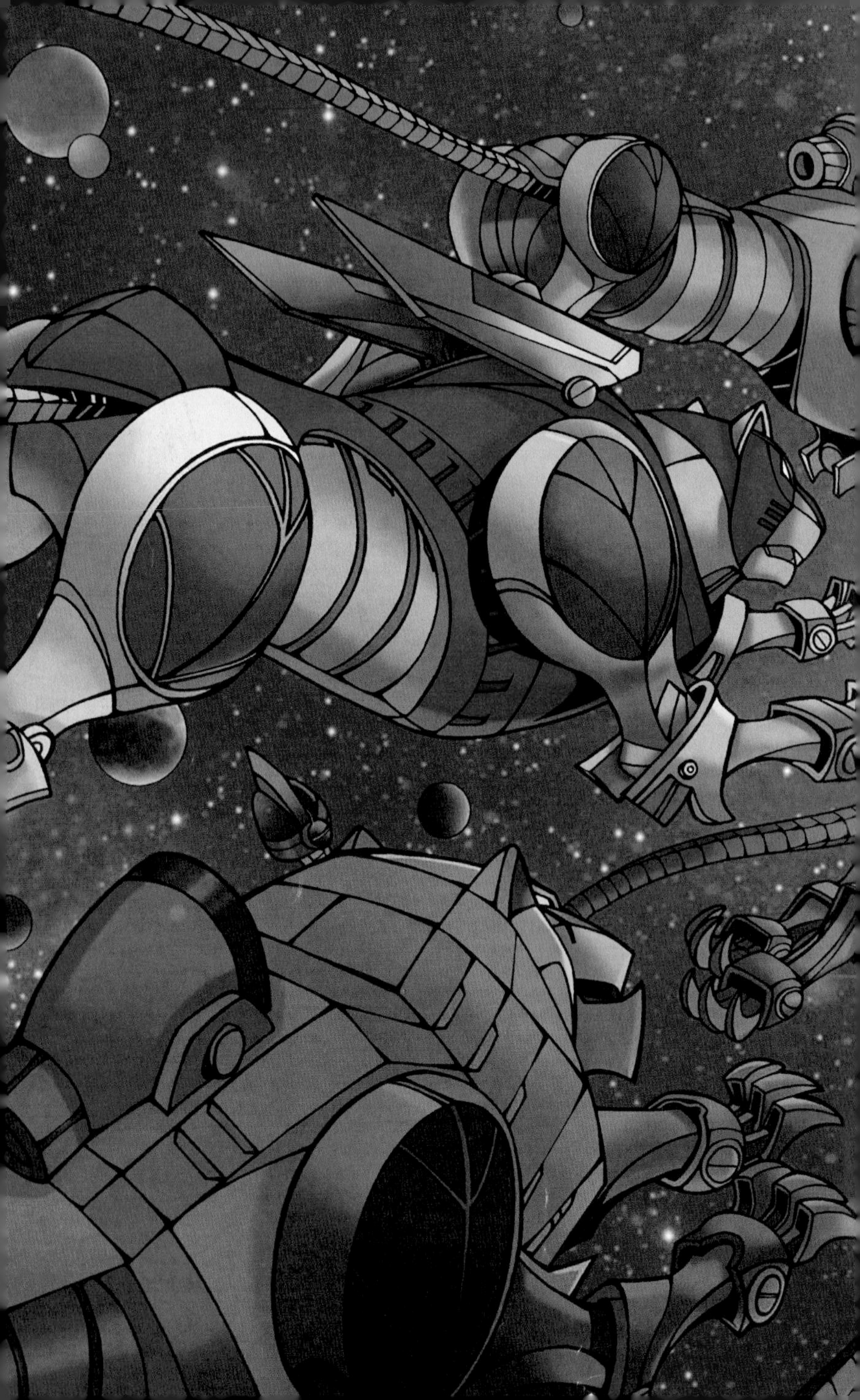

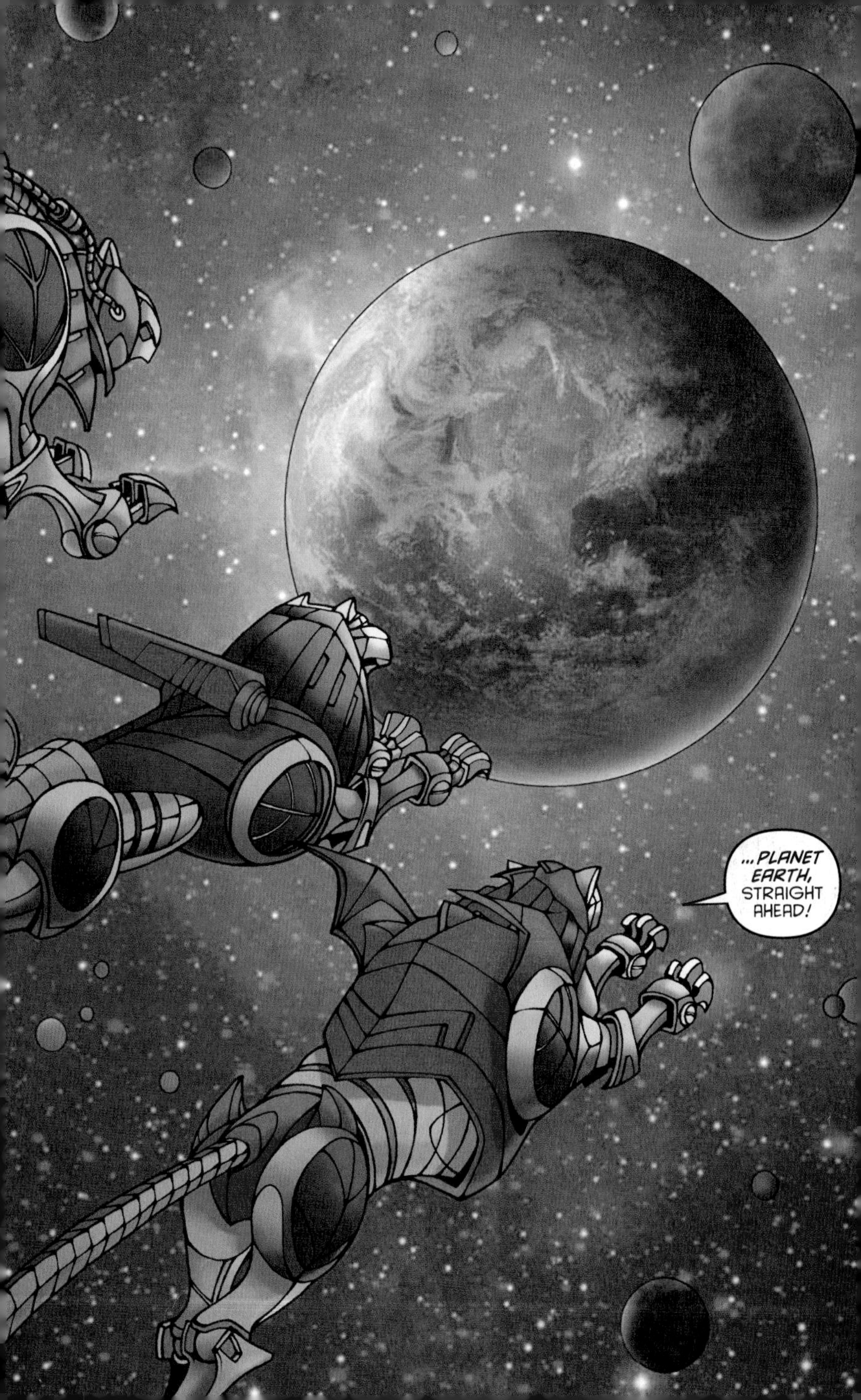
...PLANET EARTH, STRAIGHT AHEAD!

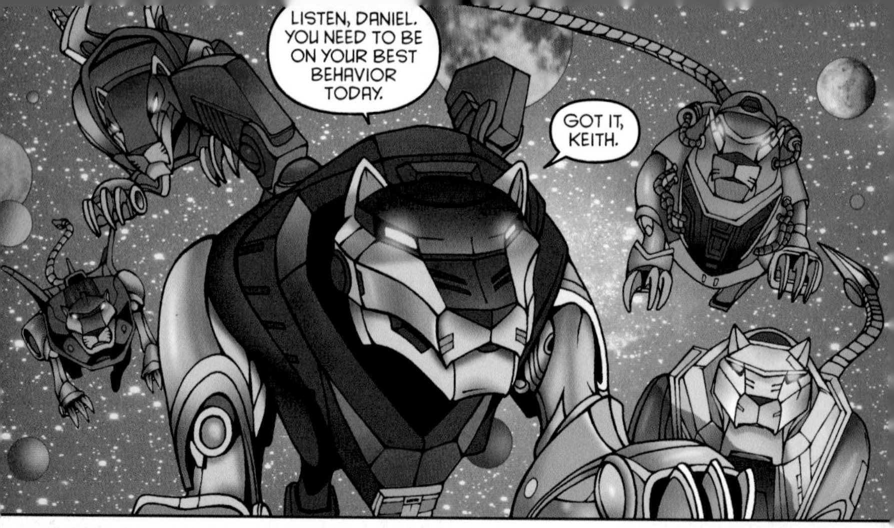
LISTEN, DANIEL. YOU NEED TO BE ON YOUR BEST BEHAVIOR TODAY.
GOT IT, KEITH.

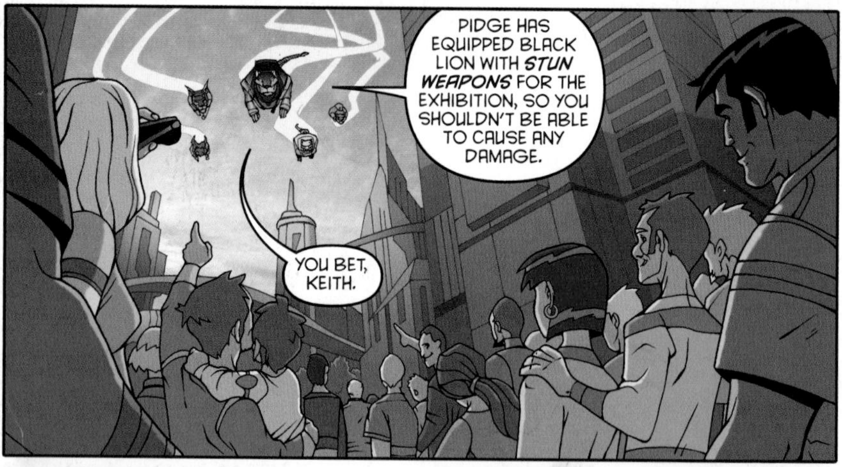
PIDGE HAS EQUIPPED BLACK LION WITH *STUN WEAPONS* FOR THE EXHIBITION, SO YOU SHOULDN'T BE ABLE TO CAUSE ANY DAMAGE.
YOU BET, KEITH.

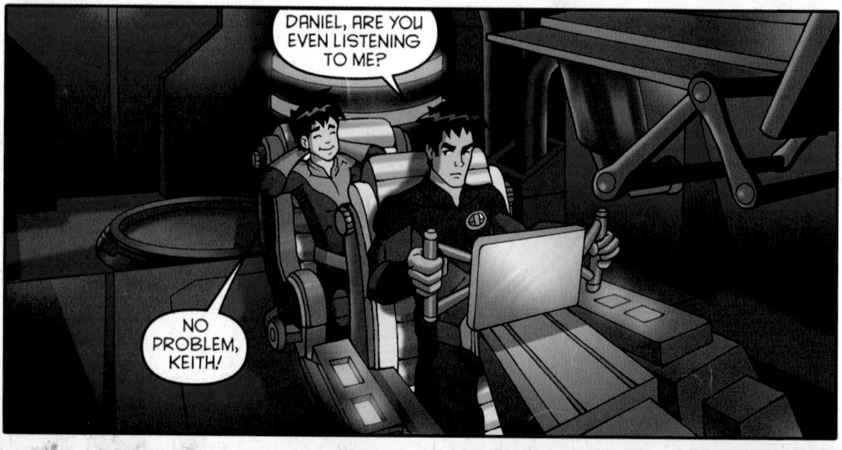
DANIEL, ARE YOU EVEN LISTENING TO ME?
NO PROBLEM, KEITH!

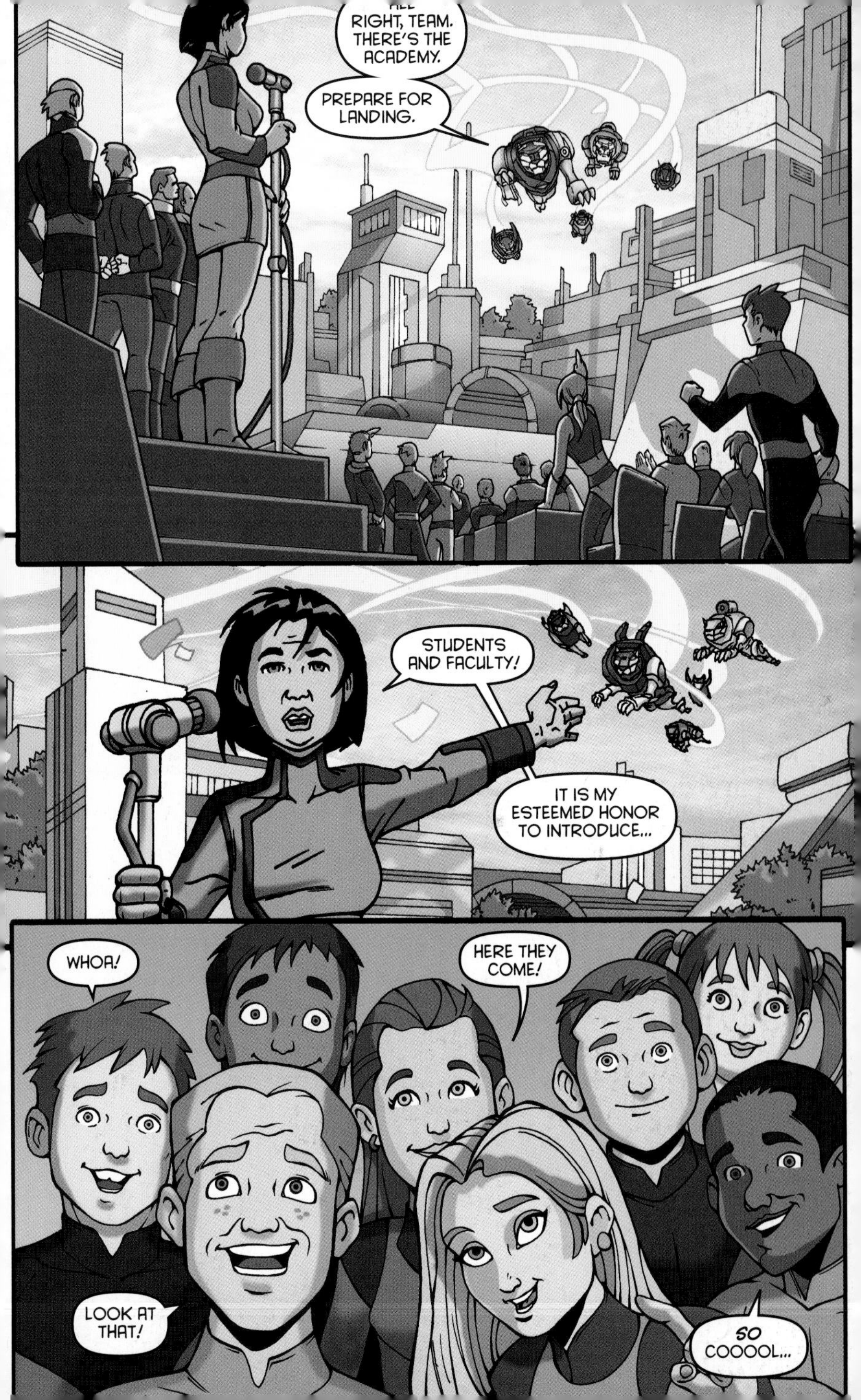
RIGHT, TEAM. THERE'S THE ACADEMY.
PREPARE FOR LANDING.
STUDENTS AND FACULTY!
IT IS MY ESTEEMED HONOR TO INTRODUCE...
WHOA!
HERE THEY COME!
LOOK AT THAT!
SO COOOOL...

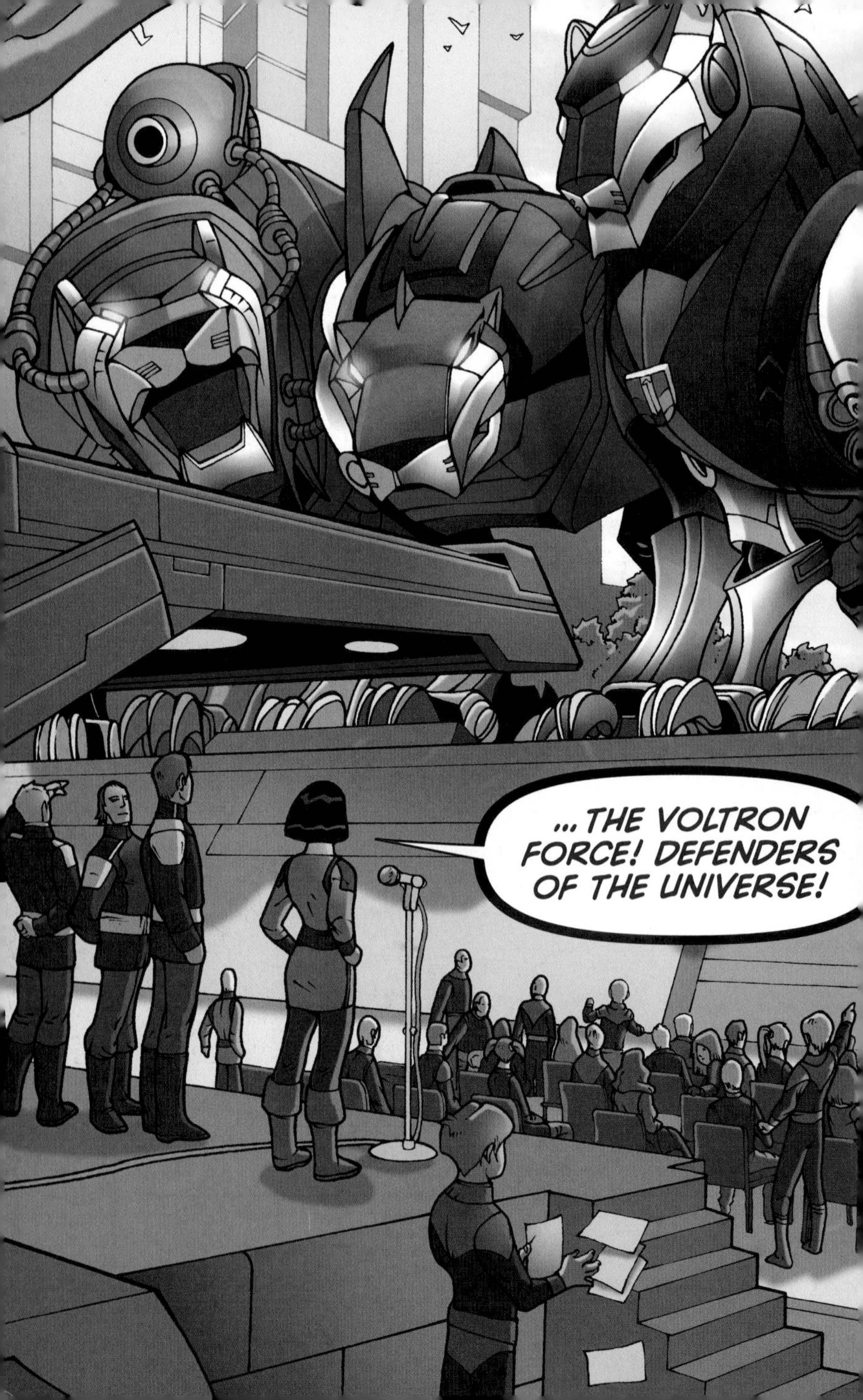
...THE VOLTRON FORCE! DEFENDERS OF THE UNIVERSE!

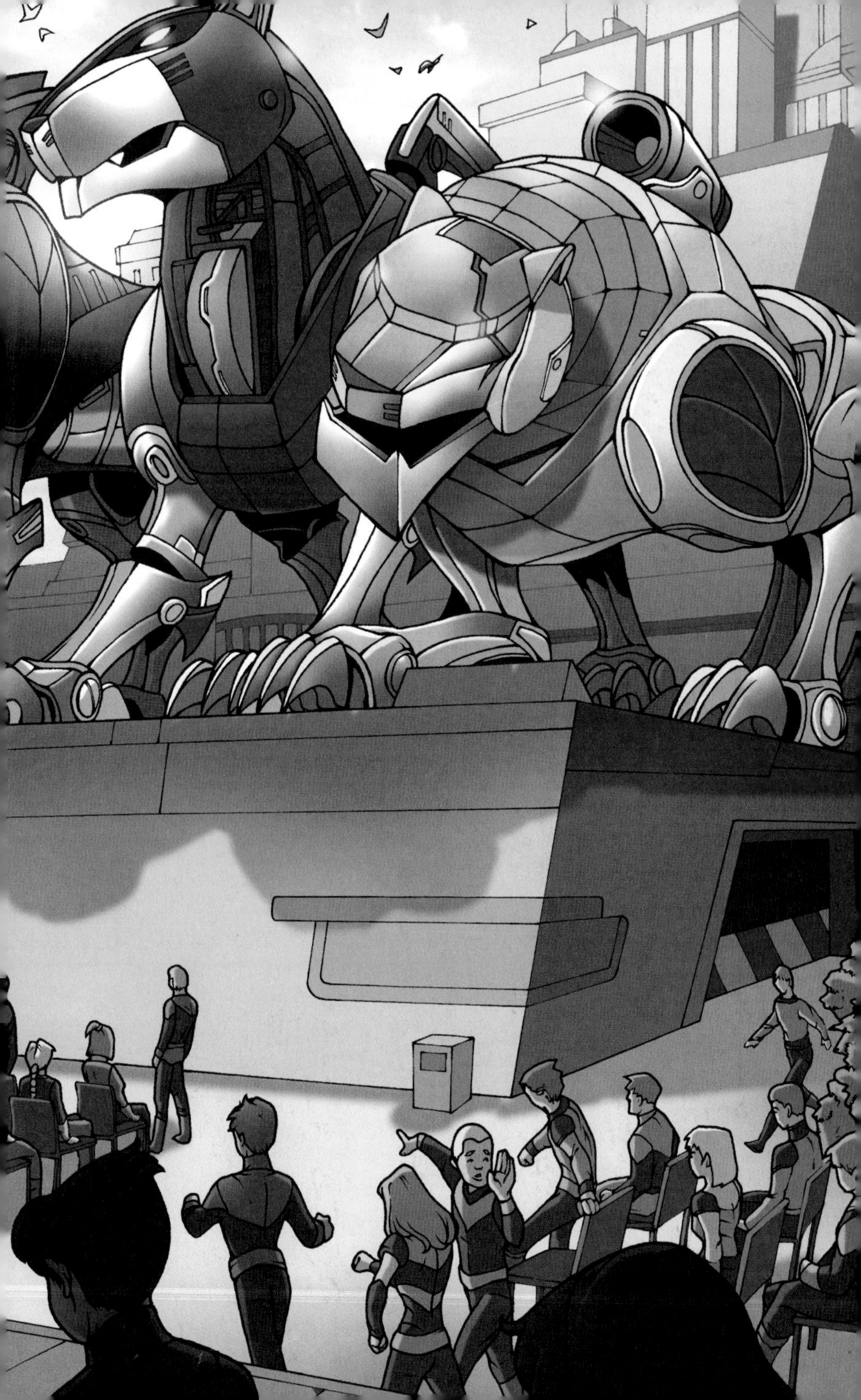

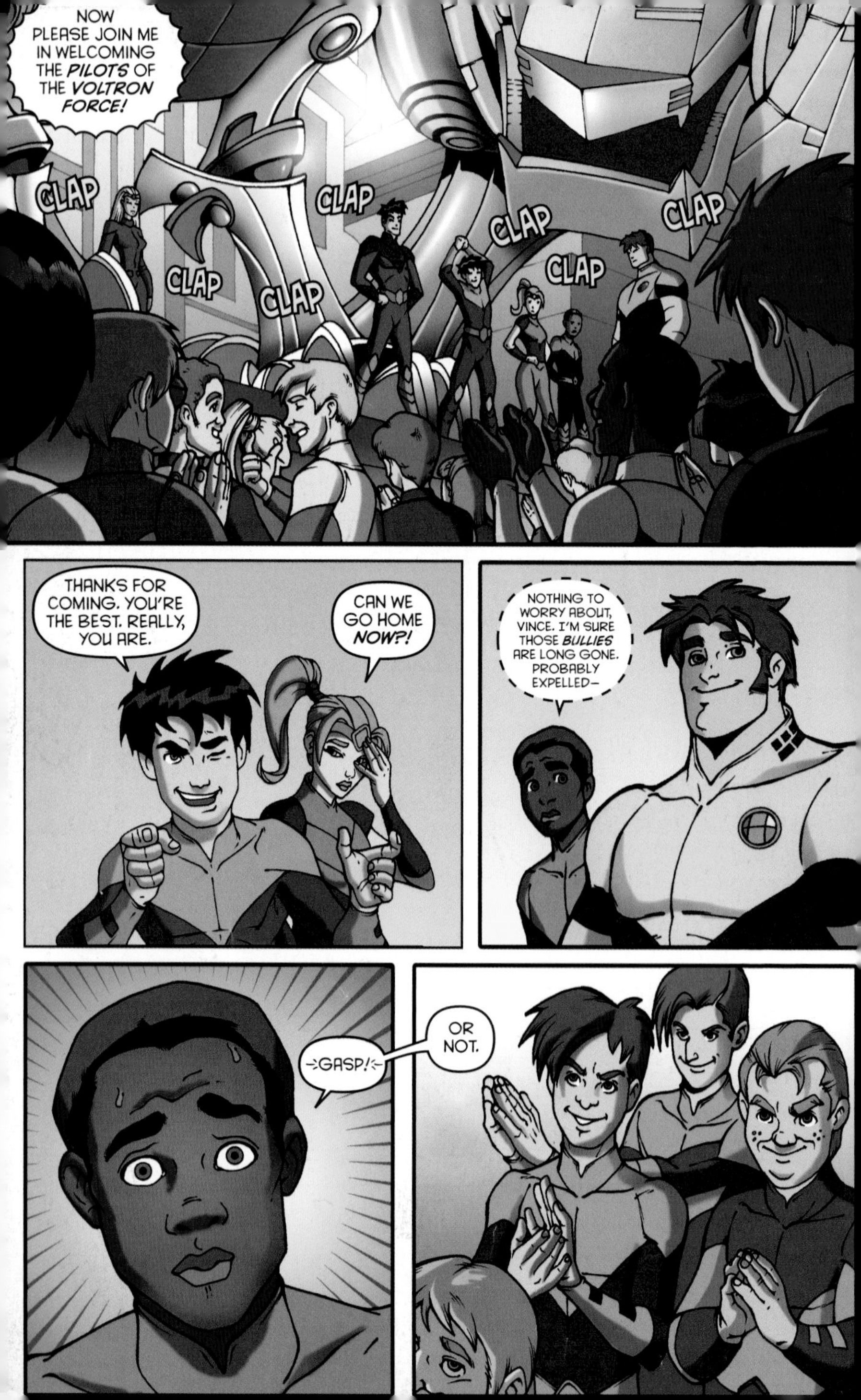
NOW PLEASE JOIN ME IN WELCOMING THE PILOTS OF THE VOLTRON FORCE!
CLAP
CLAP
CLAP
CLAP
CLAP
CLAP
CLAP
THANKS FOR COMING. YOU'RE THE BEST. REALLY, YOU ARE.
CAN WE GO HOME NOW?!
NOTHING TO WORRY ABOUT, VINCE. I'M SURE THOSE BULLIES ARE LONG GONE. PROBABLY EXPELLED—
GASP!
OR NOT.

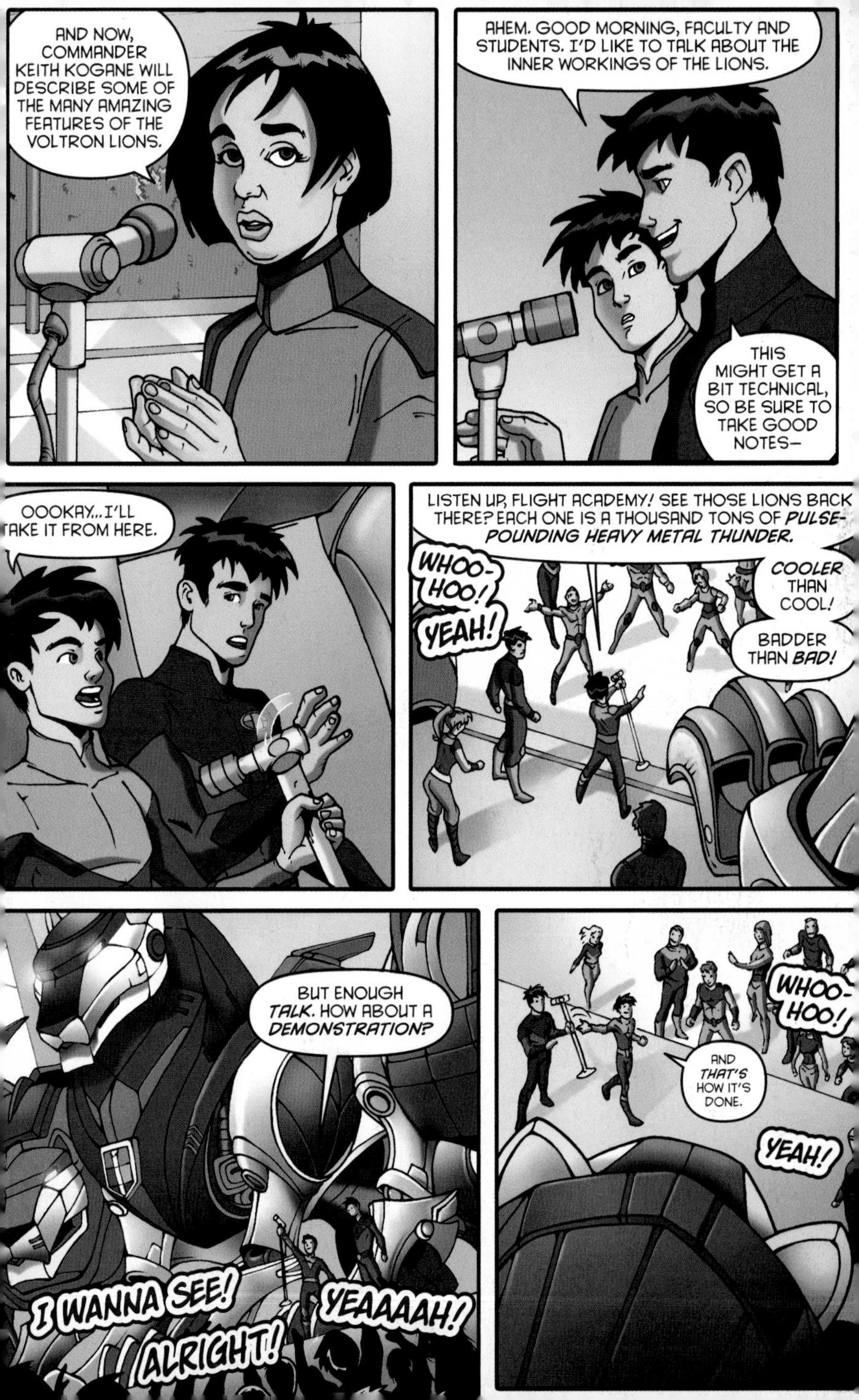
AND NOW, COMMANDER KEITH KOGANE WILL DESCRIBE SOME OF THE MANY AMAZING FEATURES OF THE VOLTRON LIONS.
AHEM. GOOD MORNING, FACULTY AND STUDENTS. I'D LIKE TO TALK ABOUT THE INNER WORKINGS OF THE LIONS.
THIS MIGHT GET A BIT TECHNICAL, SO BE SURE TO TAKE GOOD NOTES—
OOOKAY...I'LL TAKE IT FROM HERE.
LISTEN UP, FLIGHT ACADEMY! SEE THOSE LIONS BACK THERE? EACH ONE IS A THOUSAND TONS OF *PULSE-POUNDING HEAVY METAL THUNDER.*
WHOO-HOO!
YEAH!
COOLER THAN COOL!
BADDER THAN *BAD!*
BUT ENOUGH *TALK*. HOW ABOUT A *DEMONSTRATION?*
I WANNA SEE!
YEAAAAH!
ALRIGHT!
WHOO-HOO!
AND *THAT'S* HOW IT'S DONE.
YEAH!

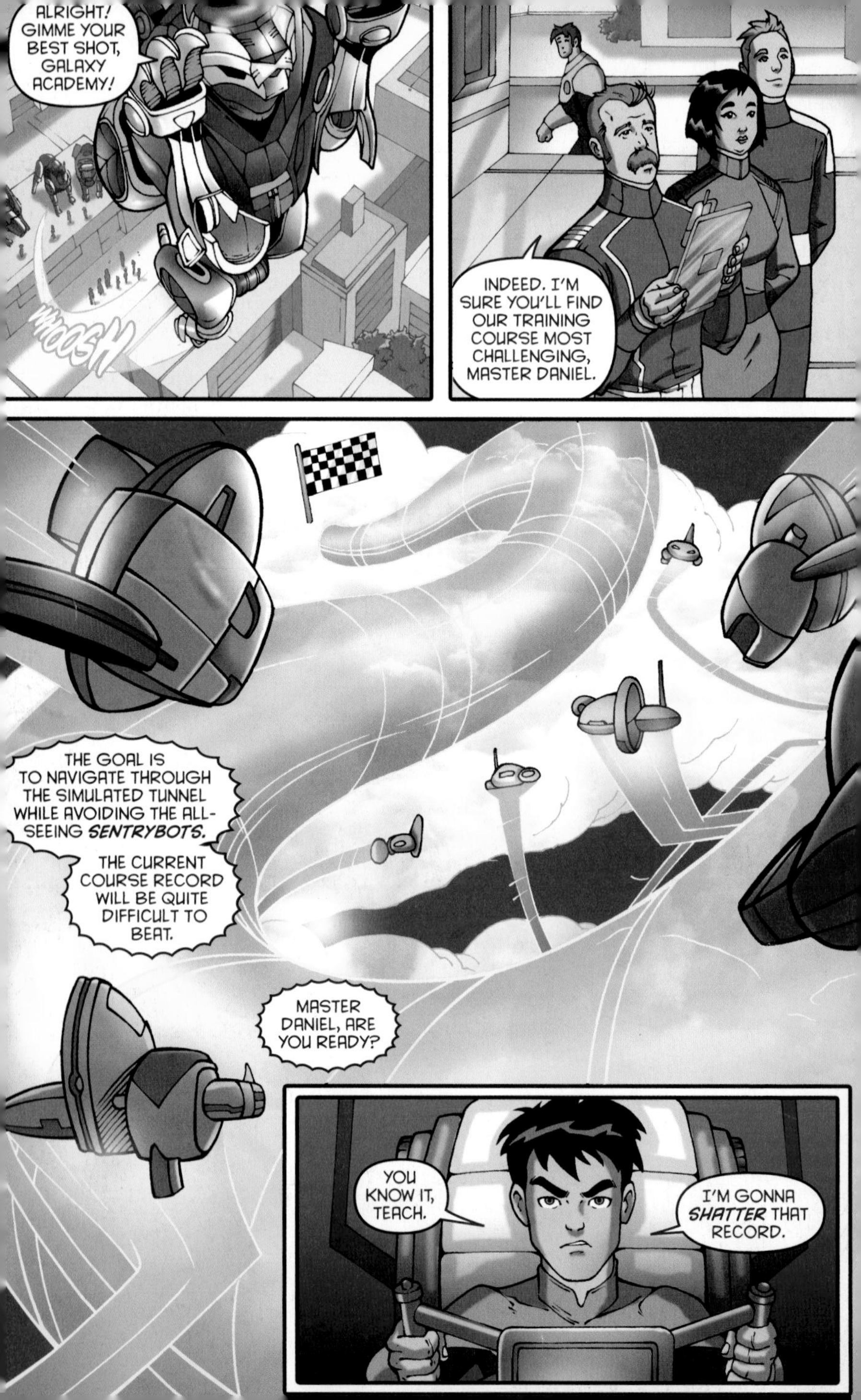
ALRIGHT! GIMME YOUR BEST SHOT, GALAXY ACADEMY!
WHOOSH
INDEED. I'M SURE YOU'LL FIND OUR TRAINING COURSE MOST CHALLENGING, MASTER DANIEL.
THE GOAL IS TO NAVIGATE THROUGH THE SIMULATED TUNNEL WHILE AVOIDING THE ALL-SEEING SENTRYBOTS.
THE CURRENT COURSE RECORD WILL BE QUITE DIFFICULT TO BEAT.
MASTER DANIEL, ARE YOU READY?
YOU KNOW IT, TEACH.
I'M GONNA SHATTER THAT RECORD.

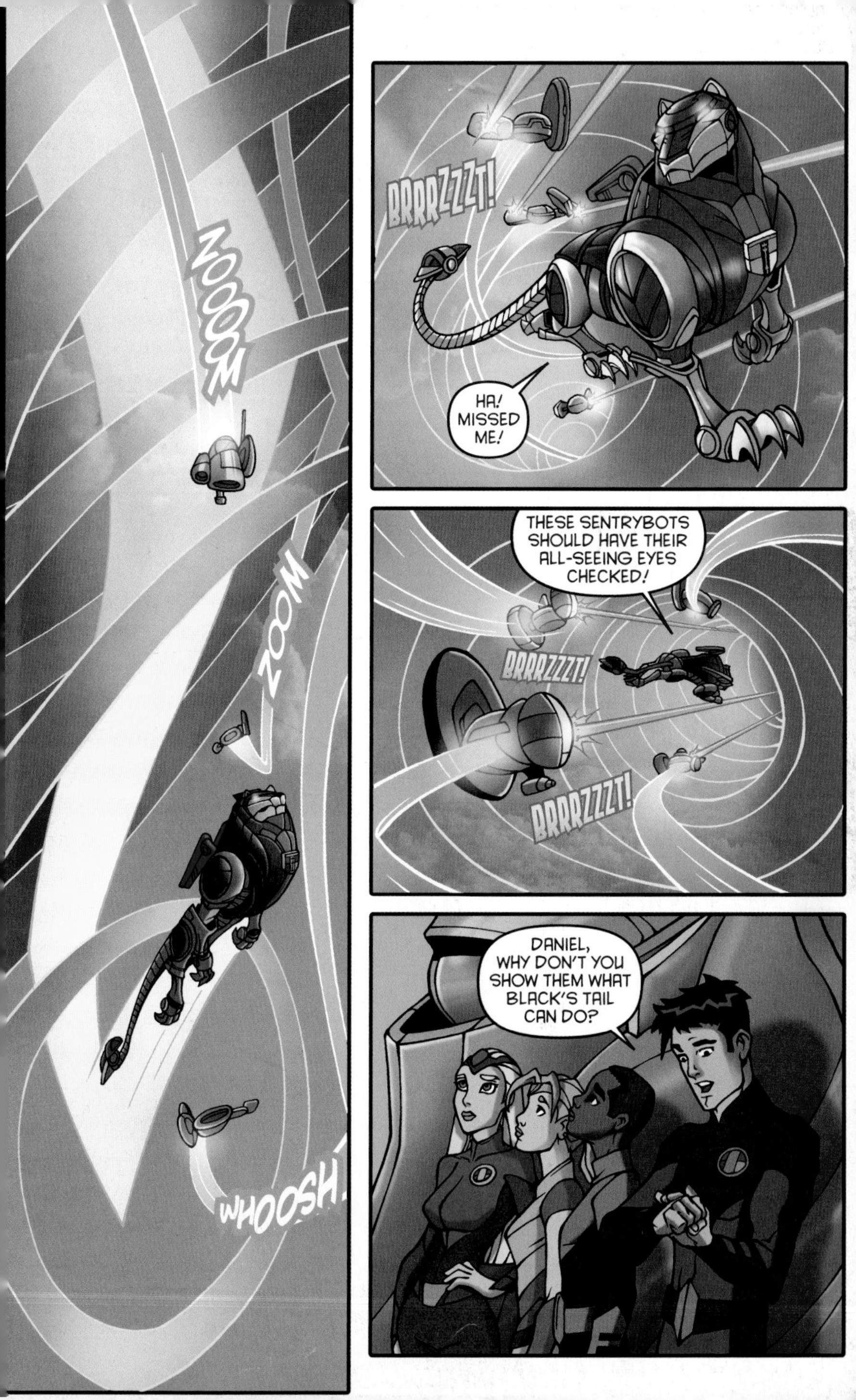
ZOOOOOM
ZOOM
WHOOSH!
BRRRZZZT!
HA! MISSED ME!
THESE SENTRYBOTS SHOULD HAVE THEIR ALL-SEEING EYES CHECKED!
BRRRZZZT!
BRRRZZZT!
DANIEL, WHY DON'T YOU SHOW THEM WHAT BLACK'S TAIL CAN DO?

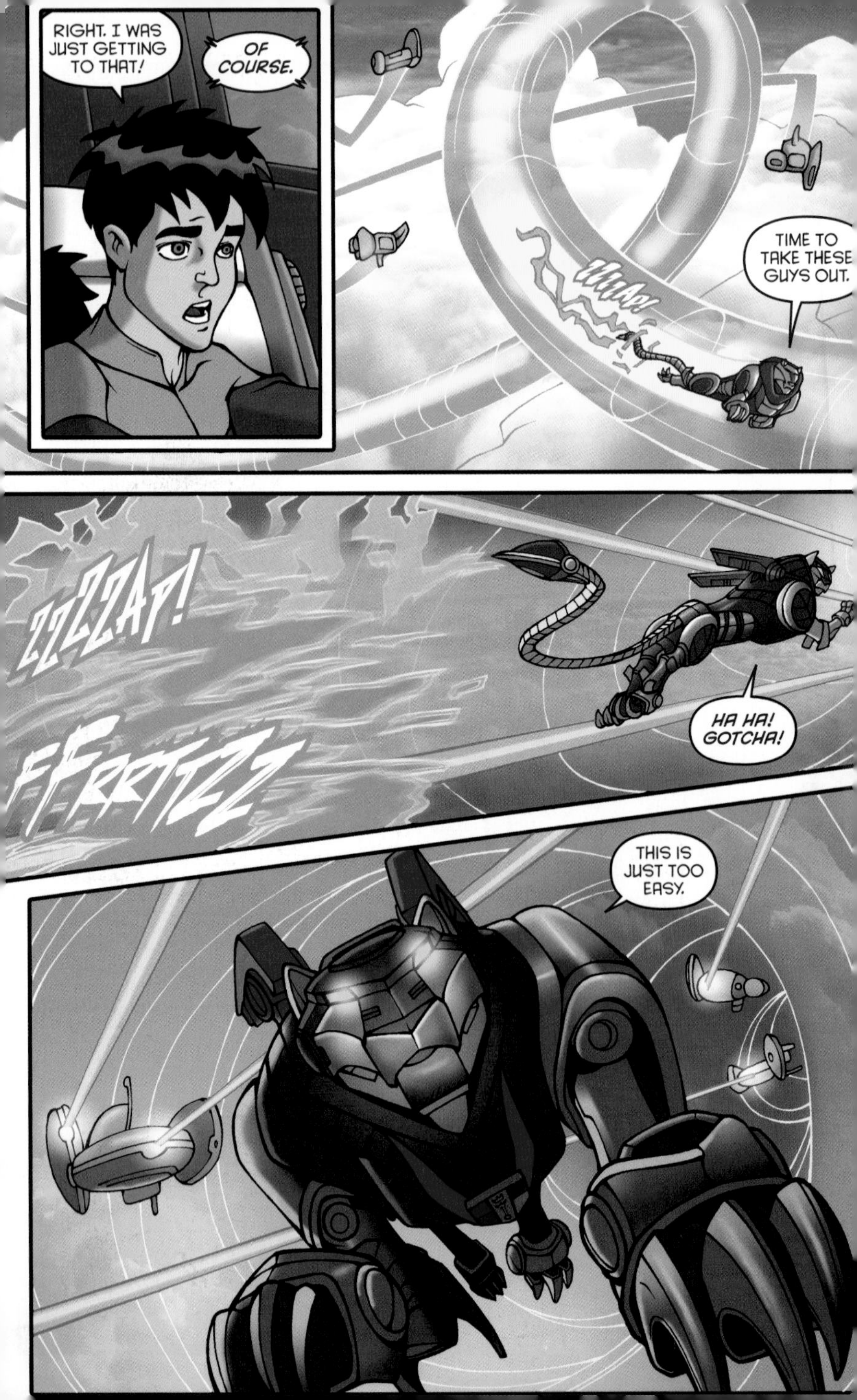
RIGHT. I WAS JUST GETTING TO THAT!
OF COURSE.
TIME TO TAKE THESE GUYS OUT.
ZZZZAP!
FFRRTZZ
HA HA! GOTCHA!
THIS IS JUST TOO EASY.

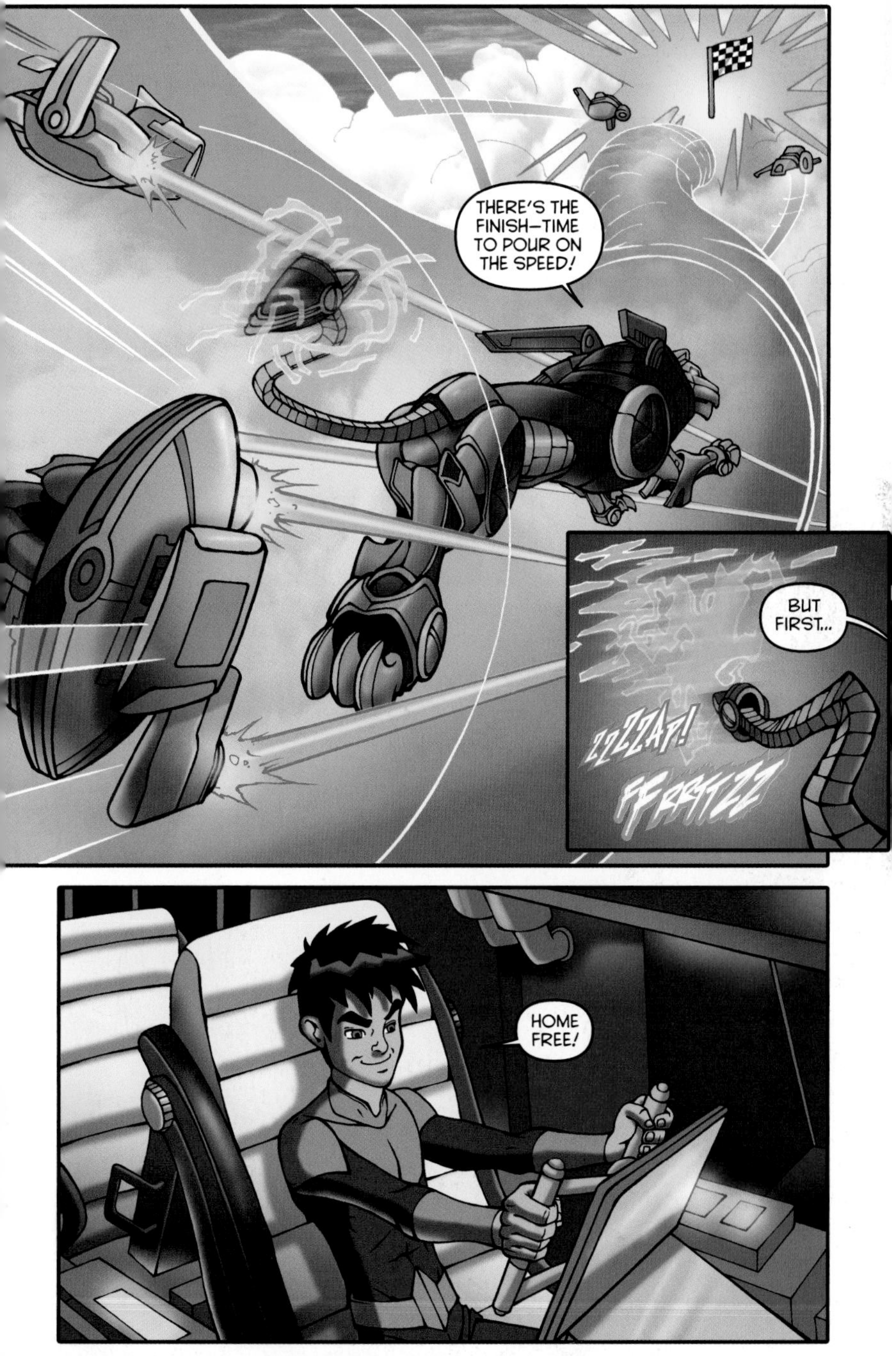
THERE'S THE FINISH—TIME TO POUR ON THE SPEED!
BUT FIRST...
ZZZZAP!
FFRRTZZ
HOME FREE!

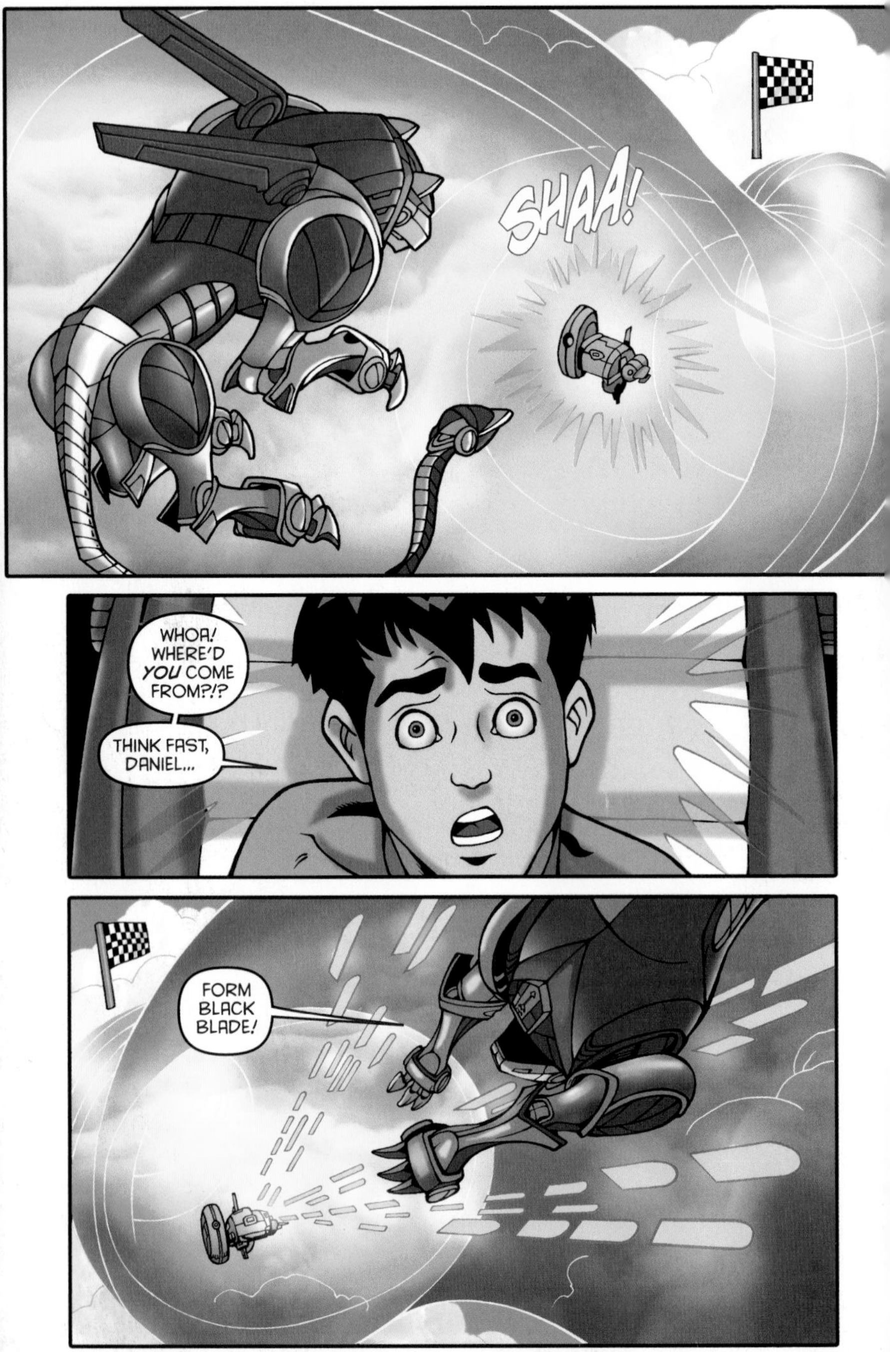
SHAA!
WHOA! WHERE'D *YOU* COME FROM?!?
THINK FAST, DANIEL...
FORM BLACK BLADE!

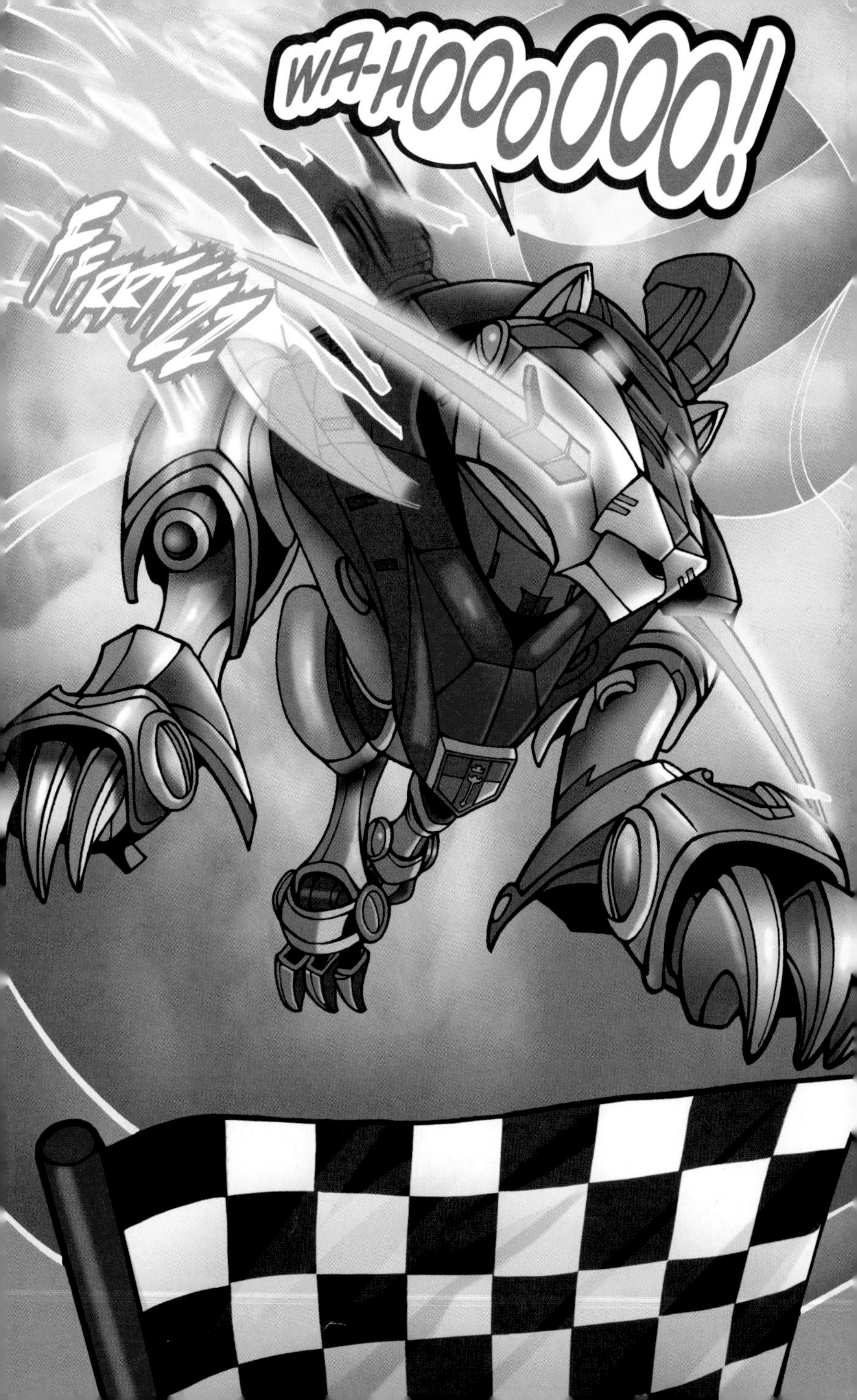
WA-HOOOOOOO!
FFFRRTZZZ

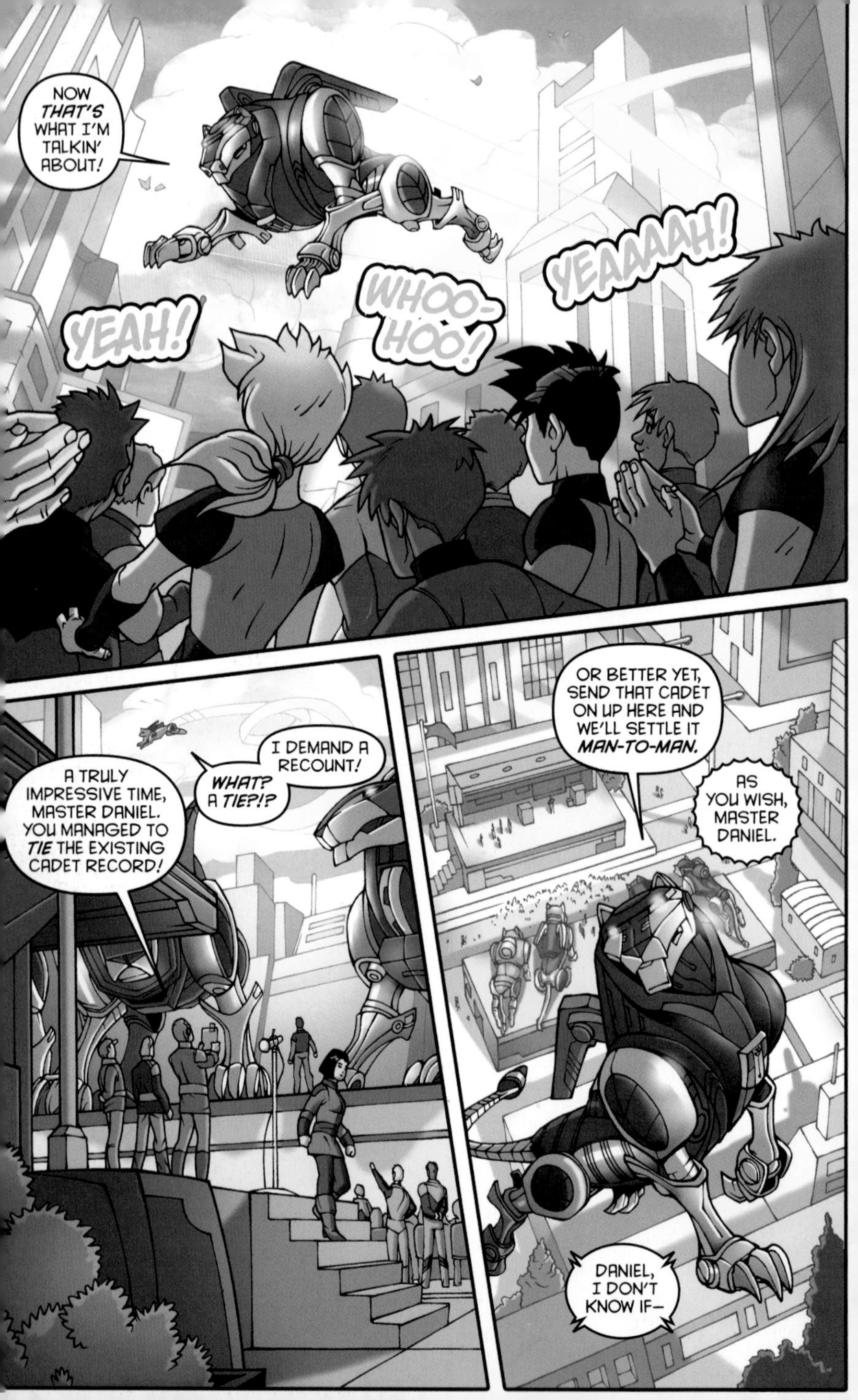
NOW THAT'S WHAT I'M TALKIN' ABOUT!
YEAH!
WHOO-HOO!
YEAAAAH!
A TRULY IMPRESSIVE TIME, MASTER DANIEL. YOU MANAGED TO TIE THE EXISTING CADET RECORD!
WHAT? A TIE?!?
I DEMAND A RECOUNT!
OR BETTER YET, SEND THAT CADET ON UP HERE AND WE'LL SETTLE IT MAN-TO-MAN.
AS YOU WISH, MASTER DANIEL.
DANIEL, I DON'T KNOW IF—

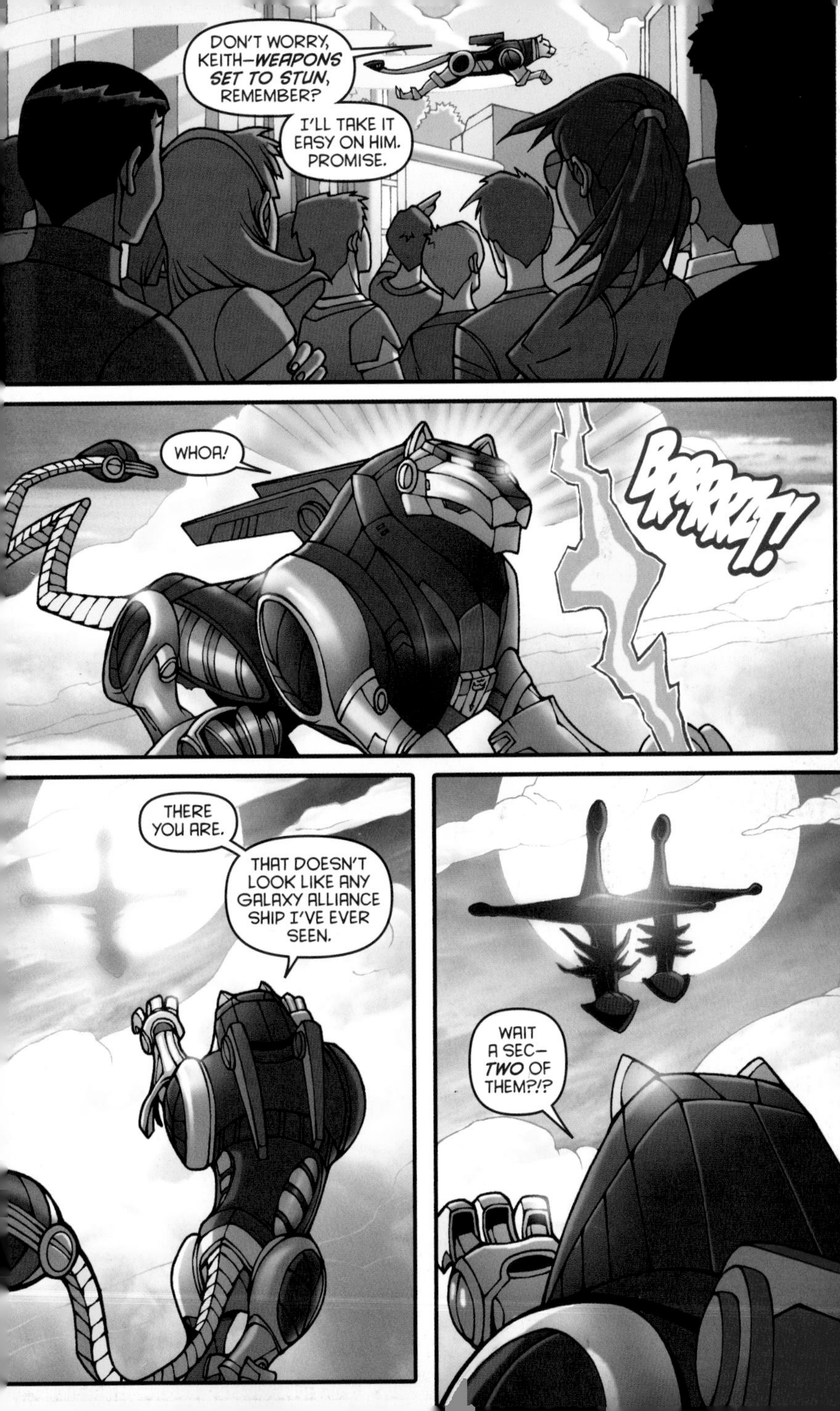
DON'T WORRY, KEITH—WEAPONS SET TO STUN, REMEMBER?
I'LL TAKE IT EASY ON HIM. PROMISE.
WHOA!
BRRRZZT!
THERE YOU ARE.
THAT DOESN'T LOOK LIKE ANY GALAXY ALLIANCE SHIP I'VE EVER SEEN.
WAIT A SEC—TWO OF THEM?!?

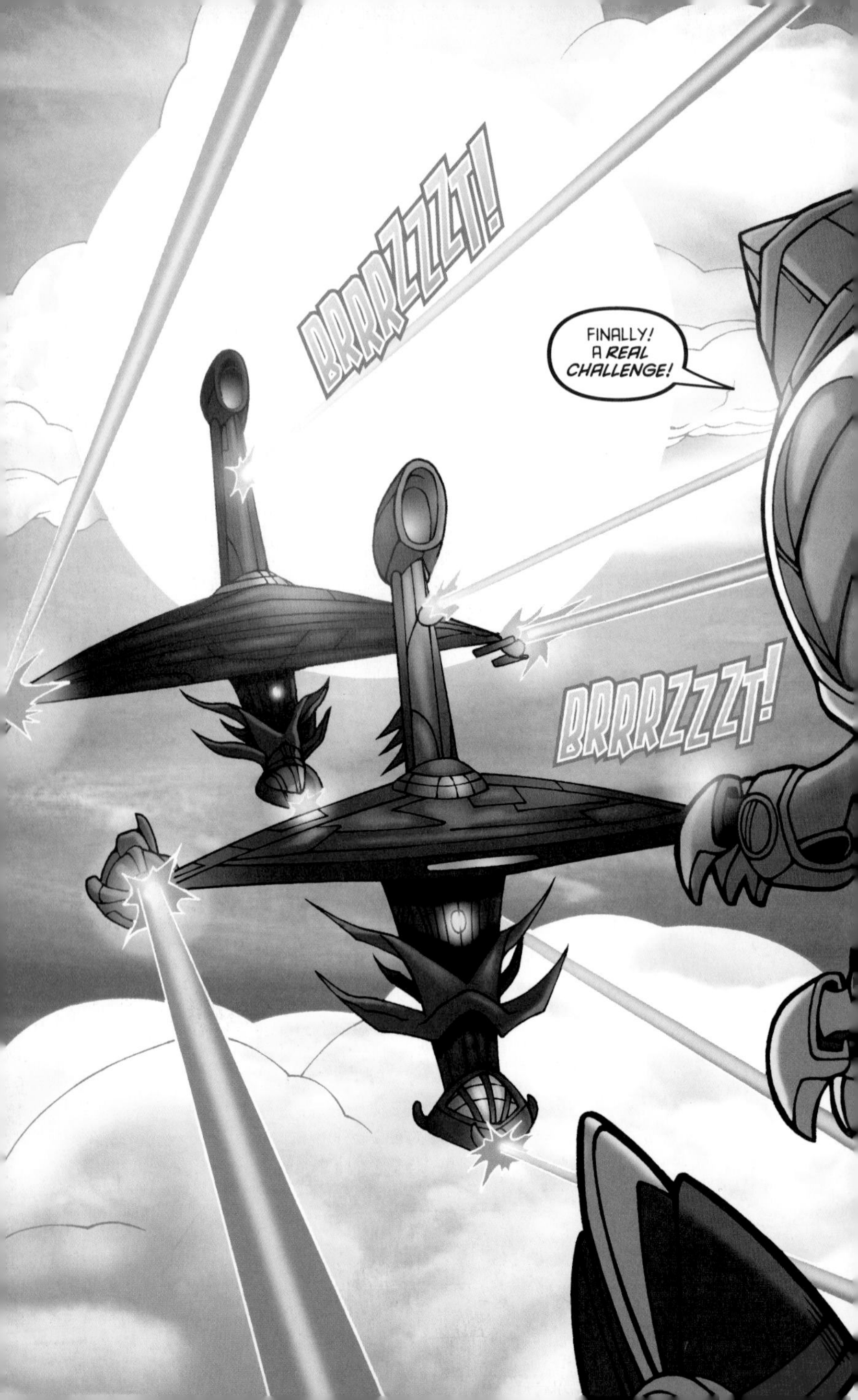
BRRRZZZZT!
FINALLY! A REAL CHALLENGE!
BRRRZZZZT!

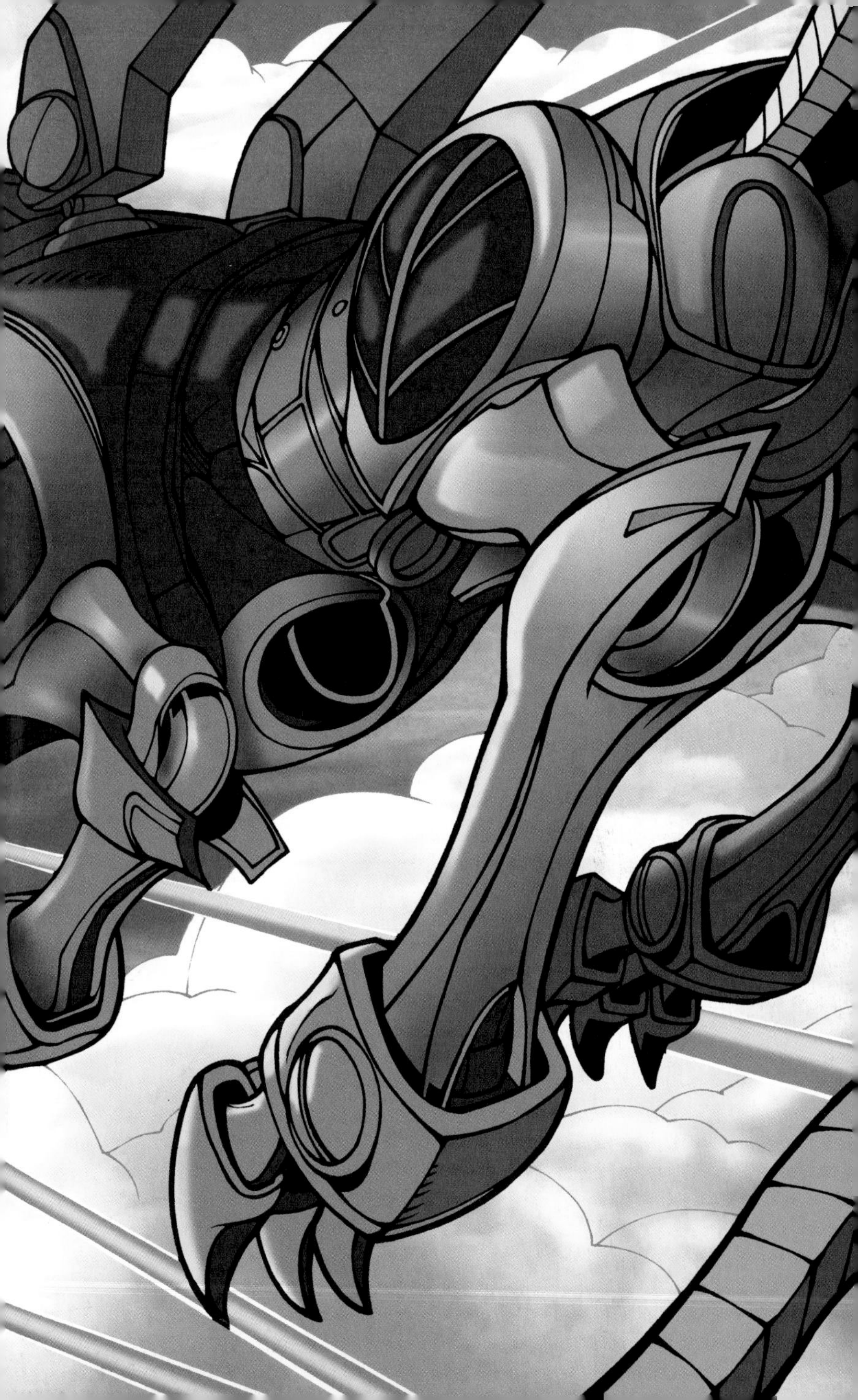

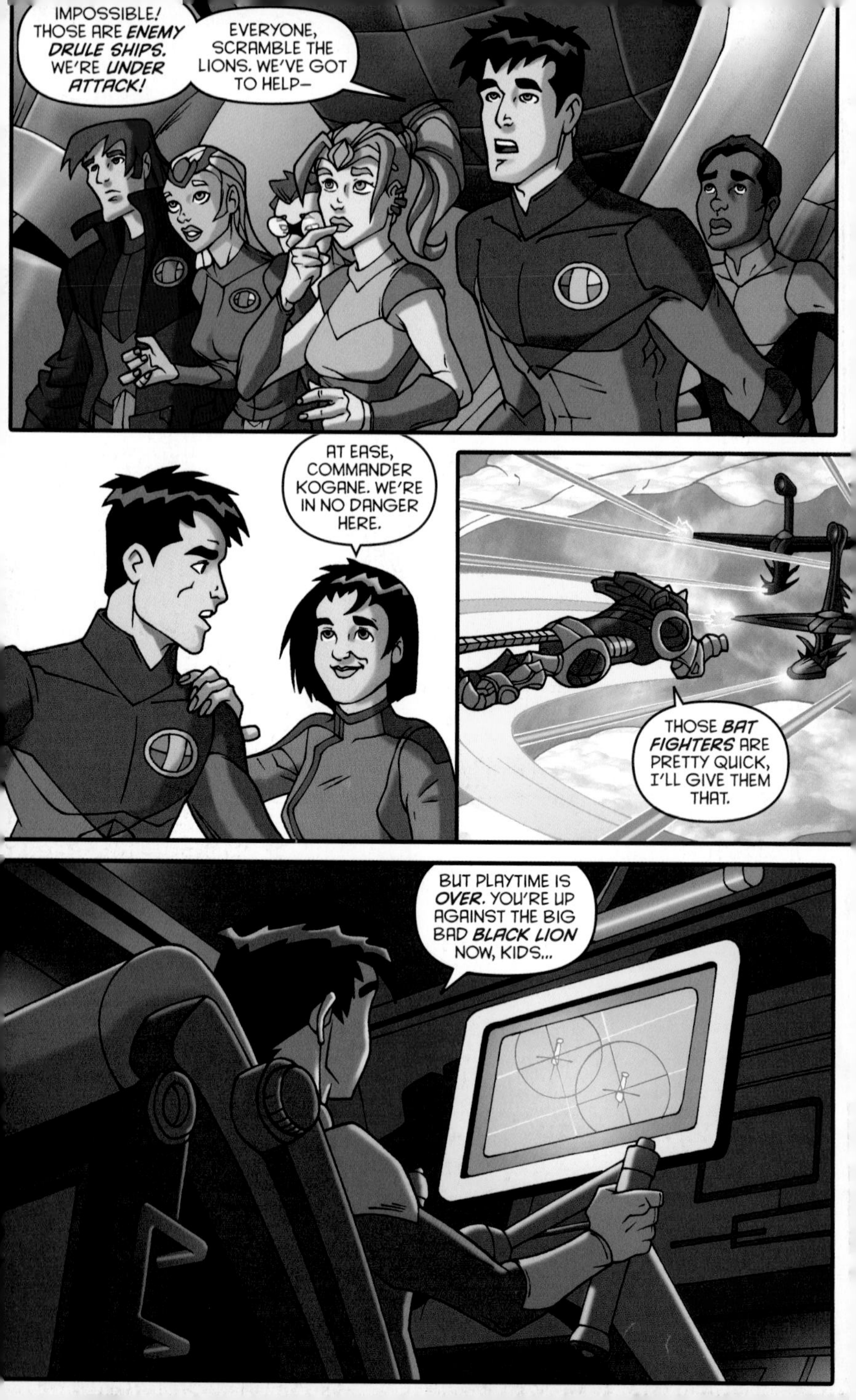
IMPOSSIBLE! THOSE ARE ENEMY DRULE SHIPS. WE'RE UNDER ATTACK!
EVERYONE, SCRAMBLE THE LIONS. WE'VE GOT TO HELP—
AT EASE, COMMANDER KOGANE. WE'RE IN NO DANGER HERE.
THOSE BAT FIGHTERS ARE PRETTY QUICK, I'LL GIVE THEM THAT.
BUT PLAYTIME IS OVER. YOU'RE UP AGAINST THE BIG BAD BLACK LION NOW, KIDS...

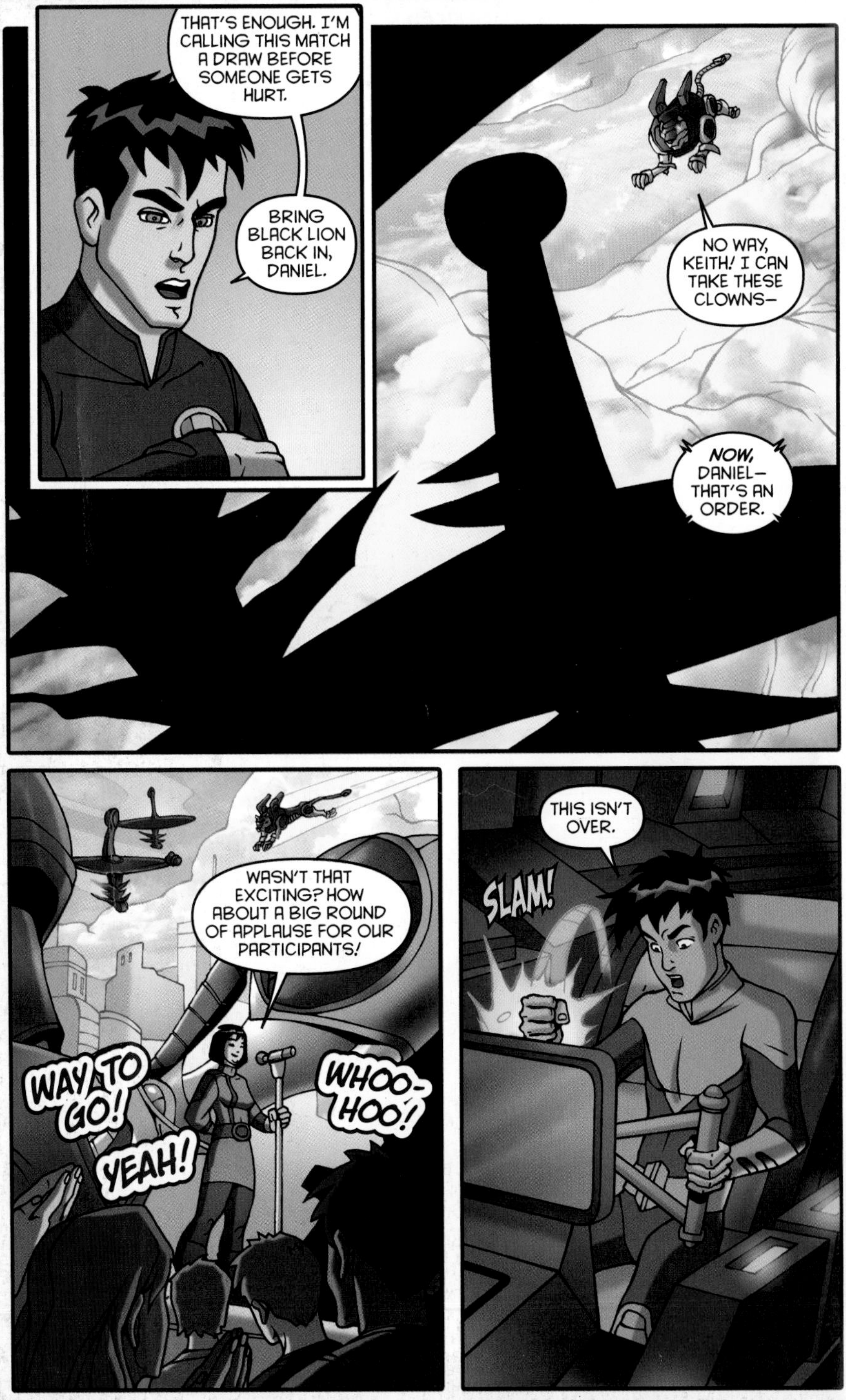
THAT'S ENOUGH. I'M CALLING THIS MATCH A DRAW BEFORE SOMEONE GETS HURT.
BRING BLACK LION BACK IN, DANIEL.
NO WAY, KEITH! I CAN TAKE THESE CLOWNS—
NOW, DANIEL— THAT'S AN ORDER.
WASN'T THAT EXCITING? HOW ABOUT A BIG ROUND OF APPLAUSE FOR OUR PARTICIPANTS!
WAY TO GO!
YEAH!
WHOO-HOO!
THIS ISN'T OVER.
SLAM!

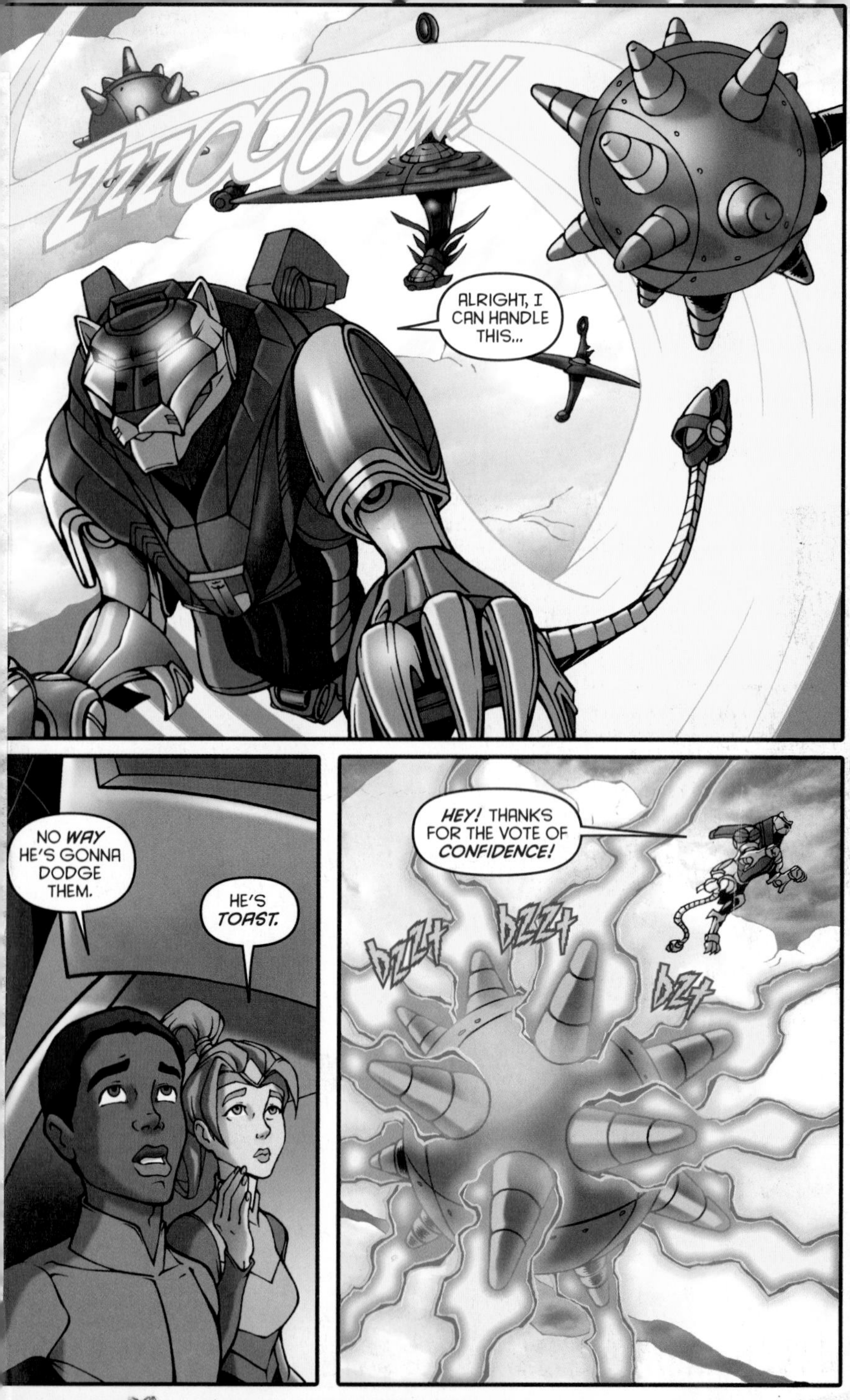

ZZZOOOOOM!
ALRIGHT, I CAN HANDLE THIS...
NO WAY HE'S GONNA DODGE THEM.
HE'S TOAST.
HEY! THANKS FOR THE VOTE OF CONFIDENCE!
bzzt
bzzt
bzzt

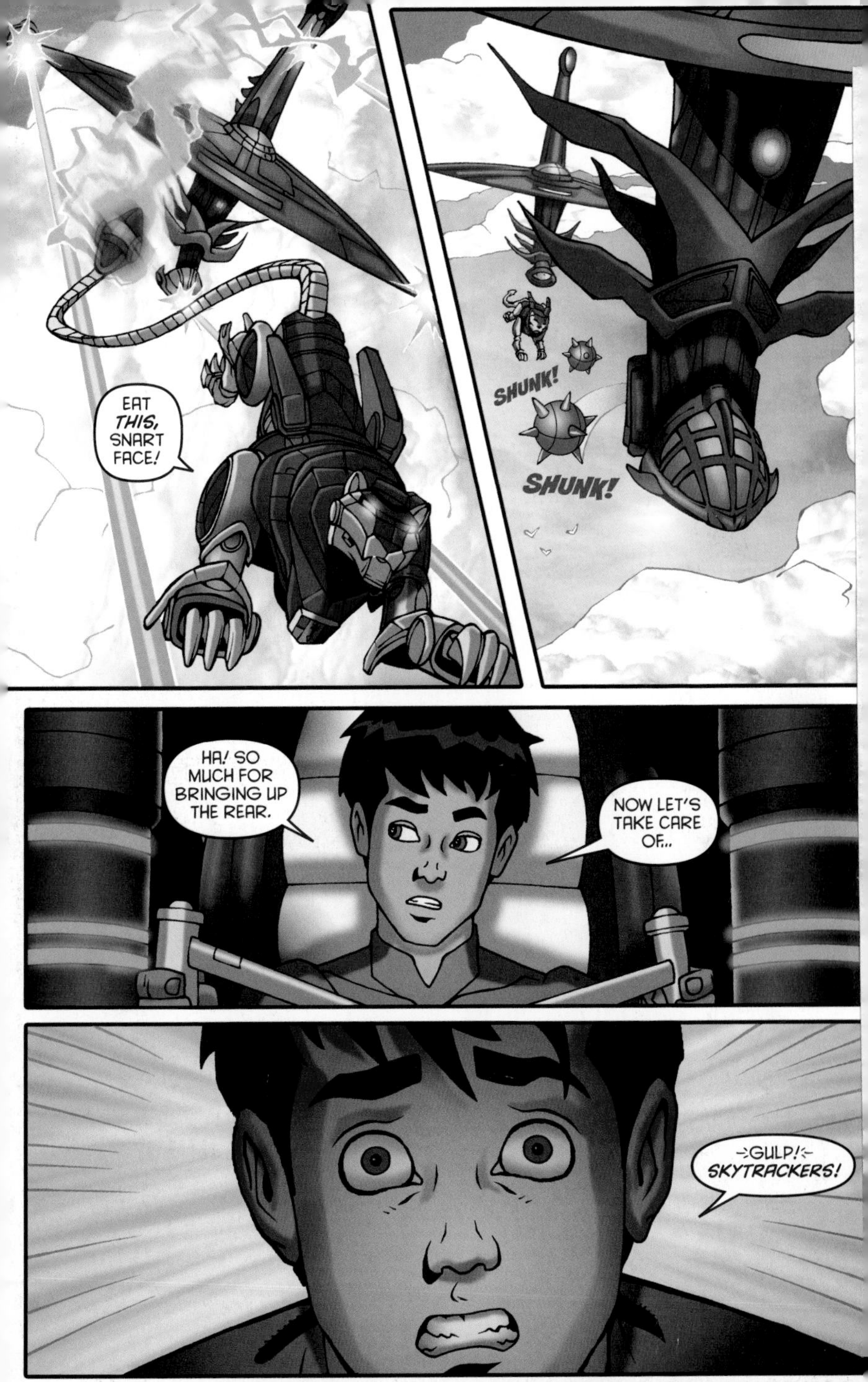
EAT THIS, SNART FACE!
SHUNK!
SHUNK!
HA! SO MUCH FOR BRINGING UP THE REAR.
NOW LET'S TAKE CARE OF...
-GULP!- SKYTRACKERS!

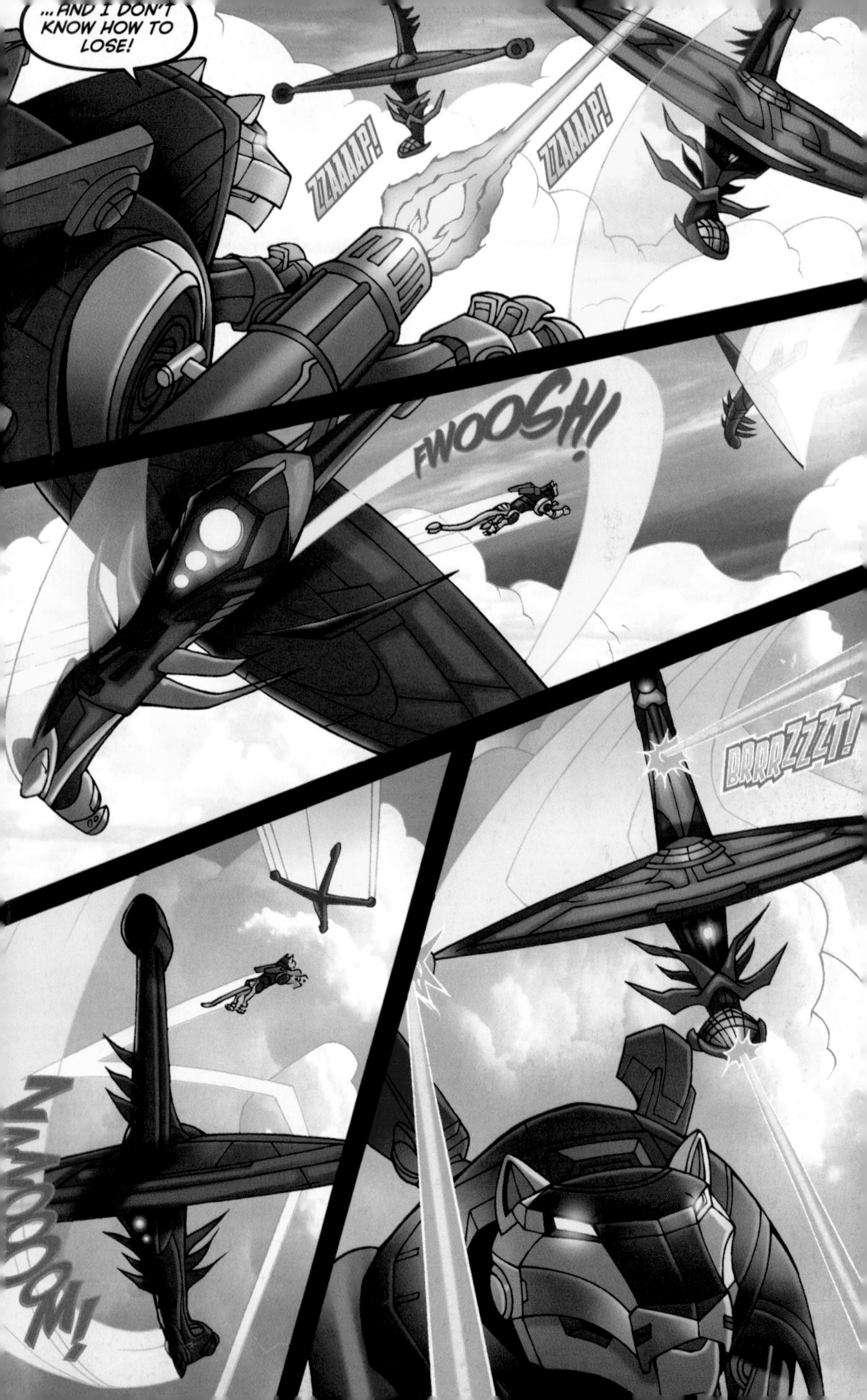
...AND I DON'T KNOW HOW TO LOSE!
ZZAAAAP!
ZZAAAAP!
FWOOSH!!
BRRRZZZT!
VVMMOOOOM!

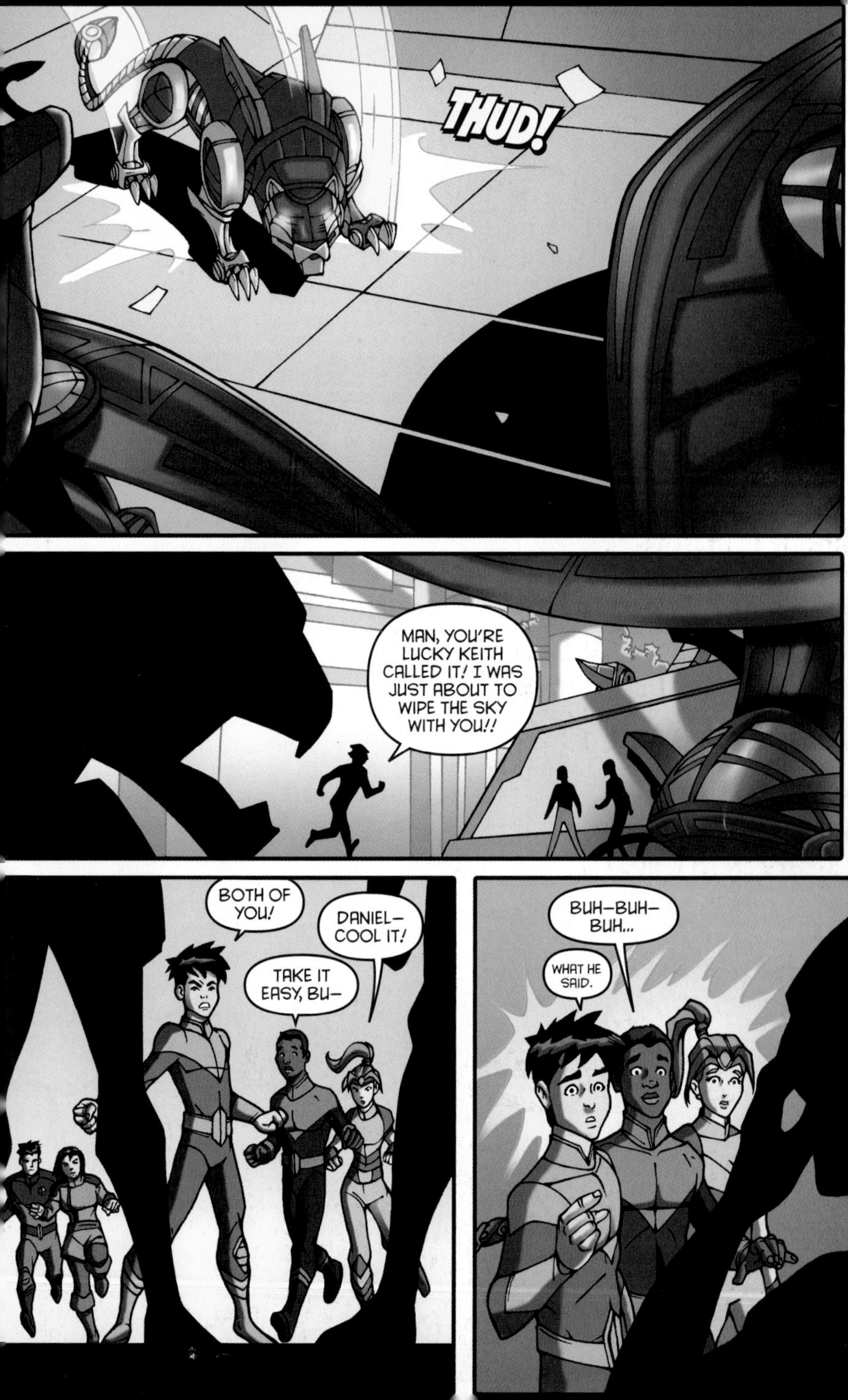
THUD!
MAN, YOU'RE LUCKY KEITH CALLED IT! I WAS JUST ABOUT TO WIPE THE SKY WITH YOU!!
BOTH OF YOU!
DANIEL— COOL IT!
TAKE IT EASY, BU—
BUH—BUH— BUH...
WHAT HE SAID.

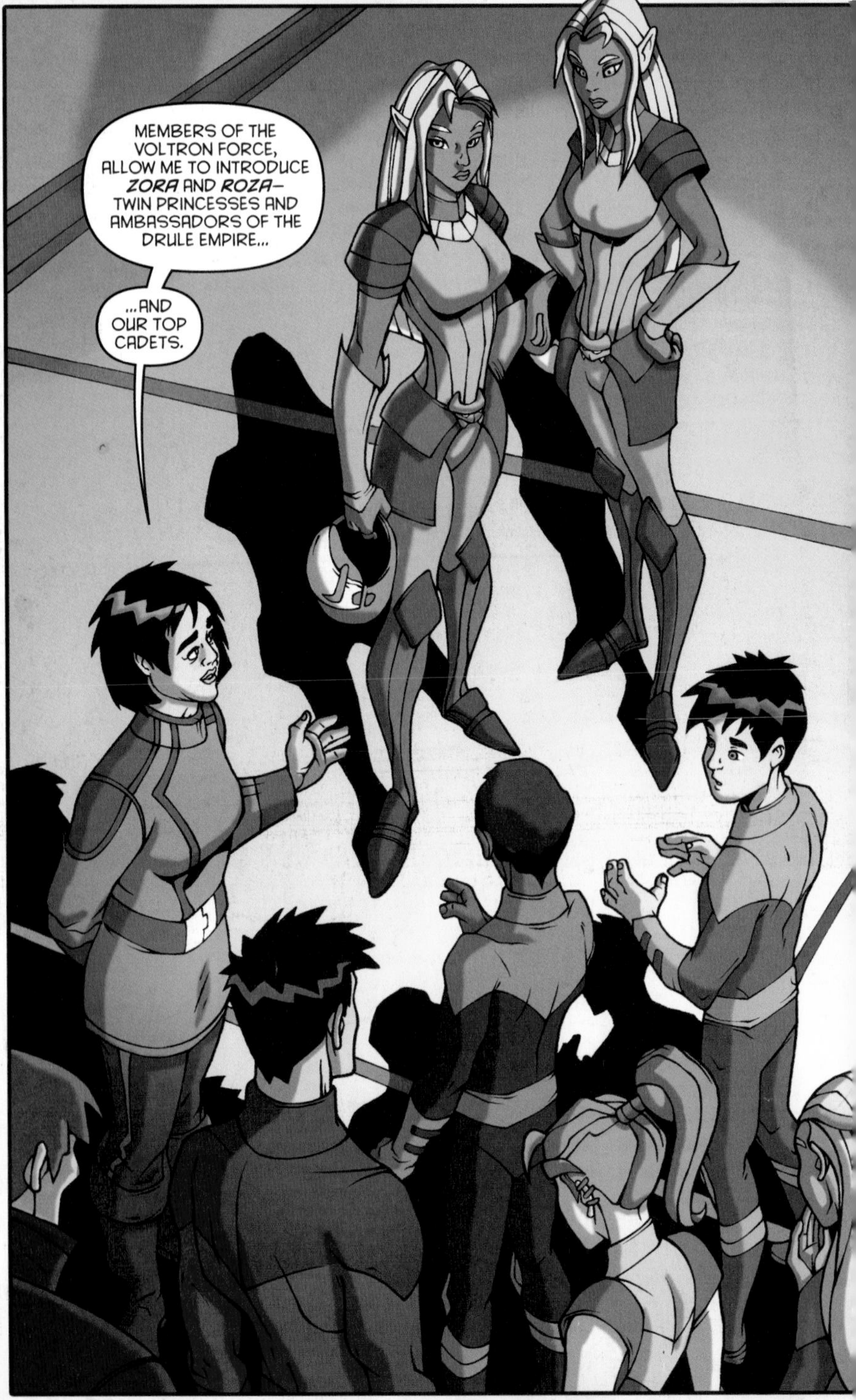
MEMBERS OF THE VOLTRON FORCE, ALLOW ME TO INTRODUCE *ZORA* AND *ROZA*— TWIN PRINCESSES AND AMBASSADORS OF THE DRULE EMPIRE...
...AND OUR TOP CADETS.

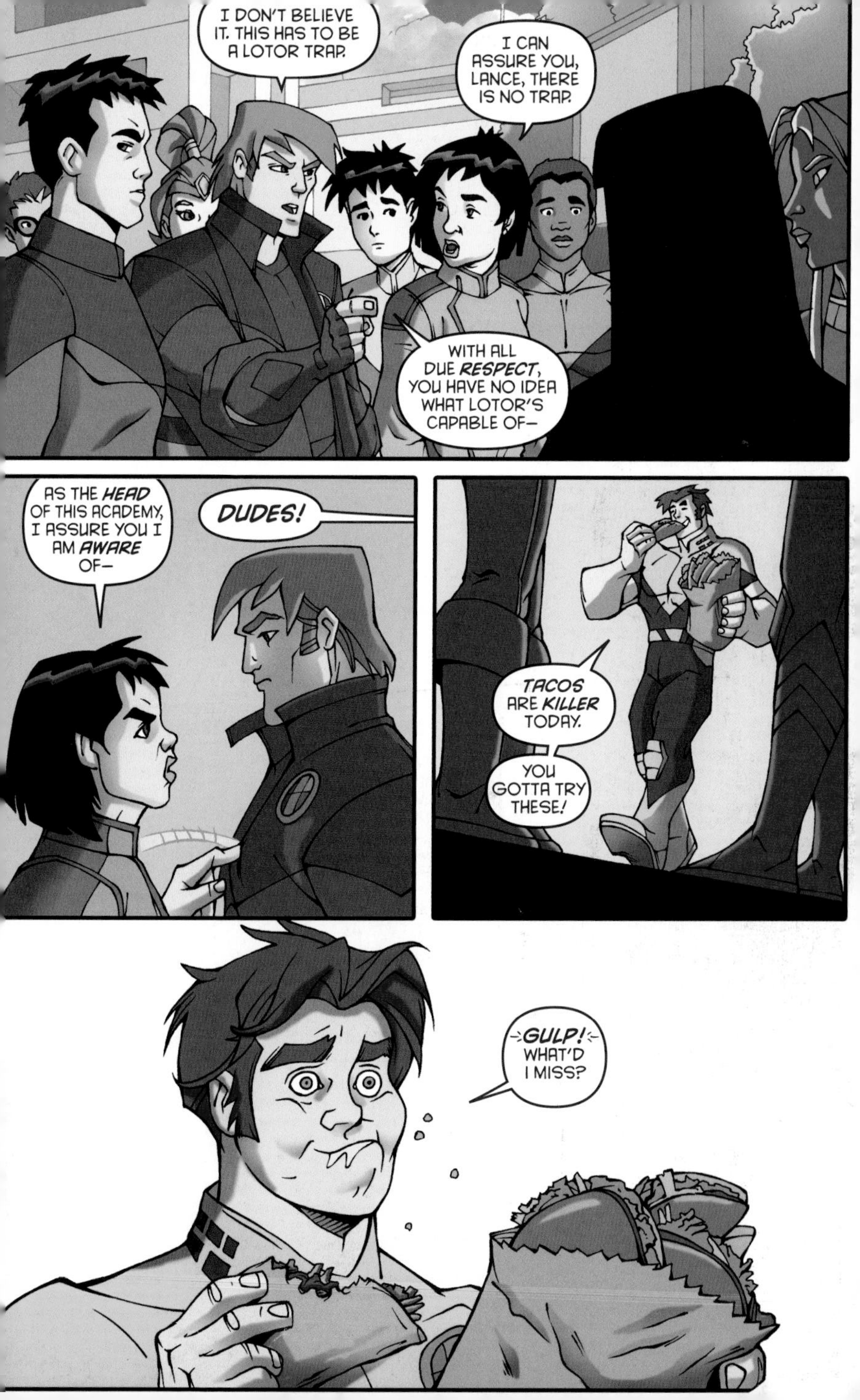
I DON'T BELIEVE IT. THIS HAS TO BE A LOTOR TRAP.
I CAN ASSURE YOU, LANCE, THERE IS NO TRAP.
WITH ALL DUE RESPECT, YOU HAVE NO IDEA WHAT LOTOR'S CAPABLE OF—
AS THE HEAD OF THIS ACADEMY, I ASSURE YOU I AM AWARE OF—
DUDES!
TACOS ARE KILLER TODAY.
YOU GOTTA TRY THESE!
GULP! WHAT'D I MISS?

LATER...

...YOU TWO DON'T SAY MUCH, DO YOU?

YOUR FLYING WAS REALLY AWESOME.

MOSTLY AWESOME.

DRULE SLIME.

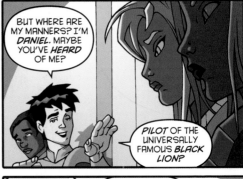

BUT WHERE ARE MY MANNERS? I'M *DANIEL.* MAYBE YOU'VE *HEARD* OF ME?

PILOT OF THE UNIVERSALLY FAMOUS *BLACK LION?*

YOU KNOW, I HELPED PIDGE DESIGN THAT COURSE. YOUR TIMES ARE QUITE IMPRESSIVE!

STOP *BORING* THE PRETTY GIRLS, *VINCE.*

AS WAS

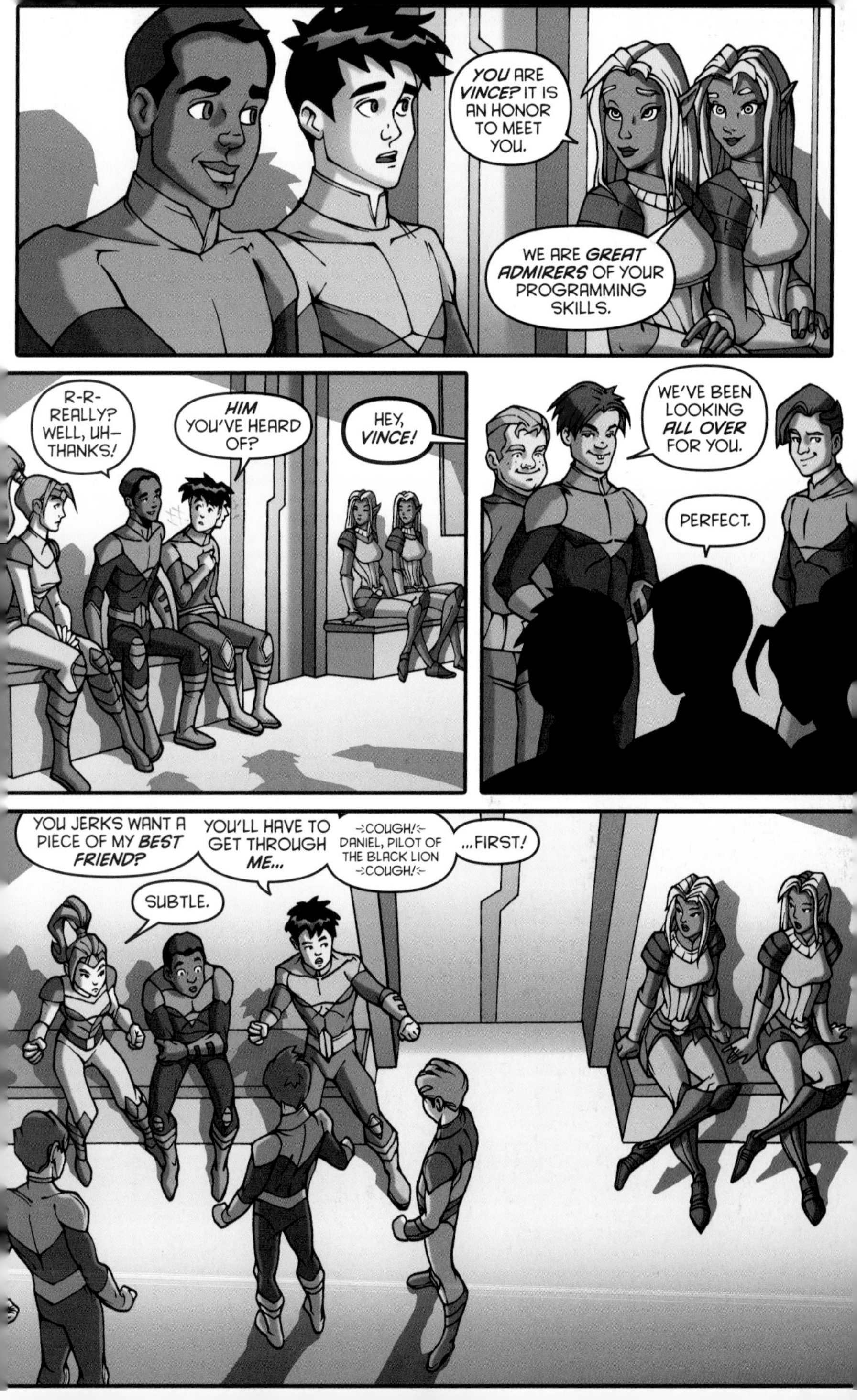
YOU ARE VINCE? IT IS AN HONOR TO MEET YOU.
WE ARE GREAT ADMIRERS OF YOUR PROGRAMMING SKILLS.
R-R-REALLY? WELL, UH— THANKS!
HIM YOU'VE HEARD OF?
HEY, VINCE!
WE'VE BEEN LOOKING ALL OVER FOR YOU.
PERFECT.
YOU JERKS WANT A PIECE OF MY BEST FRIEND?
YOU'LL HAVE TO GET THROUGH ME...
SUBTLE.
-COUGH!- DANIEL, PILOT OF THE BLACK LION -COUGH!-
...FIRST!

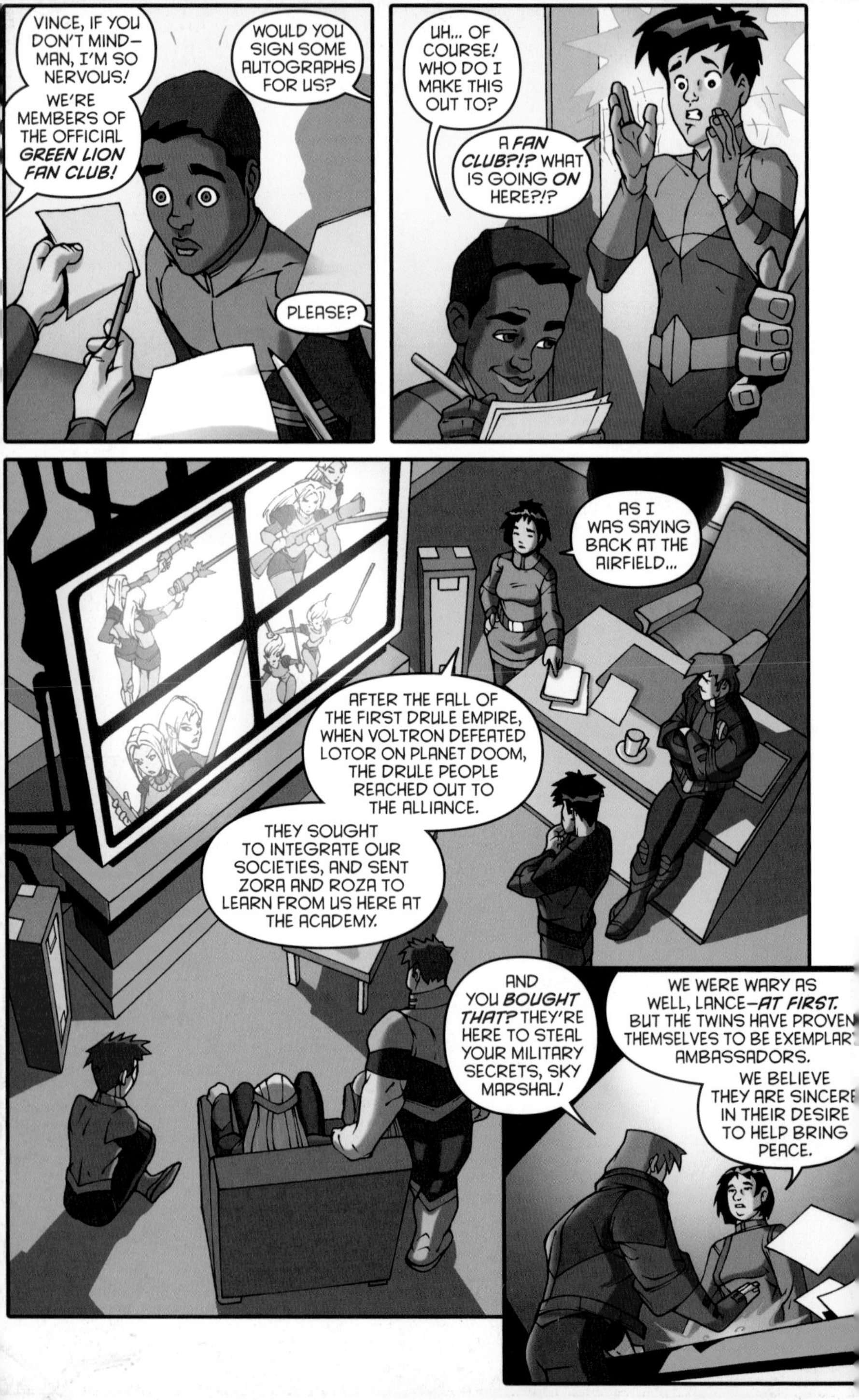

VINCE, IF YOU DON'T MIND— MAN, I'M SO NERVOUS!
WE'RE MEMBERS OF THE OFFICIAL *GREEN LION FAN CLUB!*
WOULD YOU SIGN SOME AUTOGRAPHS FOR US?
PLEASE?
UH... OF COURSE! WHO DO I MAKE THIS OUT TO?
A *FAN CLUB?!?* WHAT IS GOING *ON* HERE?!?
AS I WAS SAYING BACK AT THE AIRFIELD...
AFTER THE FALL OF THE FIRST DRULE EMPIRE, WHEN VOLTRON DEFEATED LOTOR ON PLANET DOOM, THE DRULE PEOPLE REACHED OUT TO THE ALLIANCE.
THEY SOUGHT TO INTEGRATE OUR SOCIETIES, AND SENT ZORA AND ROZA TO LEARN FROM US HERE AT THE ACADEMY.
AND YOU *BOUGHT THAT?* THEY'RE HERE TO STEAL YOUR MILITARY SECRETS, SKY MARSHAL!
WE WERE WARY AS WELL, LANCE—*AT FIRST.* BUT THE TWINS HAVE PROVEN THEMSELVES TO BE EXEMPLARY AMBASSADORS.
WE BELIEVE THEY ARE SINCERE IN THEIR DESIRE TO HELP BRING PEACE.

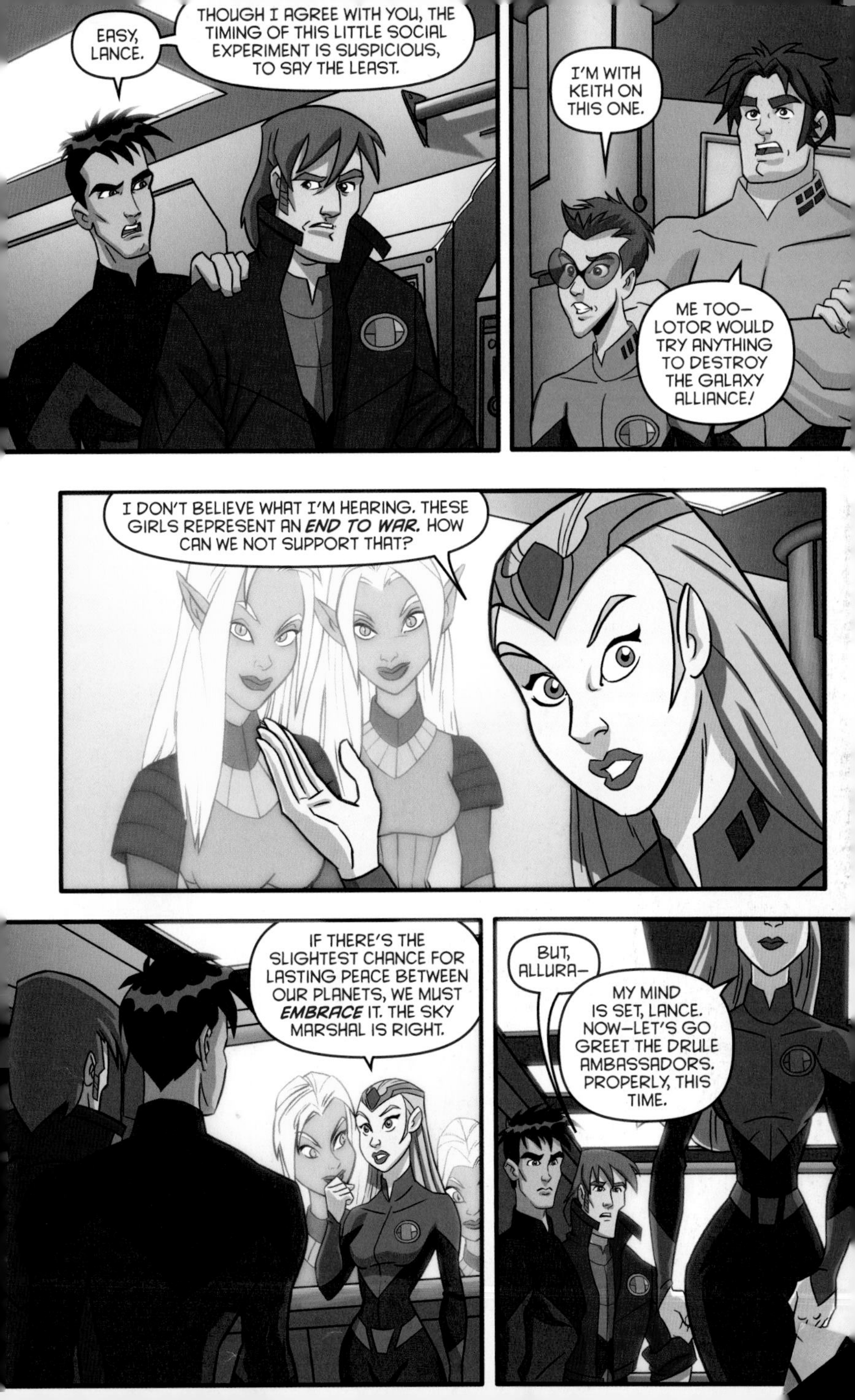
EASY, LANCE.
THOUGH I AGREE WITH YOU, THE TIMING OF THIS LITTLE SOCIAL EXPERIMENT IS SUSPICIOUS, TO SAY THE LEAST.
I'M WITH KEITH ON THIS ONE.
ME TOO— LOTOR WOULD TRY ANYTHING TO DESTROY THE GALAXY ALLIANCE!
I DON'T BELIEVE WHAT I'M HEARING. THESE GIRLS REPRESENT AN *END TO WAR.* HOW CAN WE NOT SUPPORT THAT?
IF THERE'S THE SLIGHTEST CHANCE FOR LASTING PEACE BETWEEN OUR PLANETS, WE MUST *EMBRACE* IT. THE SKY MARSHAL IS RIGHT.
BUT, ALLURA—
MY MIND IS SET, LANCE. NOW—LET'S GO GREET THE DRULE AMBASSADORS. PROPERLY, THIS TIME.

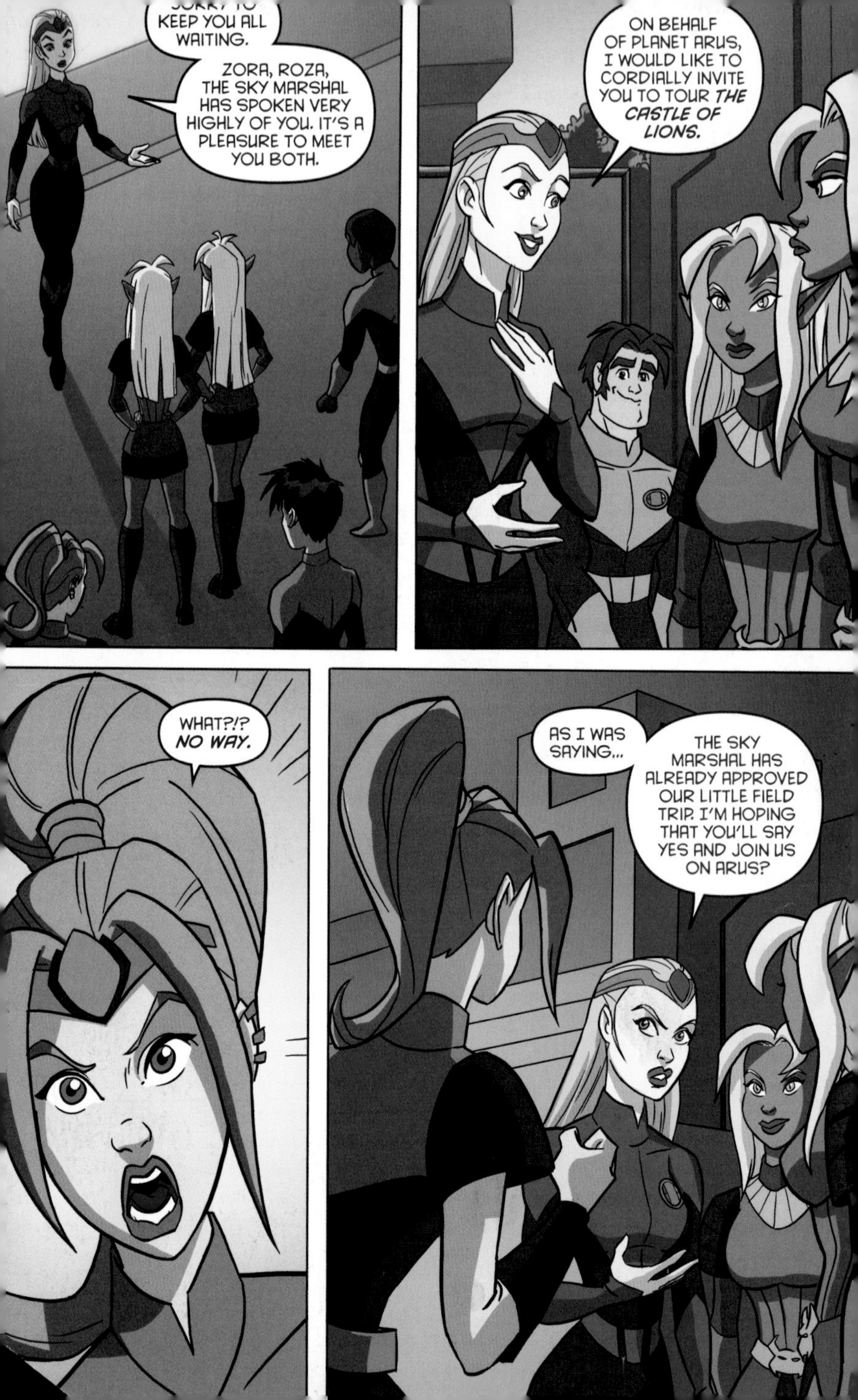
SORRY TO KEEP YOU ALL WAITING.
ZORA, ROZA, THE SKY MARSHAL HAS SPOKEN VERY HIGHLY OF YOU. IT'S A PLEASURE TO MEET YOU BOTH.
ON BEHALF OF PLANET ARUS, I WOULD LIKE TO CORDIALLY INVITE YOU TO TOUR *THE CASTLE OF LIONS.*
WHAT?!? *NO WAY.*
AS I WAS SAYING...
THE SKY MARSHAL HAS ALREADY APPROVED OUR LITTLE FIELD TRIP. I'M HOPING THAT YOU'LL SAY YES AND JOIN US ON ARUS?

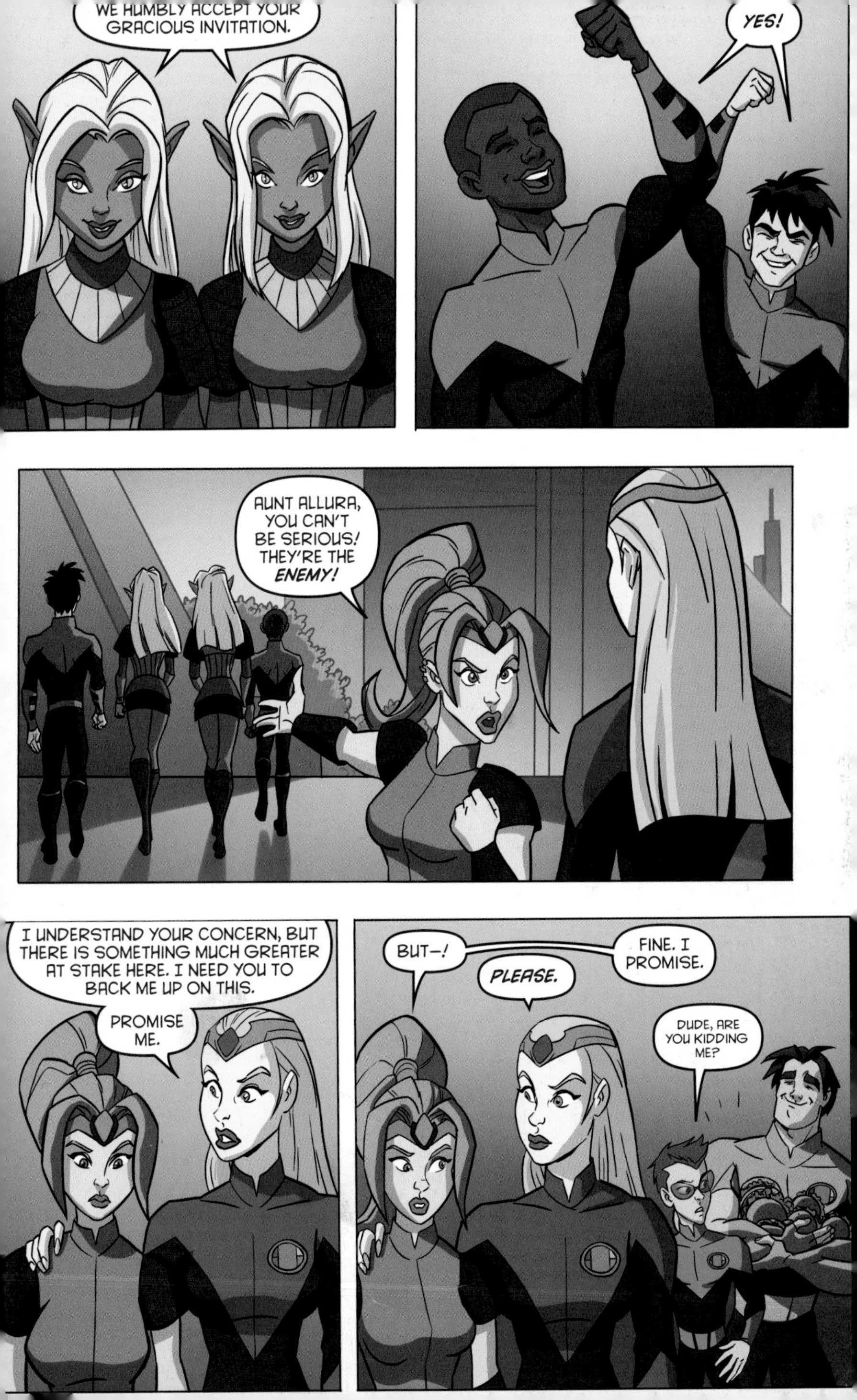
WE HUMBLY ACCEPT YOUR GRACIOUS INVITATION.
YES!
AUNT ALLURA, YOU CAN'T BE SERIOUS! THEY'RE THE ENEMY!
I UNDERSTAND YOUR CONCERN, BUT THERE IS SOMETHING MUCH GREATER AT STAKE HERE. I NEED YOU TO BACK ME UP ON THIS.
PROMISE ME.
BUT–!
PLEASE.
FINE. I PROMISE.
DUDE, ARE YOU KIDDING ME?

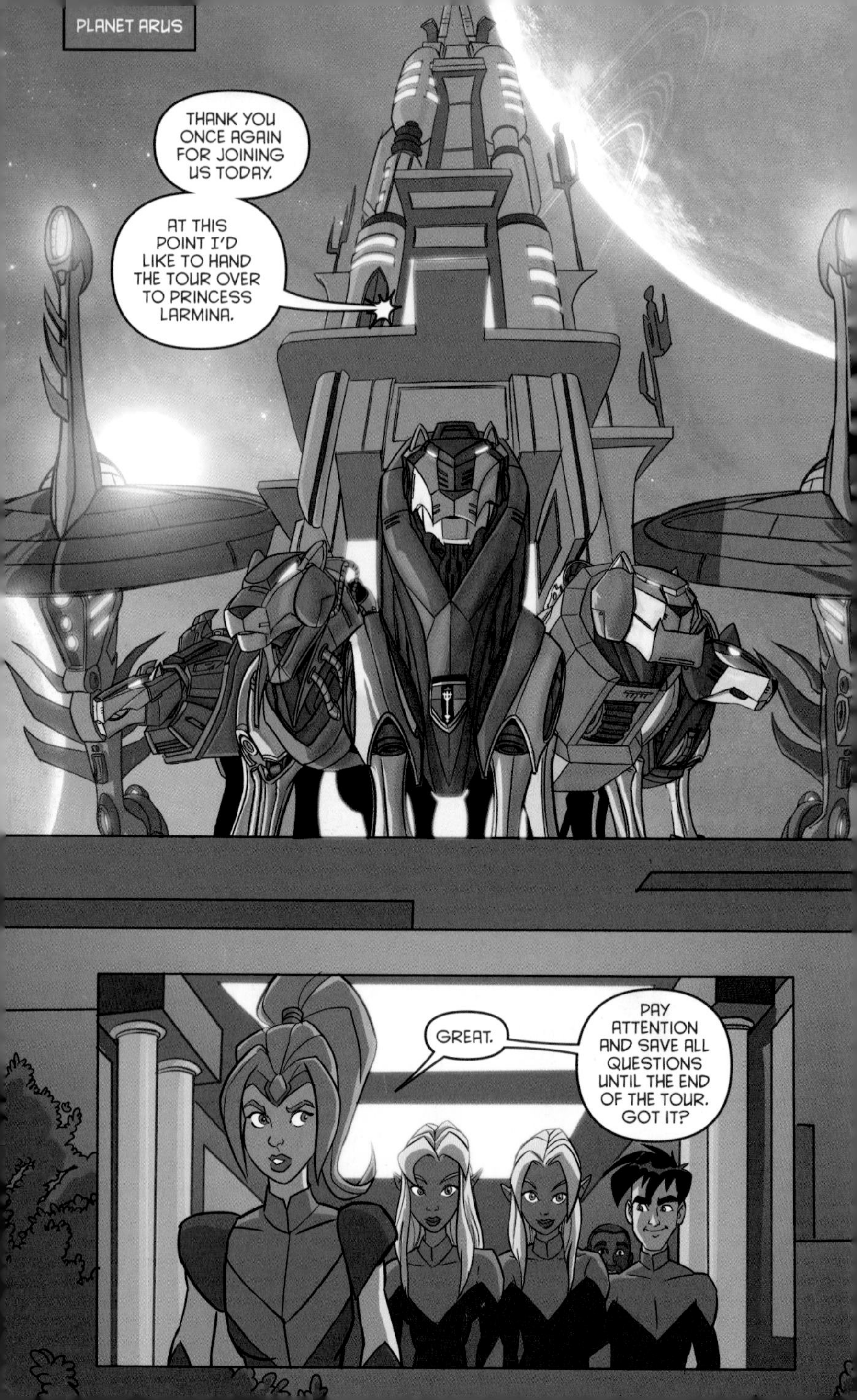
PLANET ARUS
THANK YOU ONCE AGAIN FOR JOINING US TODAY.
AT THIS POINT I'D LIKE TO HAND THE TOUR OVER TO PRINCESS LARMINA.
GREAT.
PAY ATTENTION AND SAVE ALL QUESTIONS UNTIL THE END OF THE TOUR. GOT IT?

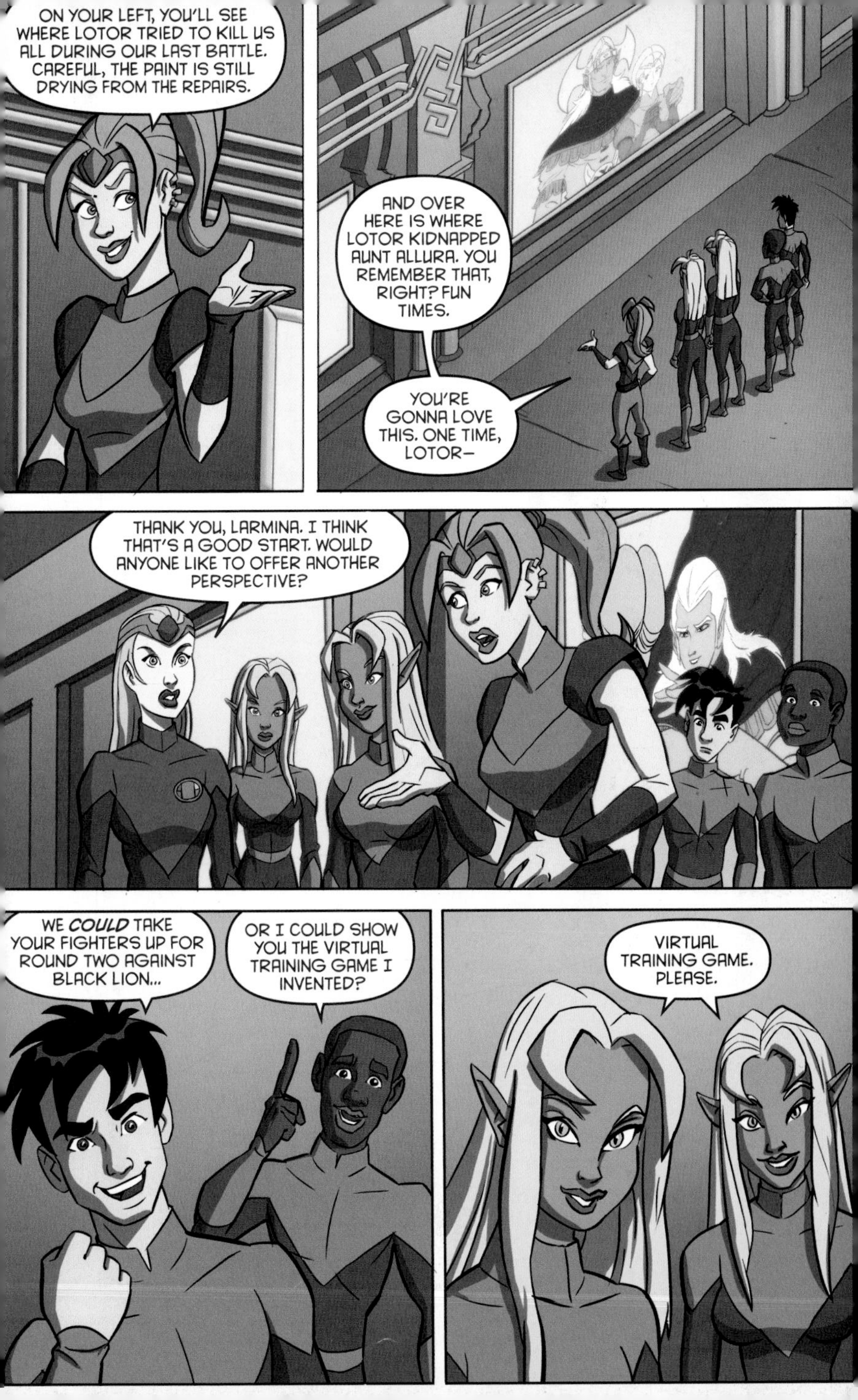
ON YOUR LEFT, YOU'LL SEE WHERE LOTOR TRIED TO KILL US ALL DURING OUR LAST BATTLE. CAREFUL, THE PAINT IS STILL DRYING FROM THE REPAIRS.
AND OVER HERE IS WHERE LOTOR KIDNAPPED AUNT ALLURA. YOU REMEMBER THAT, RIGHT? FUN TIMES.
YOU'RE GONNA LOVE THIS. ONE TIME, LOTOR—
THANK YOU, LARMINA. I THINK THAT'S A GOOD START. WOULD ANYONE LIKE TO OFFER ANOTHER PERSPECTIVE?
WE *COULD* TAKE YOUR FIGHTERS UP FOR ROUND TWO AGAINST BLACK LION...
OR I COULD SHOW YOU THE VIRTUAL TRAINING GAME I INVENTED?
VIRTUAL TRAINING GAME. PLEASE.

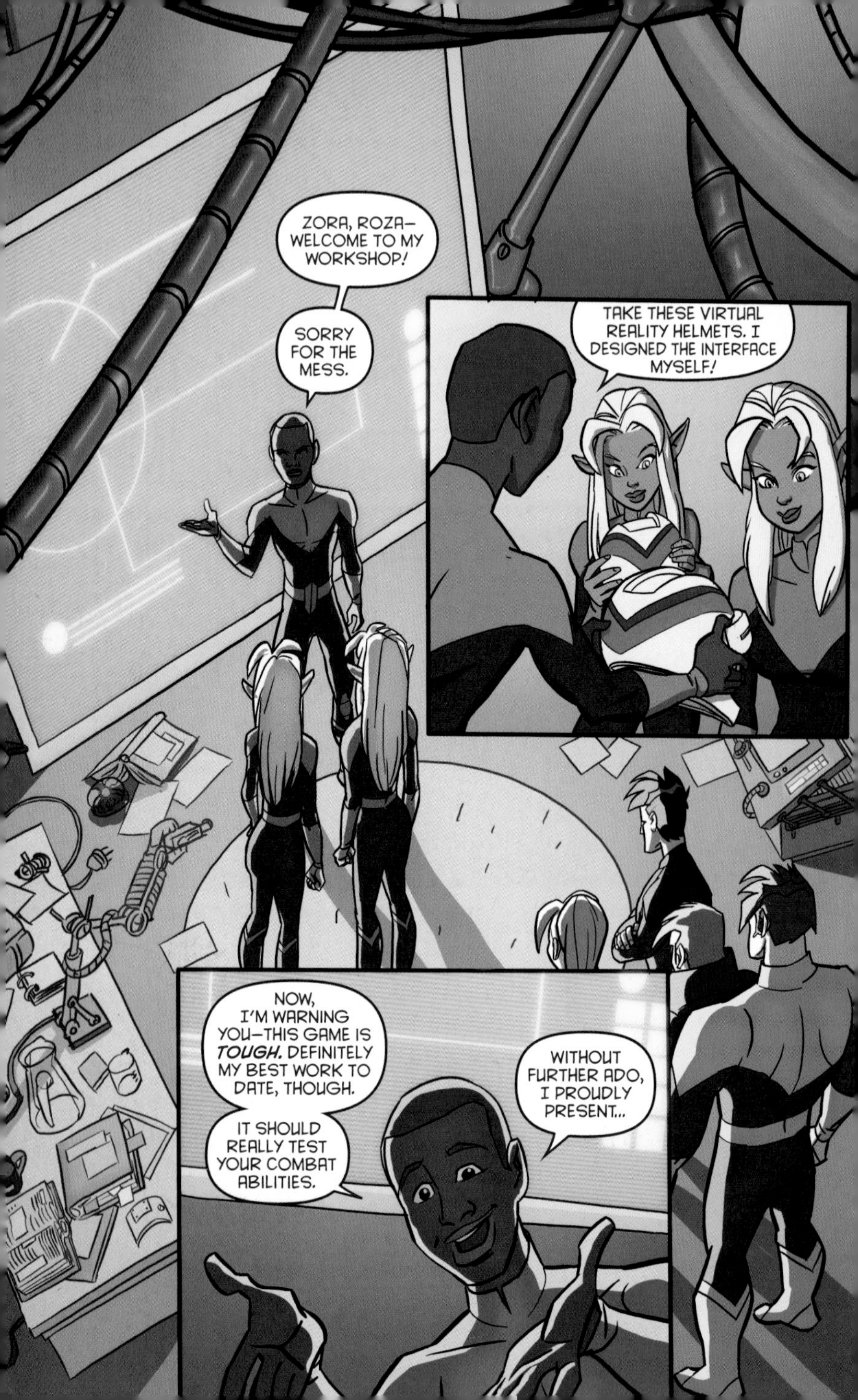
ZORA, ROZA—WELCOME TO MY WORKSHOP!
SORRY FOR THE MESS.
TAKE THESE VIRTUAL REALITY HELMETS. I DESIGNED THE INTERFACE MYSELF!
NOW, I'M WARNING YOU—THIS GAME IS *TOUGH.* DEFINITELY MY BEST WORK TO DATE, THOUGH.
IT SHOULD REALLY TEST YOUR COMBAT ABILITIES.
WITHOUT FURTHER ADO, I PROUDLY PRESENT...

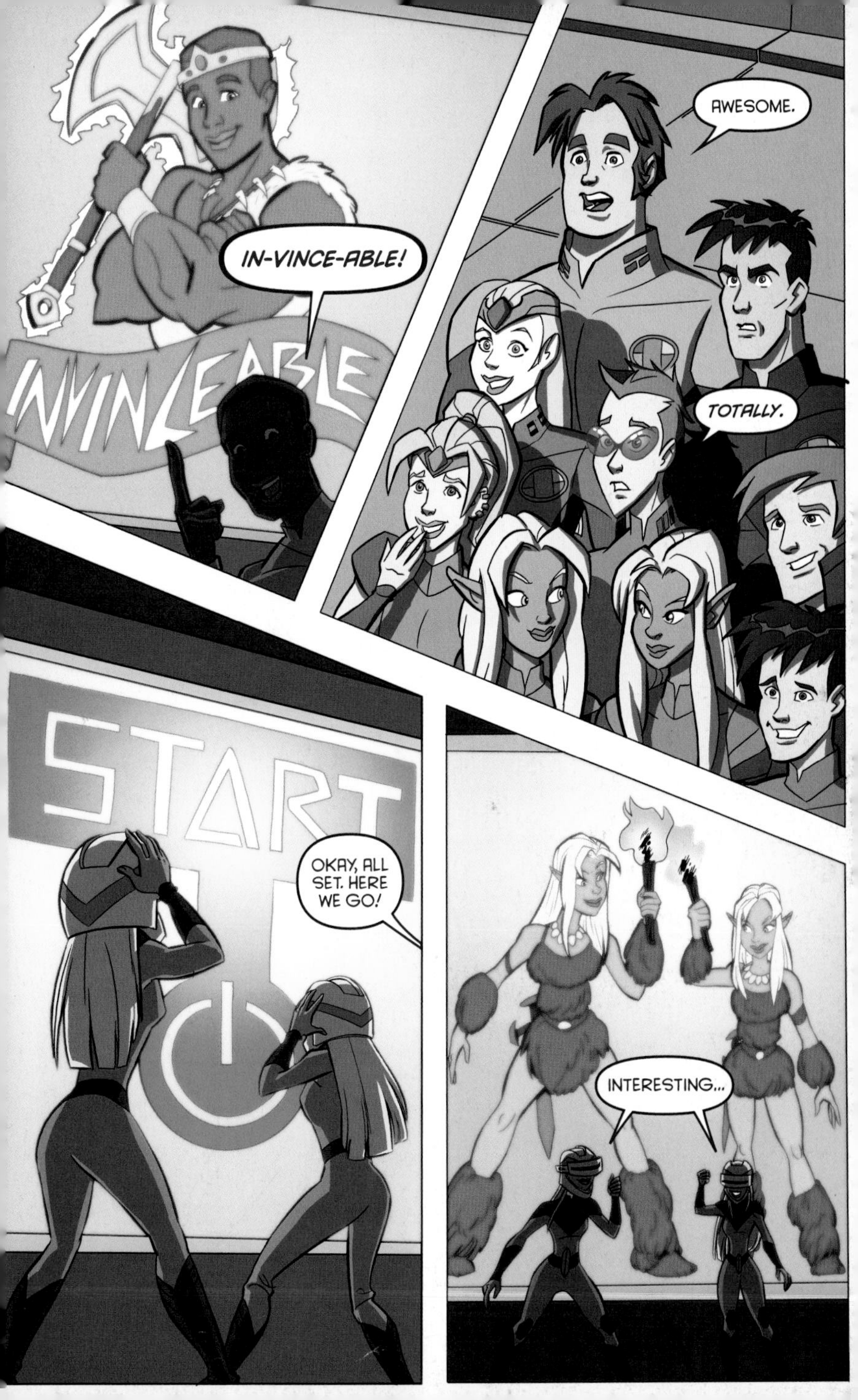
INVINCEABLE
IN-VINCE-ABLE!
AWESOME.
TOTALLY.
START
OKAY, ALL SET. HERE WE GO!
INTERESTING...

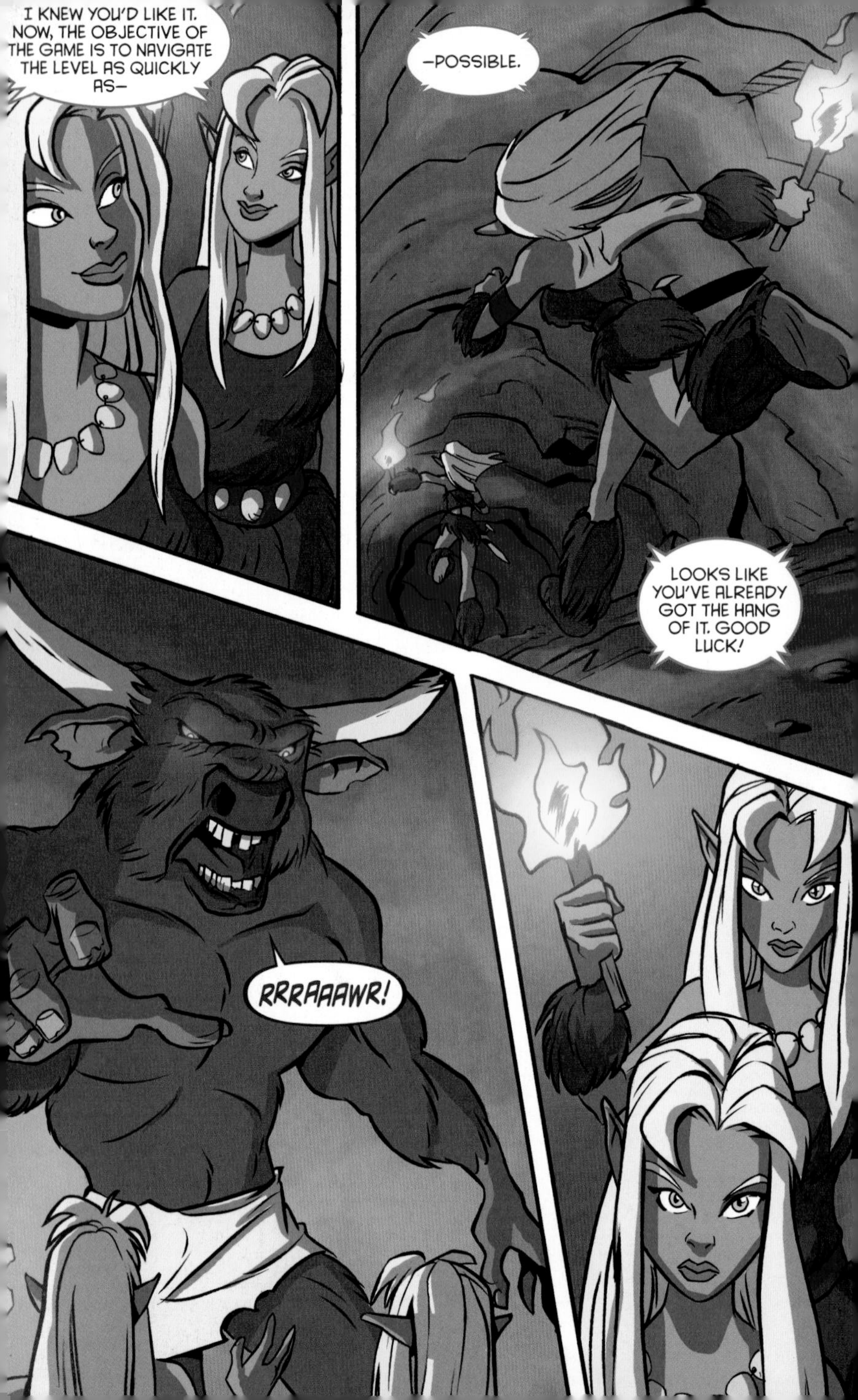
I KNEW YOU'D LIKE IT. NOW, THE OBJECTIVE OF THE GAME IS TO NAVIGATE THE LEVEL AS QUICKLY AS—
—POSSIBLE.
LOOKS LIKE YOU'VE ALREADY GOT THE HANG OF IT. GOOD LUCK!
RRRAAAWR!

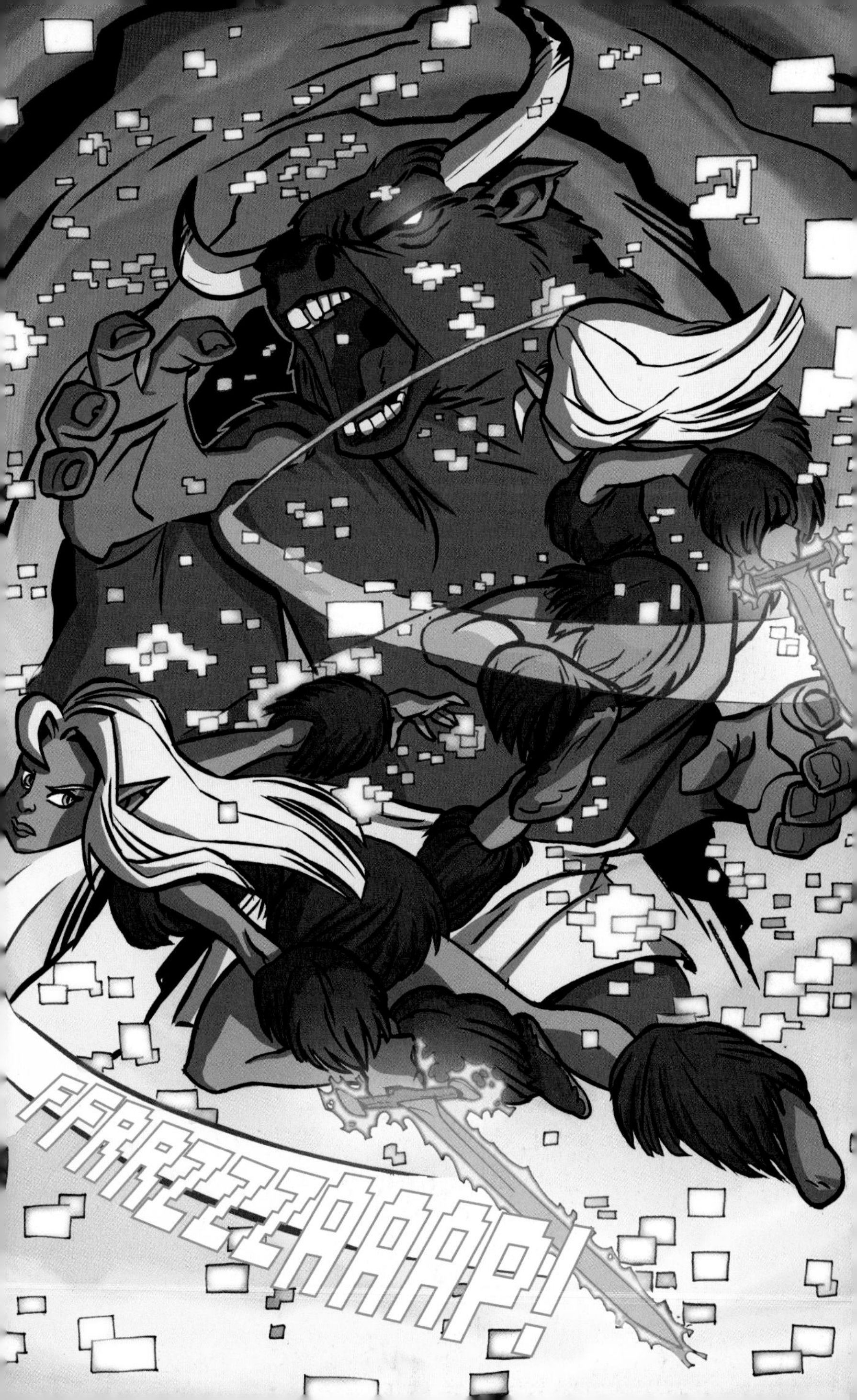
FFRRZZZZAAAAP!

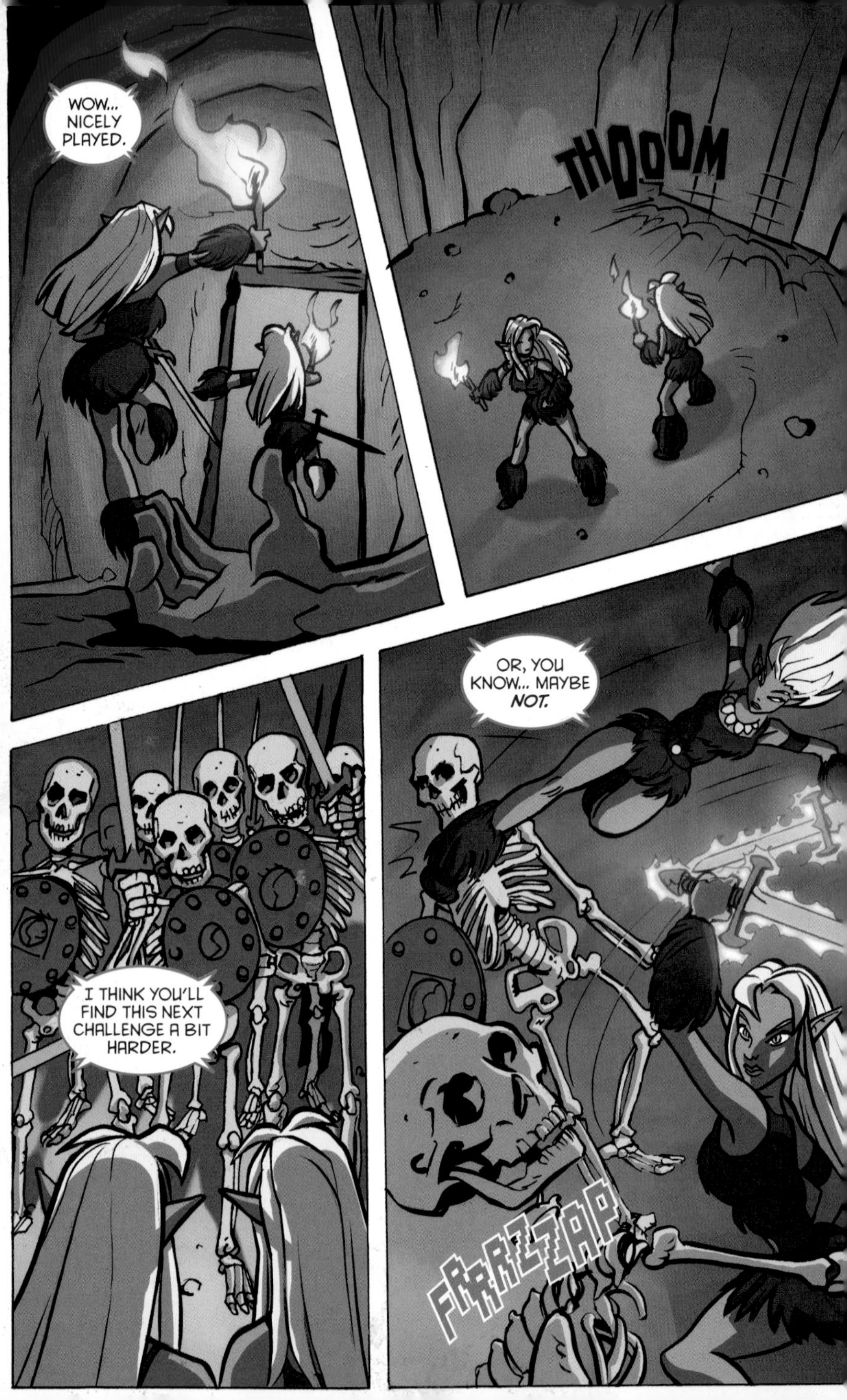
WOW... NICELY PLAYED.
THOOOM
I THINK YOU'LL FIND THIS NEXT CHALLENGE A BIT HARDER.
OR, YOU KNOW... MAYBE *NOT.*
FRRRZZAP

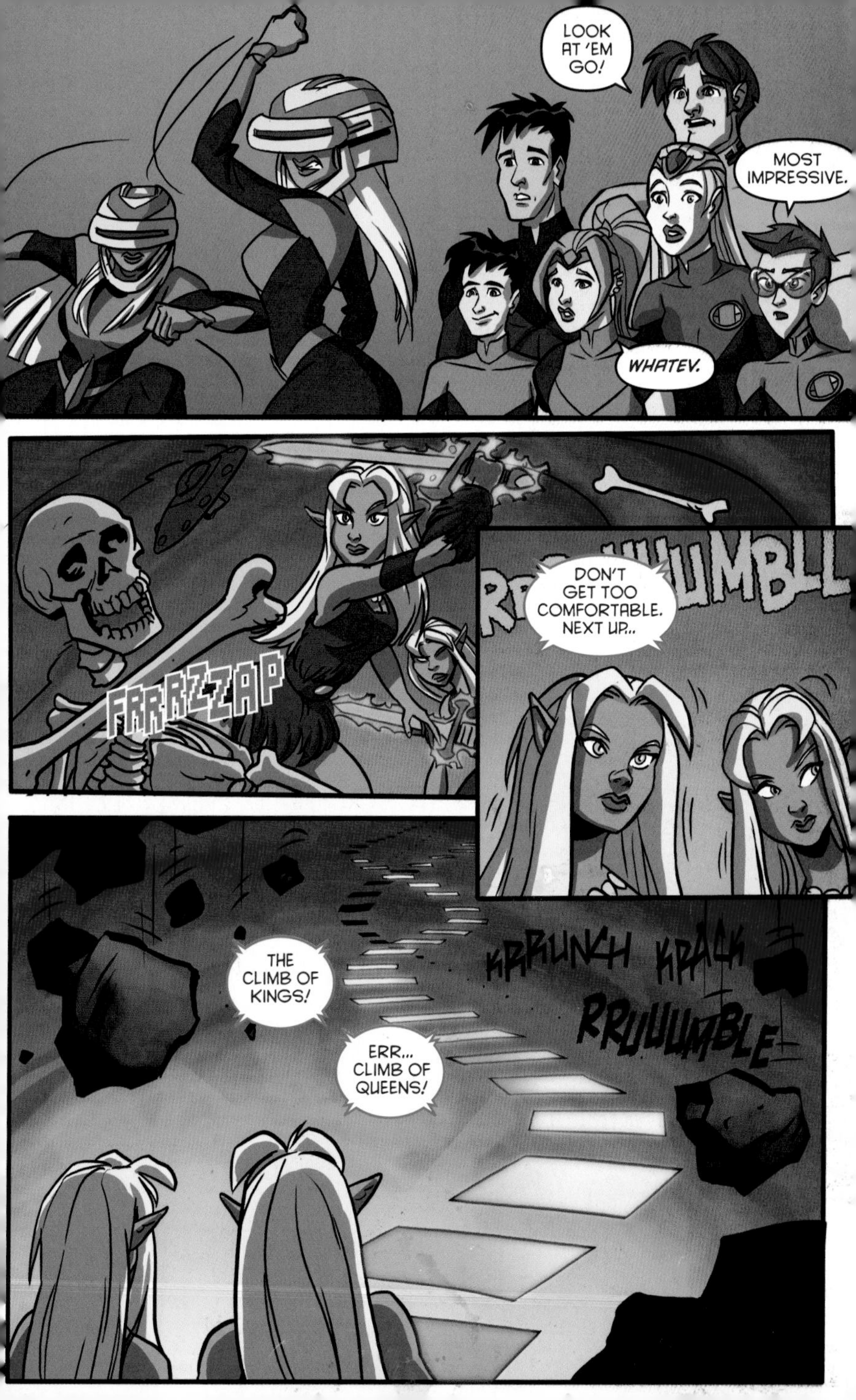
LOOK AT 'EM GO!
MOST IMPRESSIVE.
WHATEV.
FRRRZZAP
DON'T GET TOO COMFORTABLE. NEXT UP...
THE CLIMB OF KINGS!
ERR... CLIMB OF QUEENS!
KRRUNCH KRACK
RRUUUMBLE

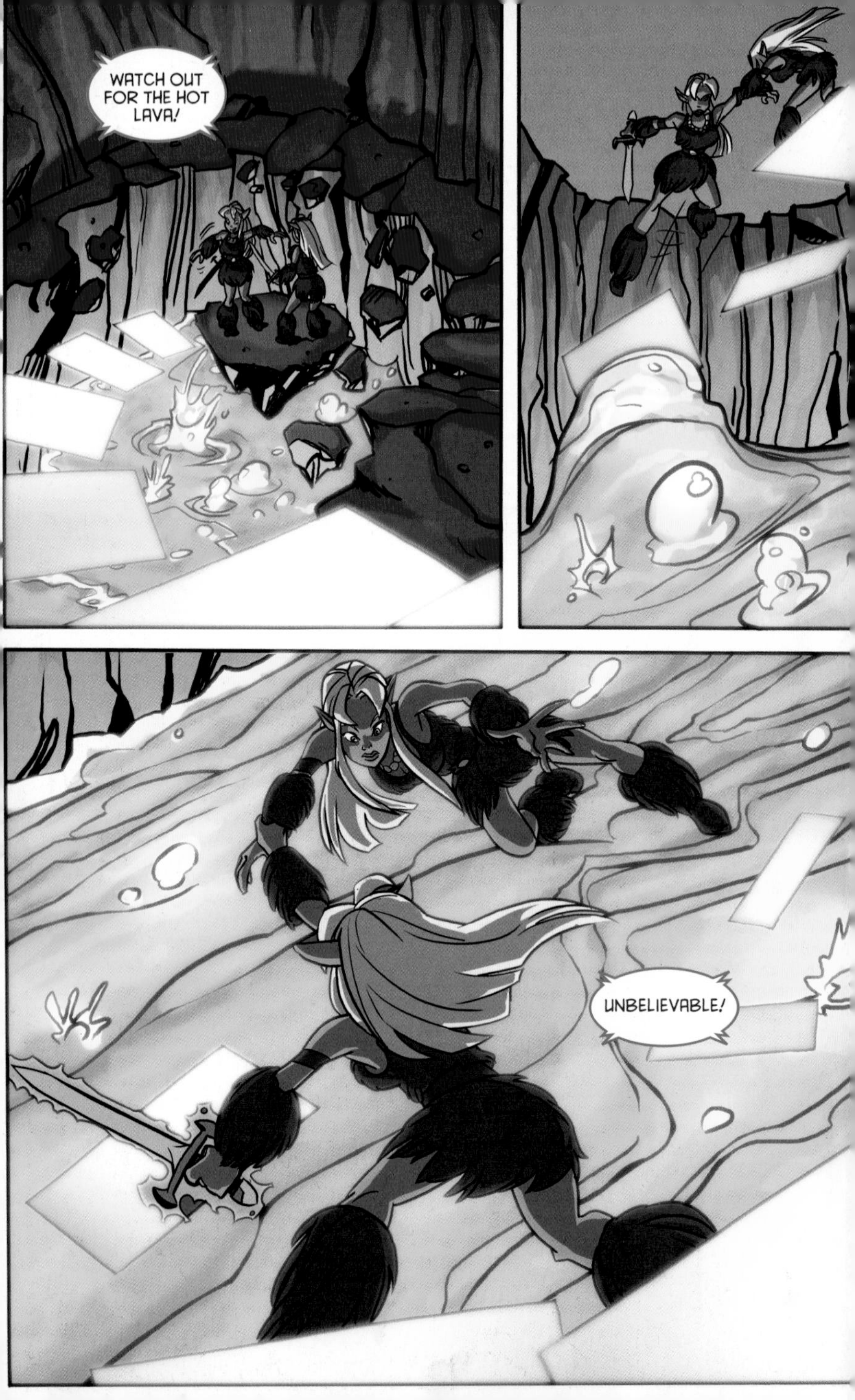
WATCH OUT FOR THE HOT LAVA!
UNBELIEVABLE!

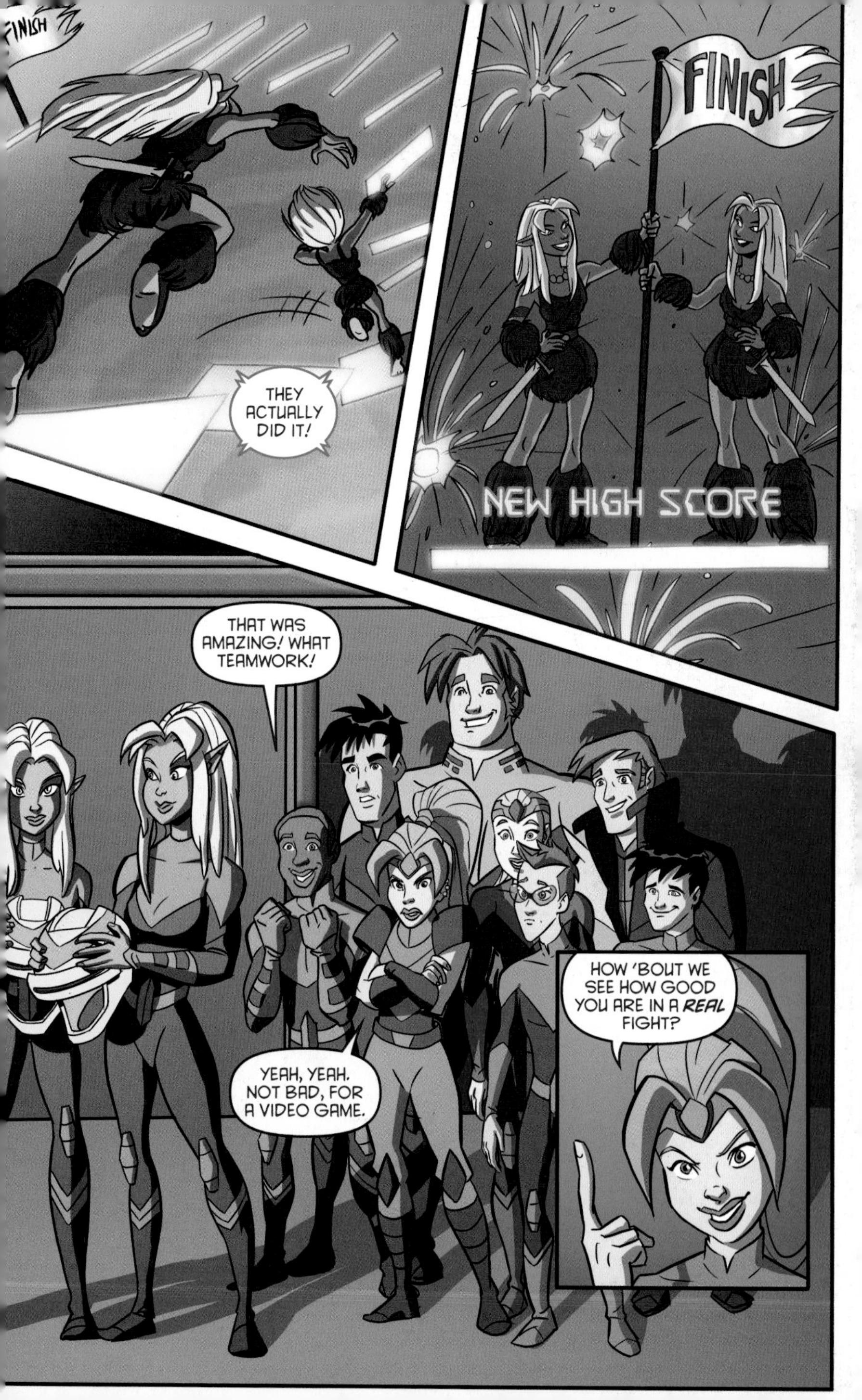
FINISH
THEY ACTUALLY DID IT!
FINISH
NEW HIGH SCORE
THAT WAS AMAZING! WHAT TEAMWORK!
YEAH, YEAH. NOT BAD, FOR A VIDEO GAME.
HOW 'BOUT WE SEE HOW GOOD YOU ARE IN A *REAL* FIGHT?

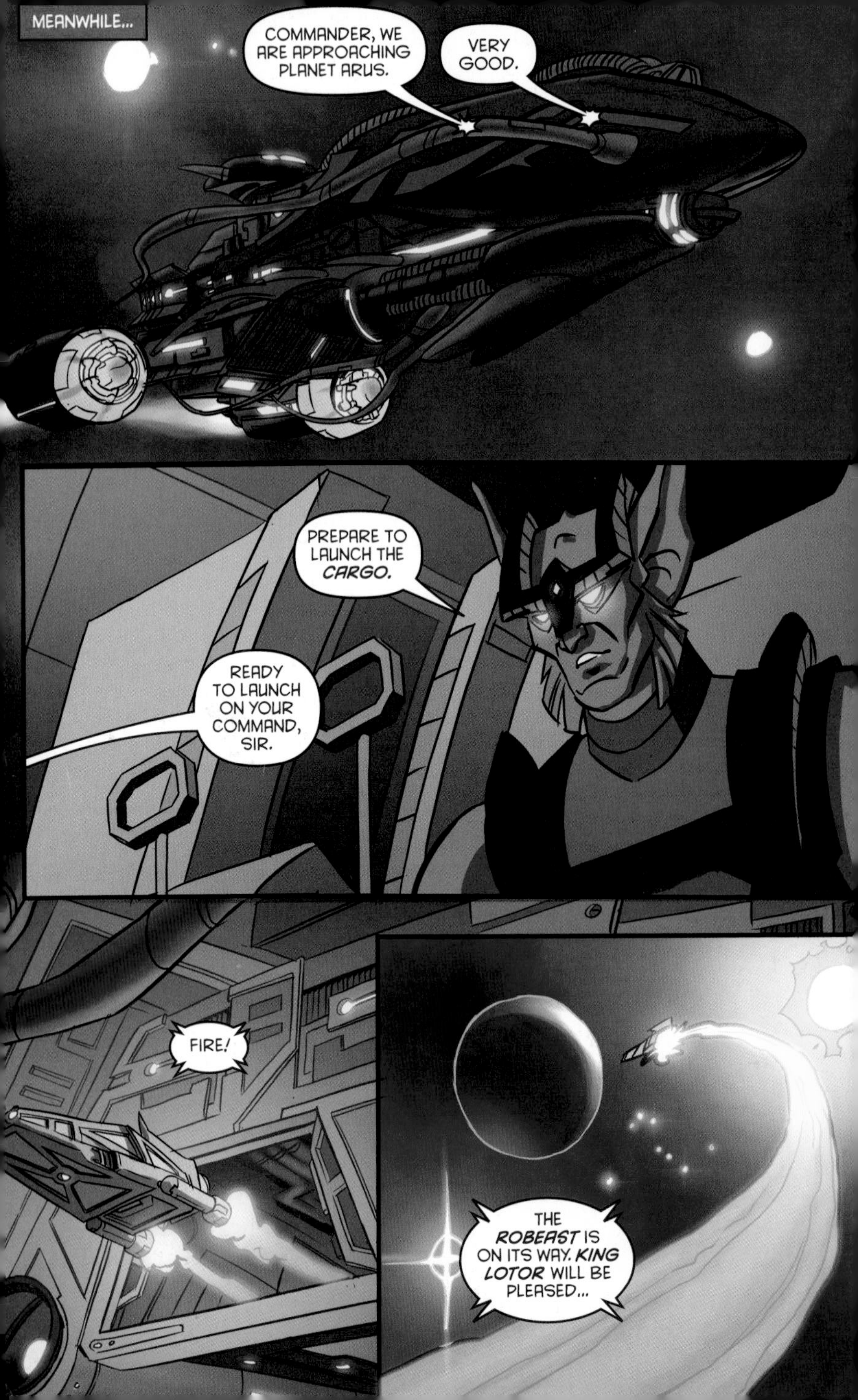
MEANWHILE...
COMMANDER, WE ARE APPROACHING PLANET ARUS.
VERY GOOD.
PREPARE TO LAUNCH THE *CARGO.*
READY TO LAUNCH ON YOUR COMMAND, SIR.
FIRE!
THE ***ROBEAST*** IS ON ITS WAY. ***KING LOTOR*** WILL BE PLEASED...

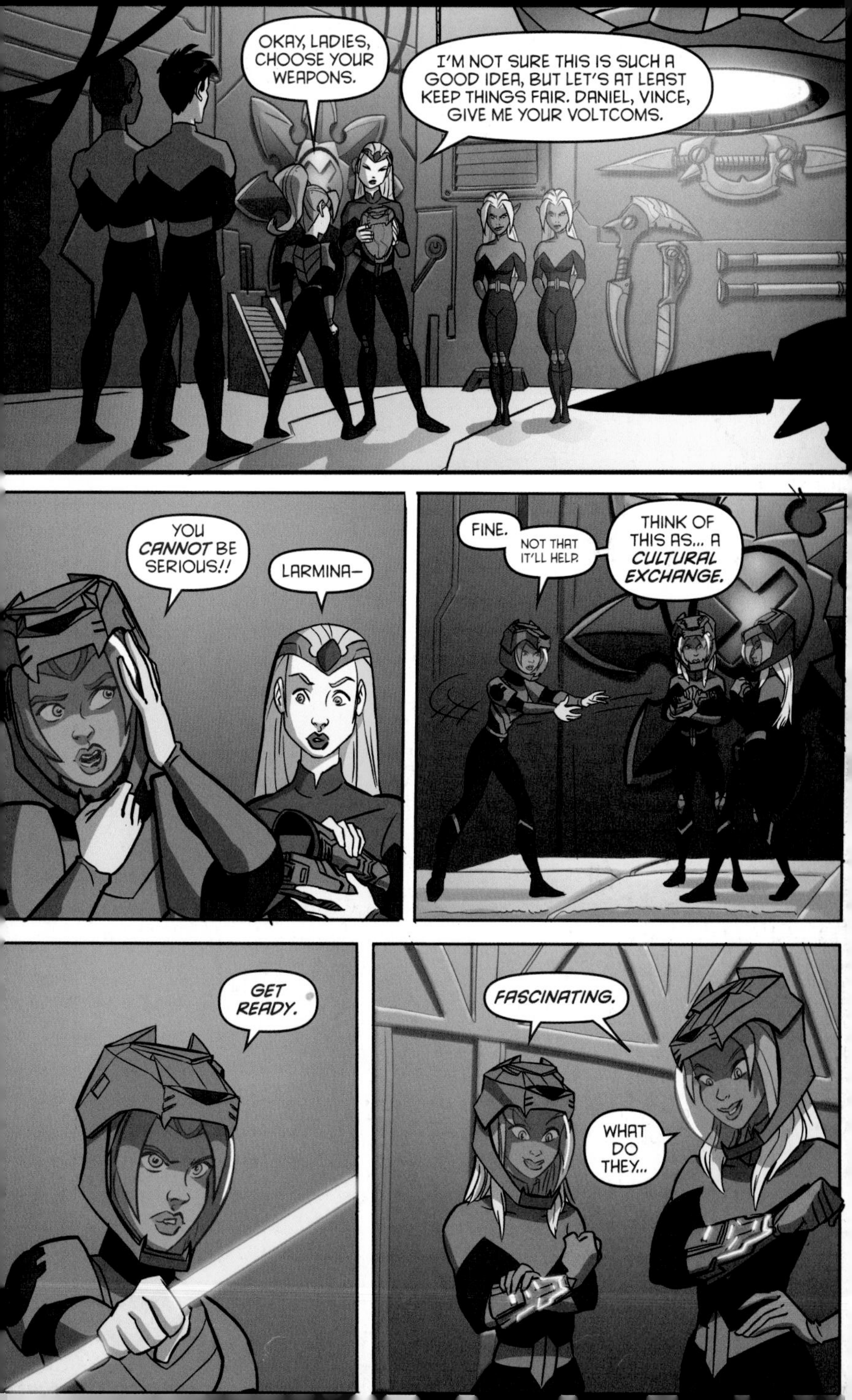
OKAY, LADIES, CHOOSE YOUR WEAPONS.
I'M NOT SURE THIS IS SUCH A GOOD IDEA, BUT LET'S AT LEAST KEEP THINGS FAIR. DANIEL, VINCE, GIVE ME YOUR VOLTCOMS.
YOU *CANNOT* BE SERIOUS!!
LARMINA—
FINE.
NOT THAT IT'LL HELP.
THINK OF THIS AS... A *CULTURAL EXCHANGE.*
GET READY.
FASCINATING.
WHAT DO THEY...

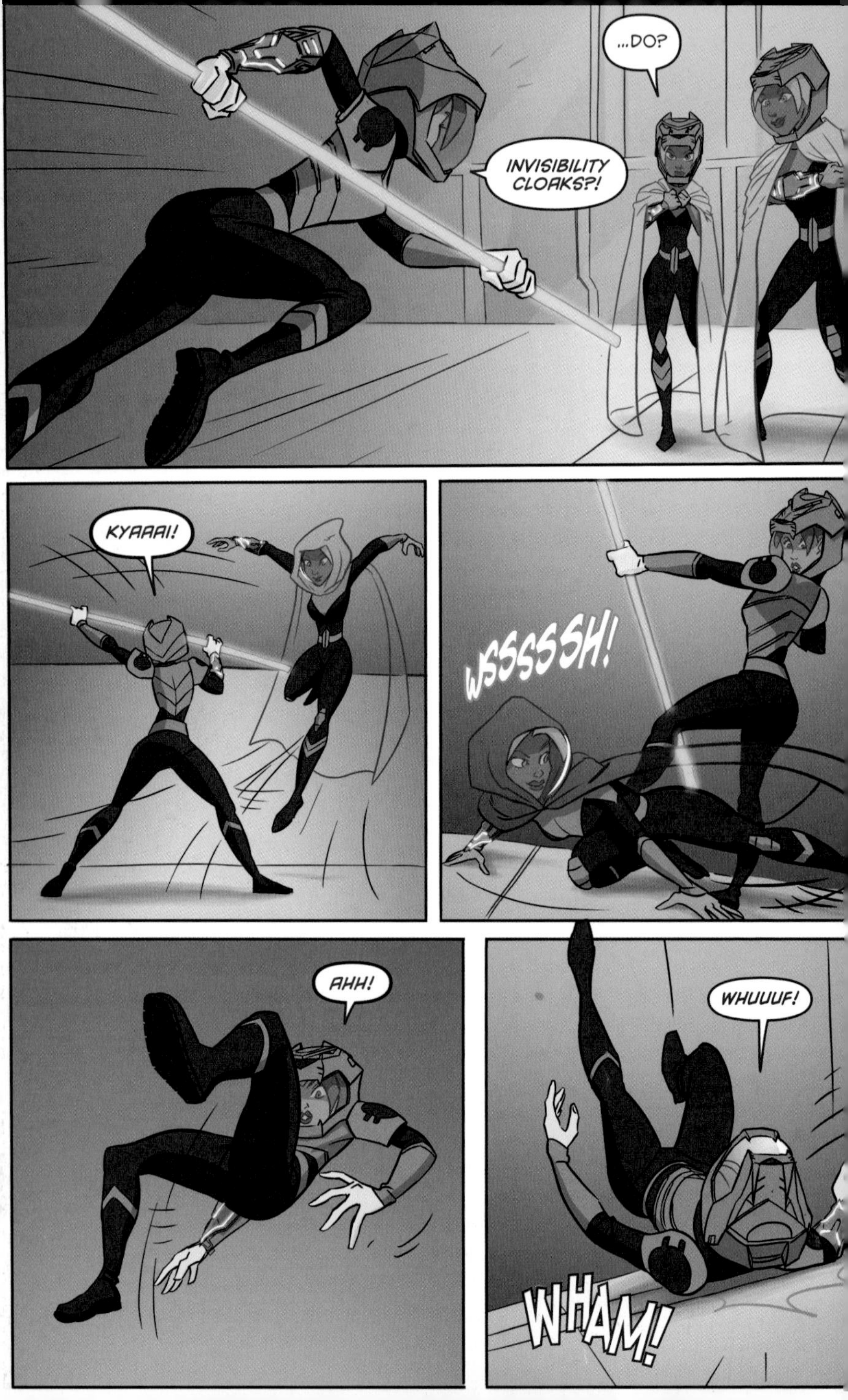
INVISIBILITY CLOAKS?!
...DO?
KYAAAI!
WSSSSSH!
AHH!
WHUUUF!
WHAM!

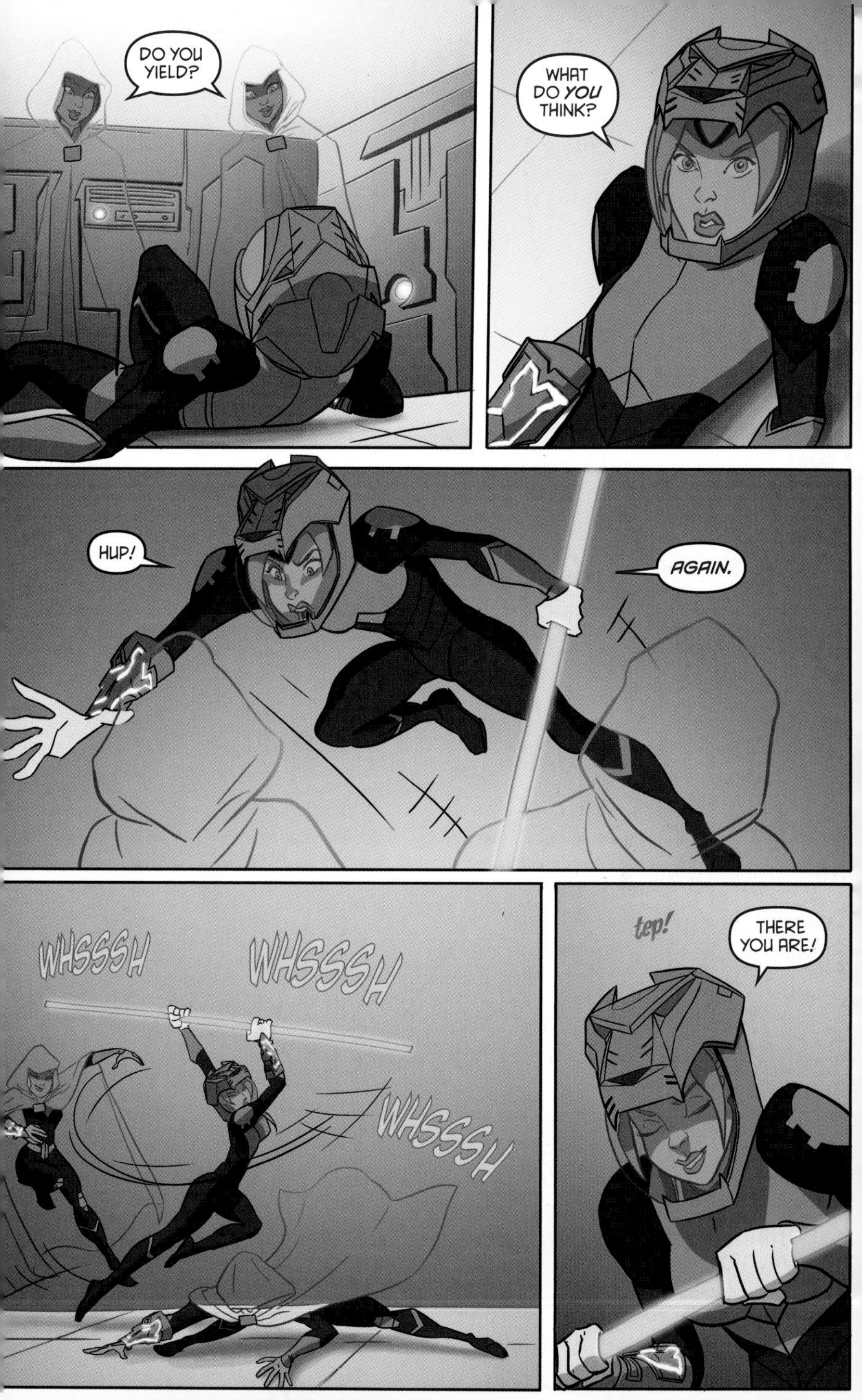
DO YOU YIELD?
WHAT DO *YOU* THINK?
HUP!
AGAIN.
WHSSSH
WHSSSH
WHSSSH
tep!
THERE YOU ARE!

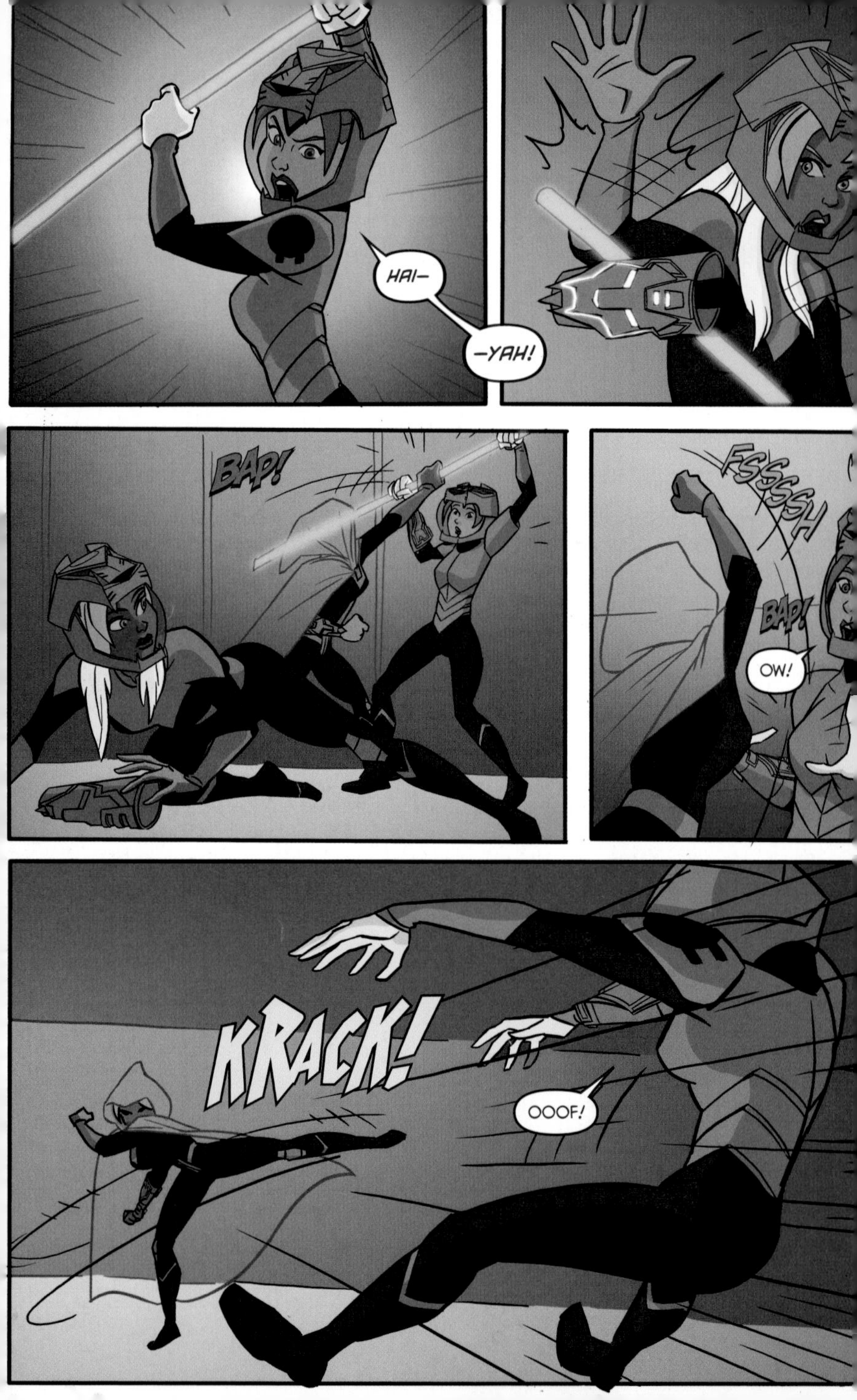
HAI—
—YAH!
BAP!
FSSSSSH
BAP!
OW!
KRACK!
OOOF!

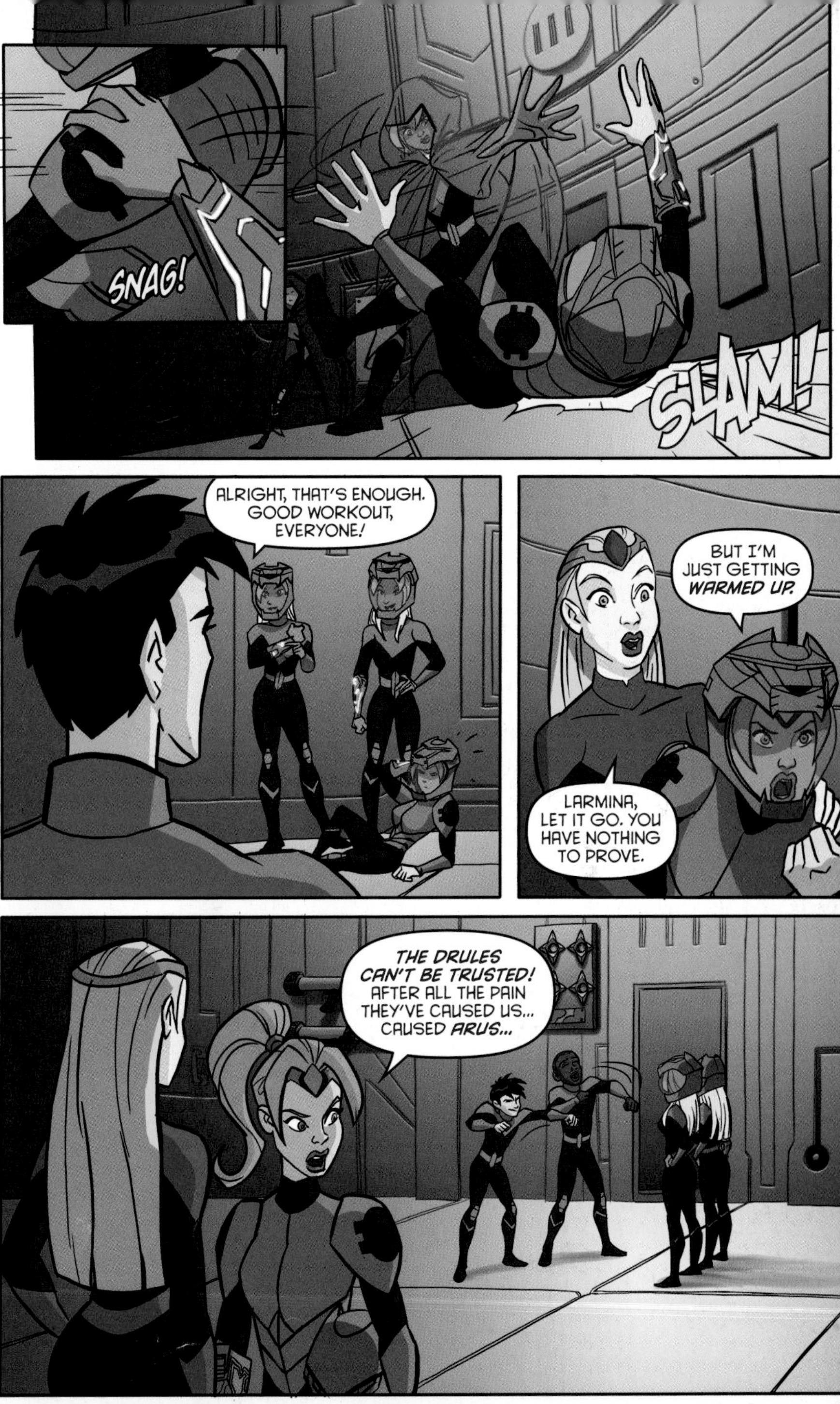
SNAG!
SLAM!
ALRIGHT, THAT'S ENOUGH. GOOD WORKOUT, EVERYONE!
BUT I'M JUST GETTING WARMED UP.
LARMINA, LET IT GO. YOU HAVE NOTHING TO PROVE.
THE DRULES CAN'T BE TRUSTED! AFTER ALL THE PAIN THEY'VE CAUSED US... CAUSED ARUS...

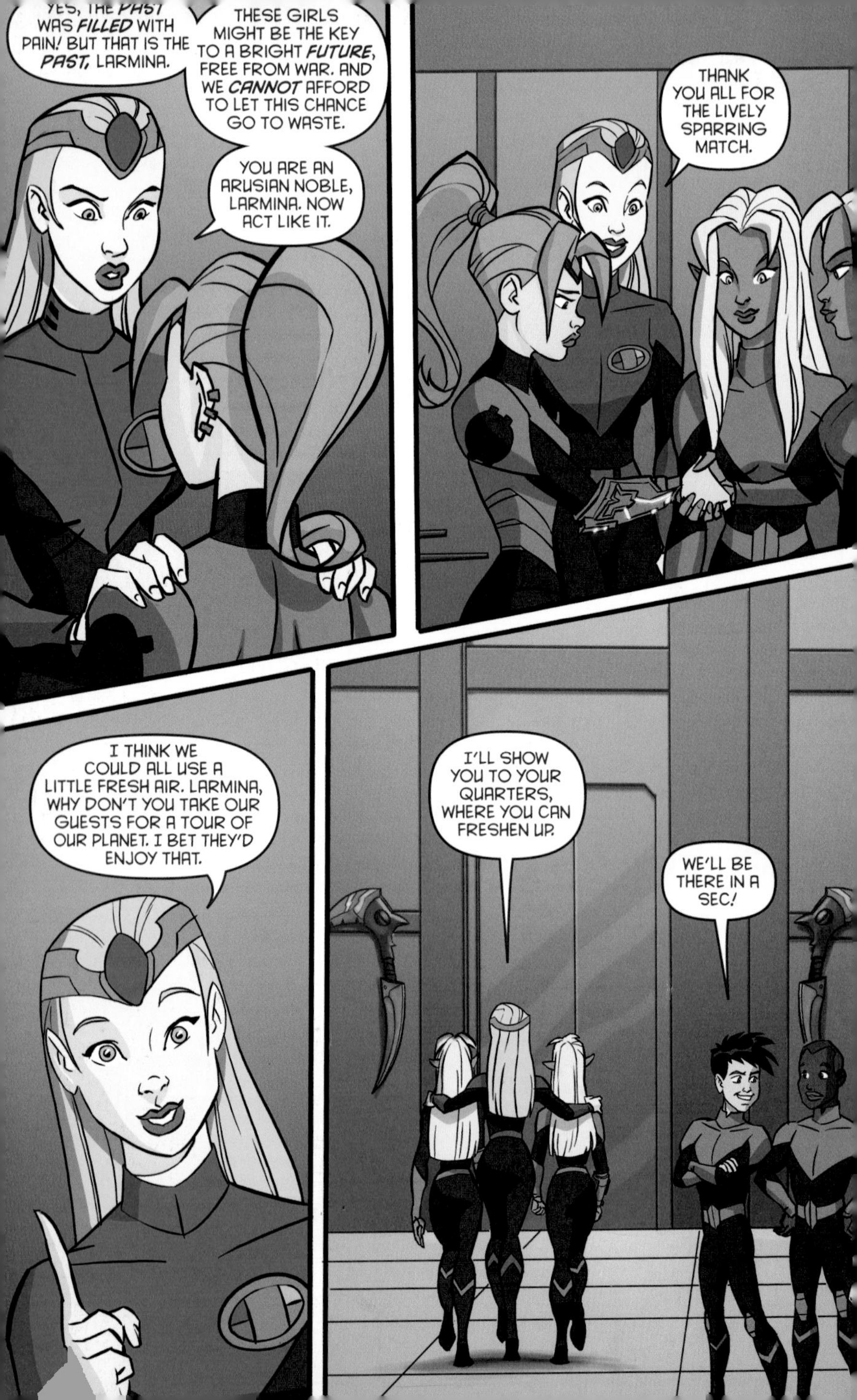
YES, THE PAST WAS FILLED WITH PAIN! BUT THAT IS THE PAST, LARMINA.
THESE GIRLS MIGHT BE THE KEY TO A BRIGHT FUTURE, FREE FROM WAR. AND WE CANNOT AFFORD TO LET THIS CHANCE GO TO WASTE.
YOU ARE AN ARUSIAN NOBLE, LARMINA. NOW ACT LIKE IT.
THANK YOU ALL FOR THE LIVELY SPARRING MATCH.
I THINK WE COULD ALL USE A LITTLE FRESH AIR. LARMINA, WHY DON'T YOU TAKE OUR GUESTS FOR A TOUR OF OUR PLANET. I BET THEY'D ENJOY THAT.
I'LL SHOW YOU TO YOUR QUARTERS, WHERE YOU CAN FRESHEN UP.
WE'LL BE THERE IN A SEC!

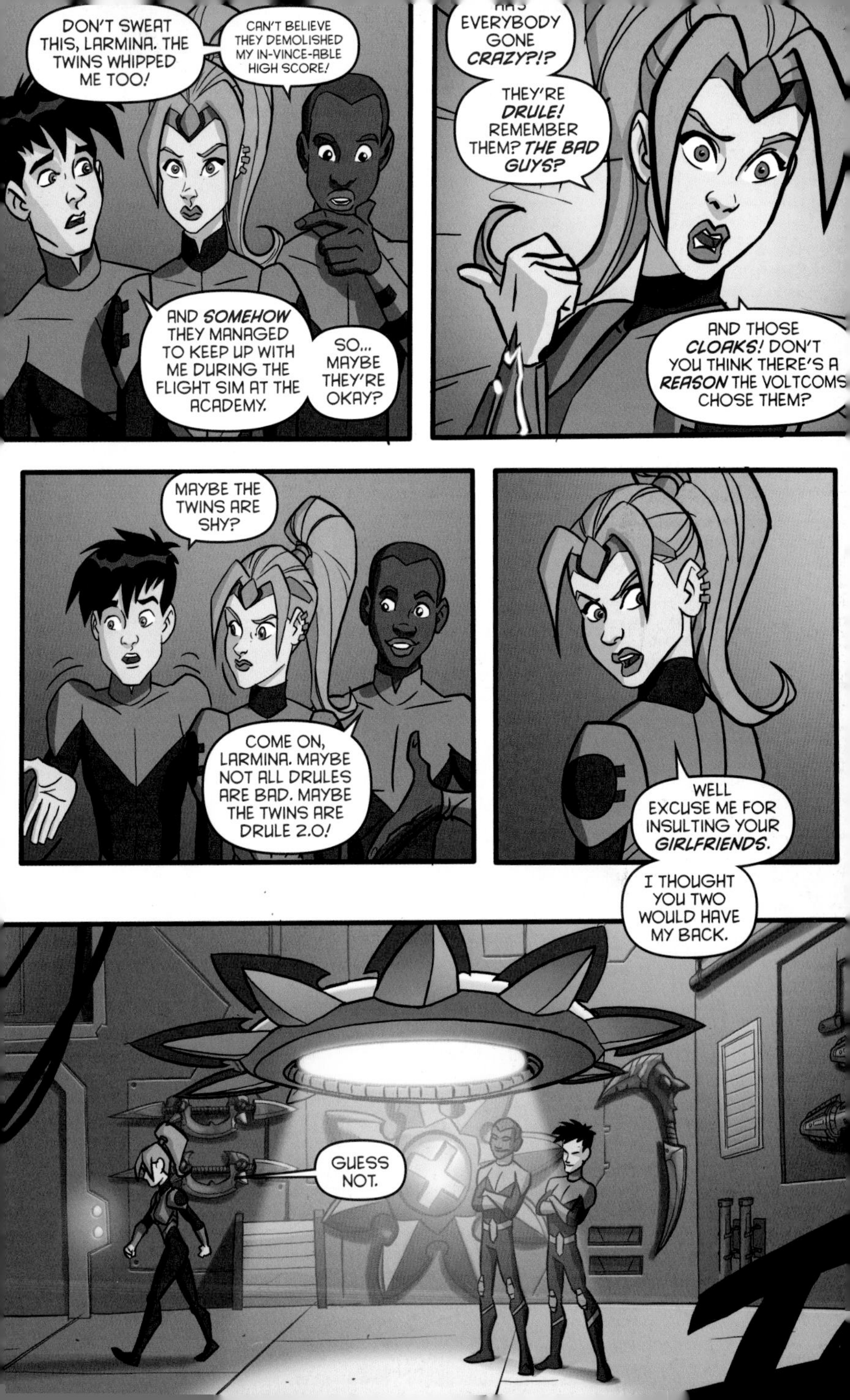
DON'T SWEAT THIS, LARMINA. THE TWINS WHIPPED ME TOO!
CAN'T BELIEVE THEY DEMOLISHED MY IN-VINCE-ABLE HIGH SCORE!
AND *SOMEHOW* THEY MANAGED TO KEEP UP WITH ME DURING THE FLIGHT SIM AT THE ACADEMY.
SO... MAYBE THEY'RE OKAY?
EVERYBODY GONE *CRAZY?!?*
THEY'RE *DRULE!* REMEMBER THEM? *THE BAD GUYS?*
AND THOSE *CLOAKS!* DON'T YOU THINK THERE'S A *REASON* THE VOLTCOMS CHOSE THEM?
MAYBE THE TWINS ARE SHY?
COME ON, LARMINA. MAYBE NOT ALL DRULES ARE BAD. MAYBE THE TWINS ARE DRULE 2.0!
WELL EXCUSE ME FOR INSULTING YOUR *GIRLFRIENDS*.
I THOUGHT YOU TWO WOULD HAVE MY BACK.
GUESS NOT.

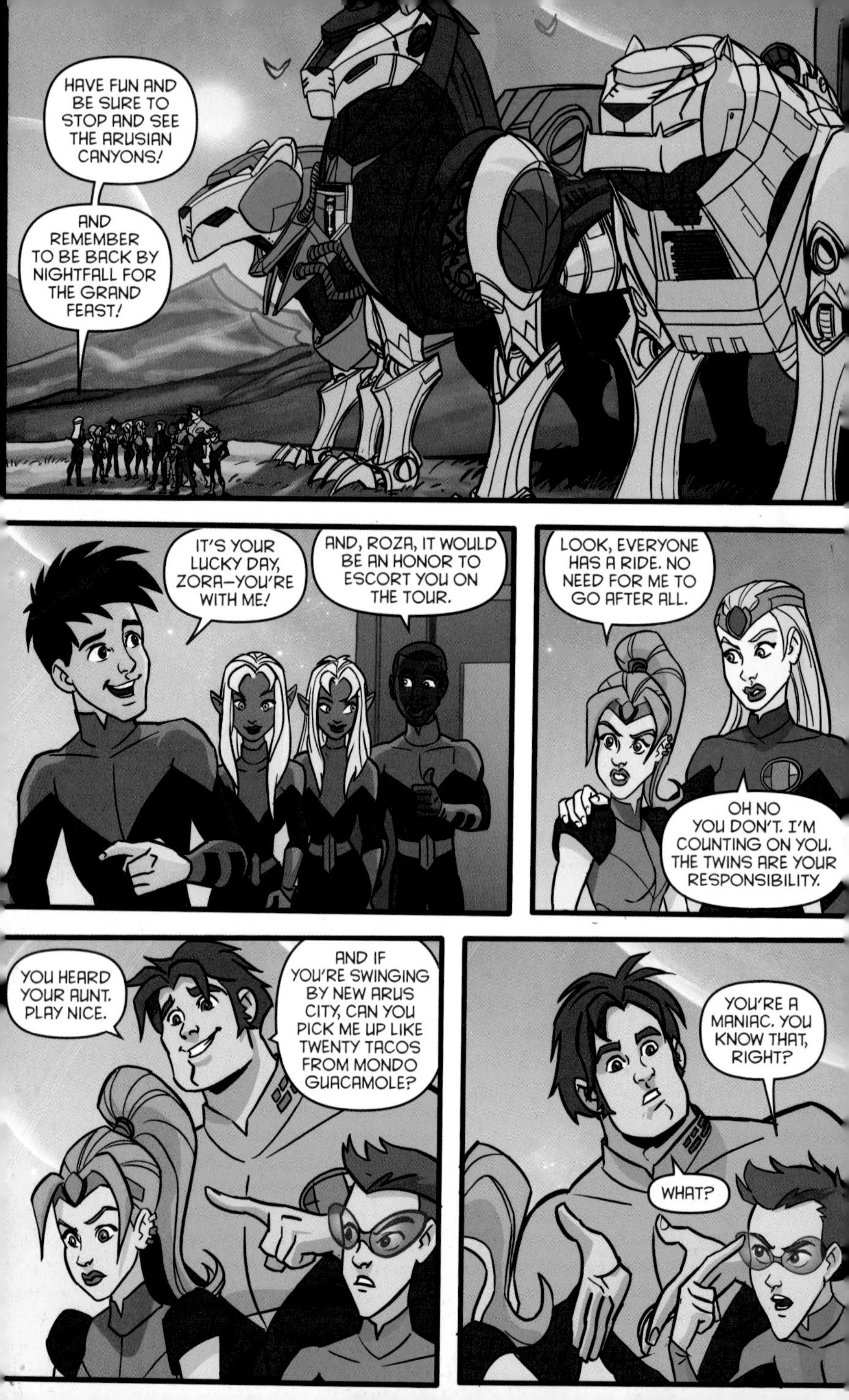
HAVE FUN AND BE SURE TO STOP AND SEE THE ARUSIAN CANYONS!
AND REMEMBER TO BE BACK BY NIGHTFALL FOR THE GRAND FEAST!
IT'S YOUR LUCKY DAY, ZORA—YOU'RE WITH ME!
AND, ROZA, IT WOULD BE AN HONOR TO ESCORT YOU ON THE TOUR.
LOOK, EVERYONE HAS A RIDE. NO NEED FOR ME TO GO AFTER ALL.
OH NO YOU DON'T. I'M COUNTING ON YOU. THE TWINS ARE YOUR RESPONSIBILITY.
YOU HEARD YOUR AUNT. PLAY NICE.
AND IF YOU'RE SWINGING BY NEW ARUS CITY, CAN YOU PICK ME UP LIKE TWENTY TACOS FROM MONDO GUACAMOLE?
YOU'RE A MANIAC. YOU KNOW THAT, RIGHT?
WHAT?

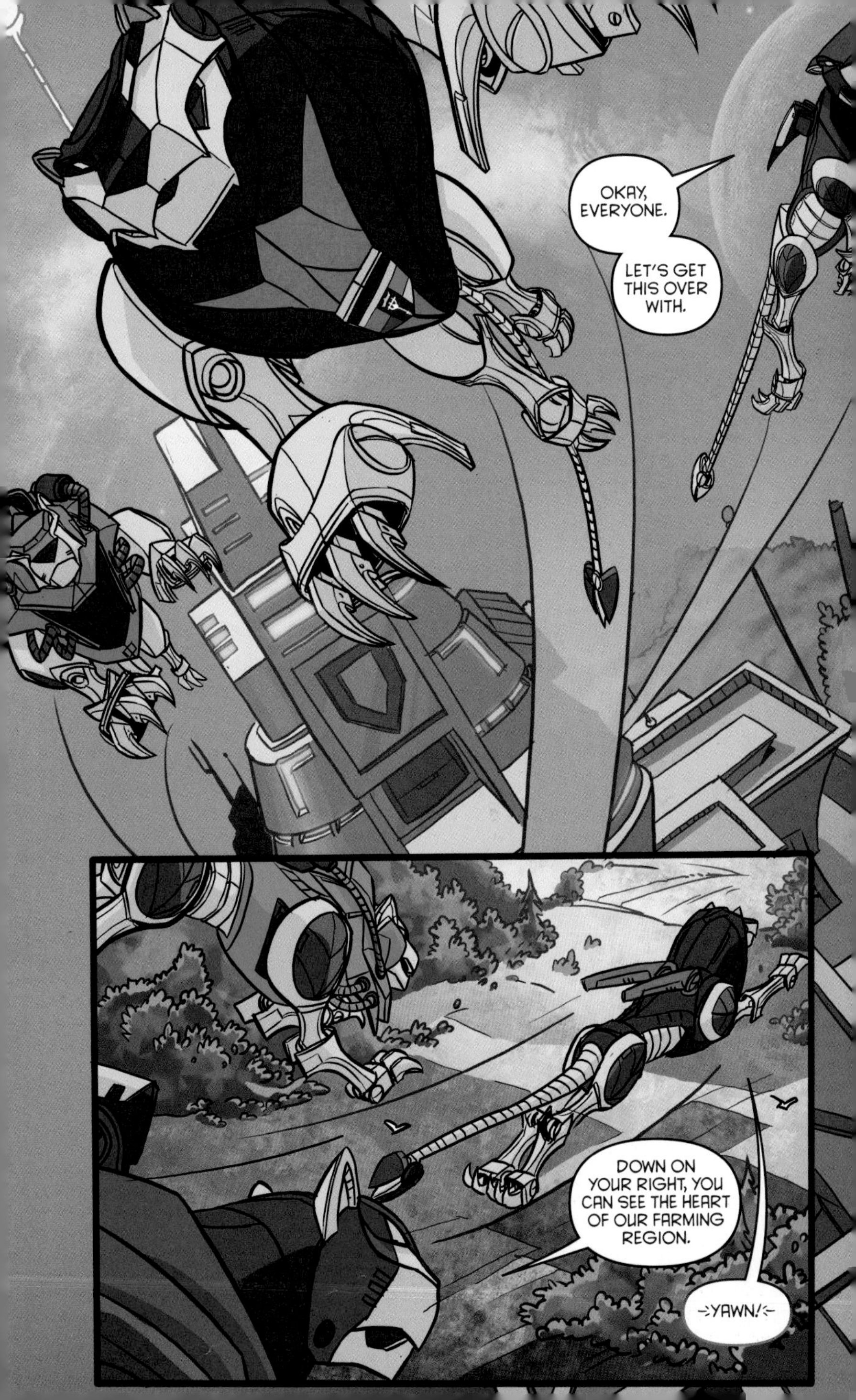
OKAY, EVERYONE.
LET'S GET THIS OVER WITH.
DOWN ON YOUR RIGHT, YOU CAN SEE THE HEART OF OUR FARMING REGION.
-YAWN!-

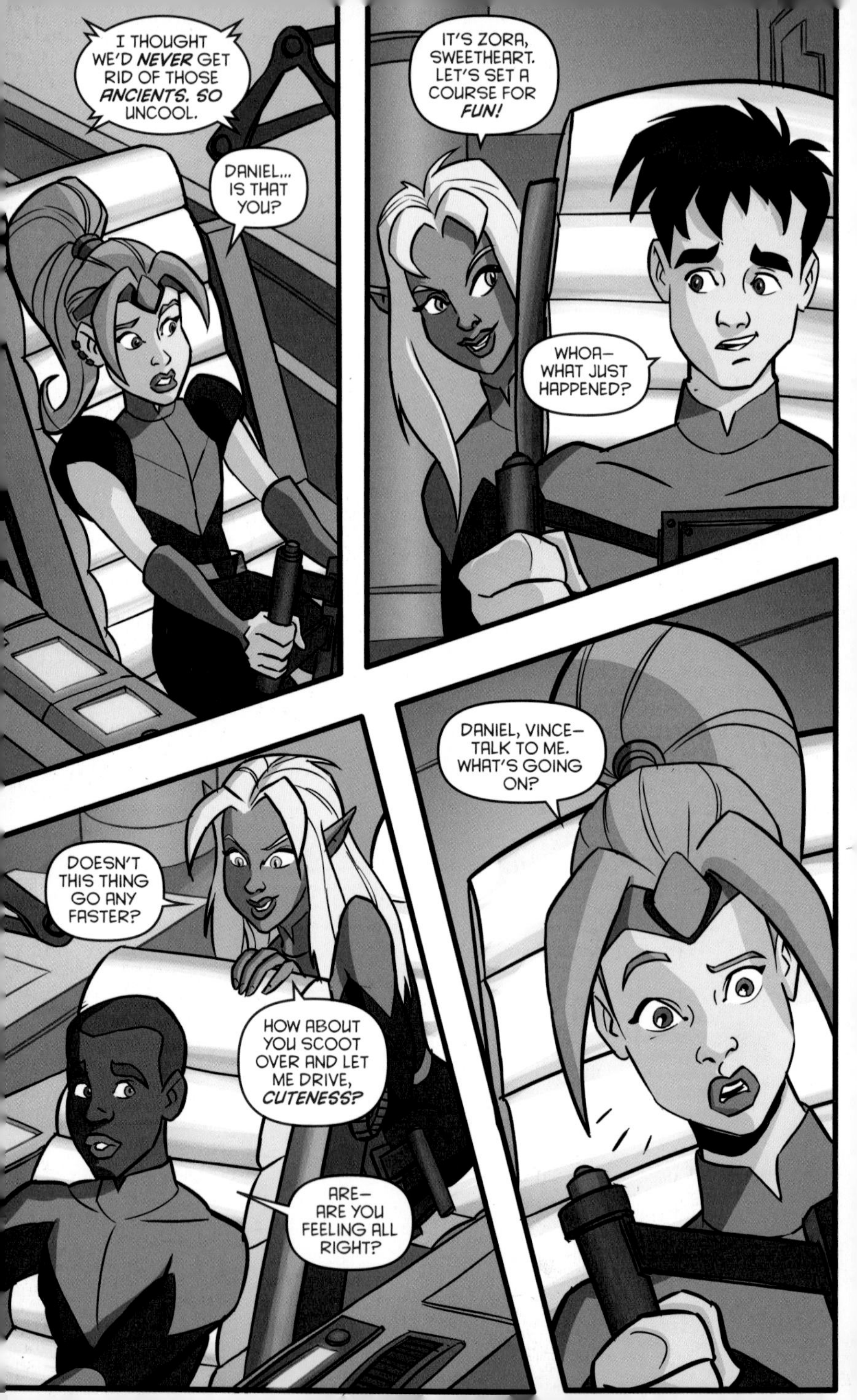
I THOUGHT WE'D NEVER GET RID OF THOSE ANCIENTS. SO UNCOOL.
DANIEL... IS THAT YOU?
IT'S ZORA, SWEETHEART. LET'S SET A COURSE FOR FUN!
WHOA— WHAT JUST HAPPENED?
DOESN'T THIS THING GO ANY FASTER?
HOW ABOUT YOU SCOOT OVER AND LET ME DRIVE, CUTENESS?
ARE— ARE YOU FEELING ALL RIGHT?
DANIEL, VINCE— TALK TO ME. WHAT'S GOING ON?

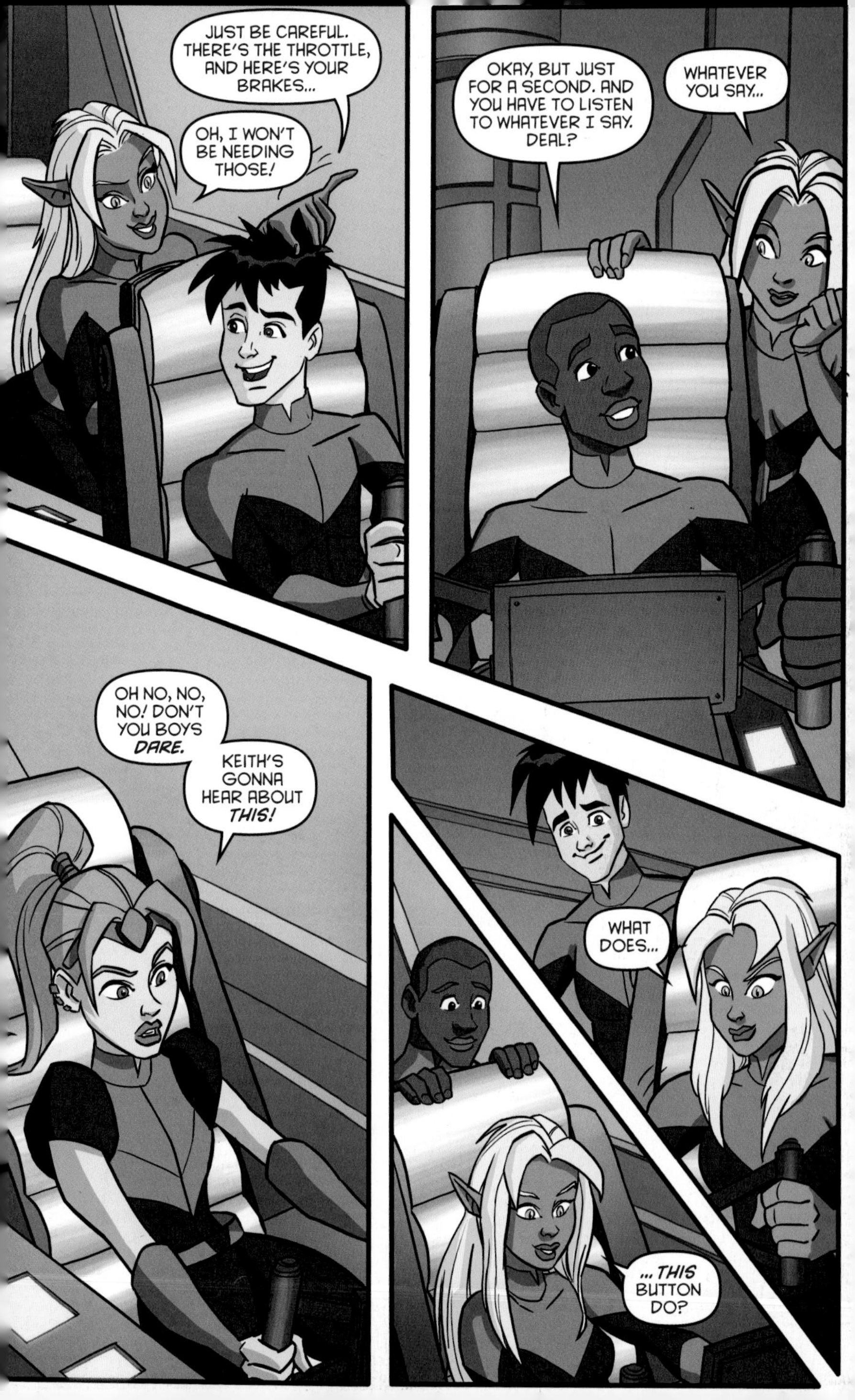
JUST BE CAREFUL. THERE'S THE THROTTLE, AND HERE'S YOUR BRAKES...
OH, I WON'T BE NEEDING THOSE!
OKAY, BUT JUST FOR A SECOND. AND YOU HAVE TO LISTEN TO WHATEVER I SAY. DEAL?
WHATEVER YOU SAY...
OH NO, NO, NO! DON'T YOU BOYS DARE.
KEITH'S GONNA HEAR ABOUT THIS!
WHAT DOES...
...THIS BUTTON DO?

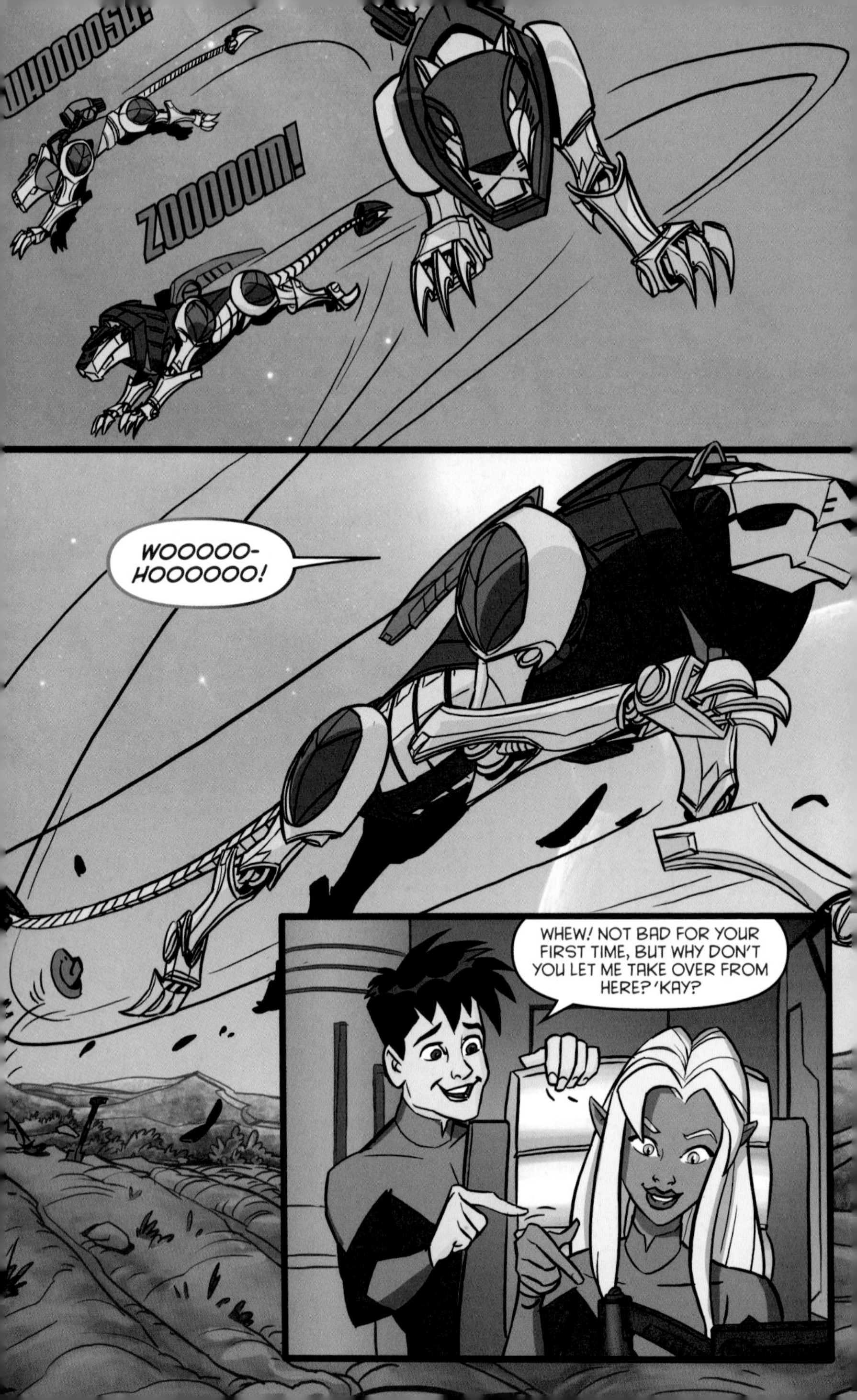
WHOOOOSH!
ZOOOOOM!
WOOOOO-HOOOOOO!
WHEW! NOT BAD FOR YOUR FIRST TIME, BUT WHY DON'T YOU LET ME TAKE OVER FROM HERE? 'KAY?

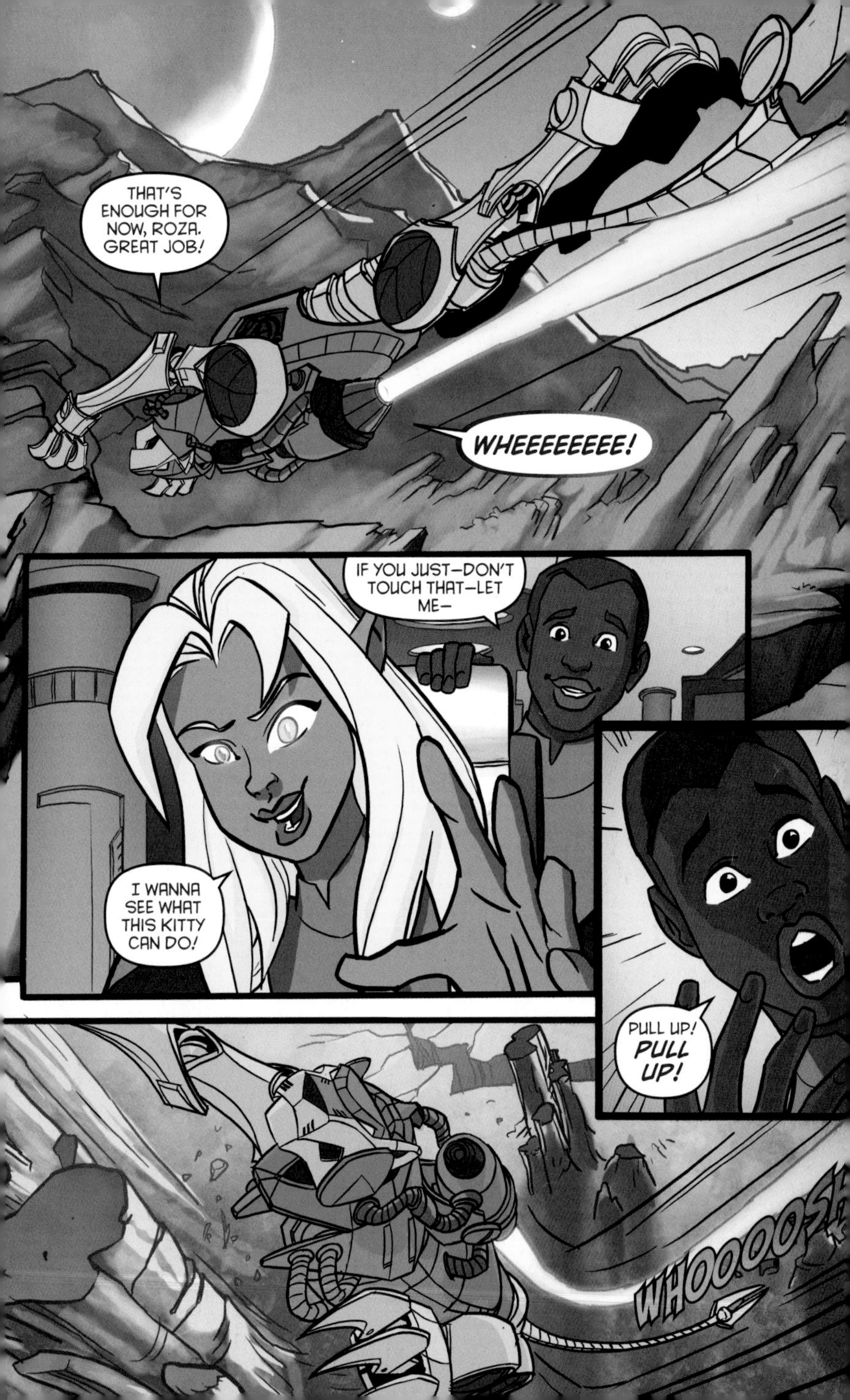

THAT'S ENOUGH FOR NOW, ROZA. GREAT JOB!
WHEEEEEEEE!
IF YOU JUST—DON'T TOUCH THAT—LET ME—
I WANNA SEE WHAT THIS KITTY CAN DO!
PULL UP! PULL UP!
WHOOOOSH

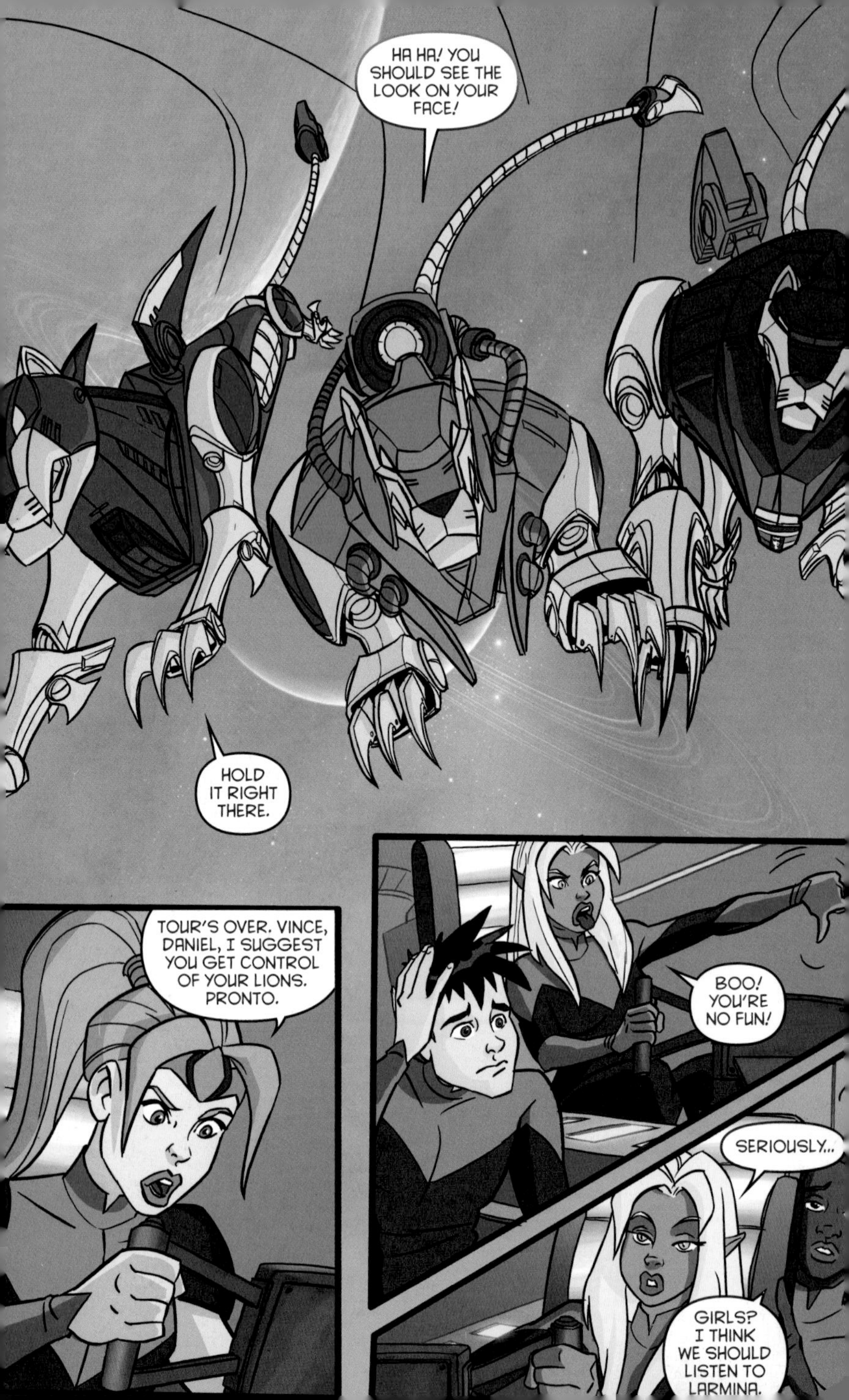
HA HA! YOU SHOULD SEE THE LOOK ON YOUR FACE!
HOLD IT RIGHT THERE.
TOUR'S OVER. VINCE, DANIEL, I SUGGEST YOU GET CONTROL OF YOUR LIONS. PRONTO.
BOO! YOU'RE NO FUN!
SERIOUSLY...
GIRLS? I THINK WE SHOULD LISTEN TO LARMINA.

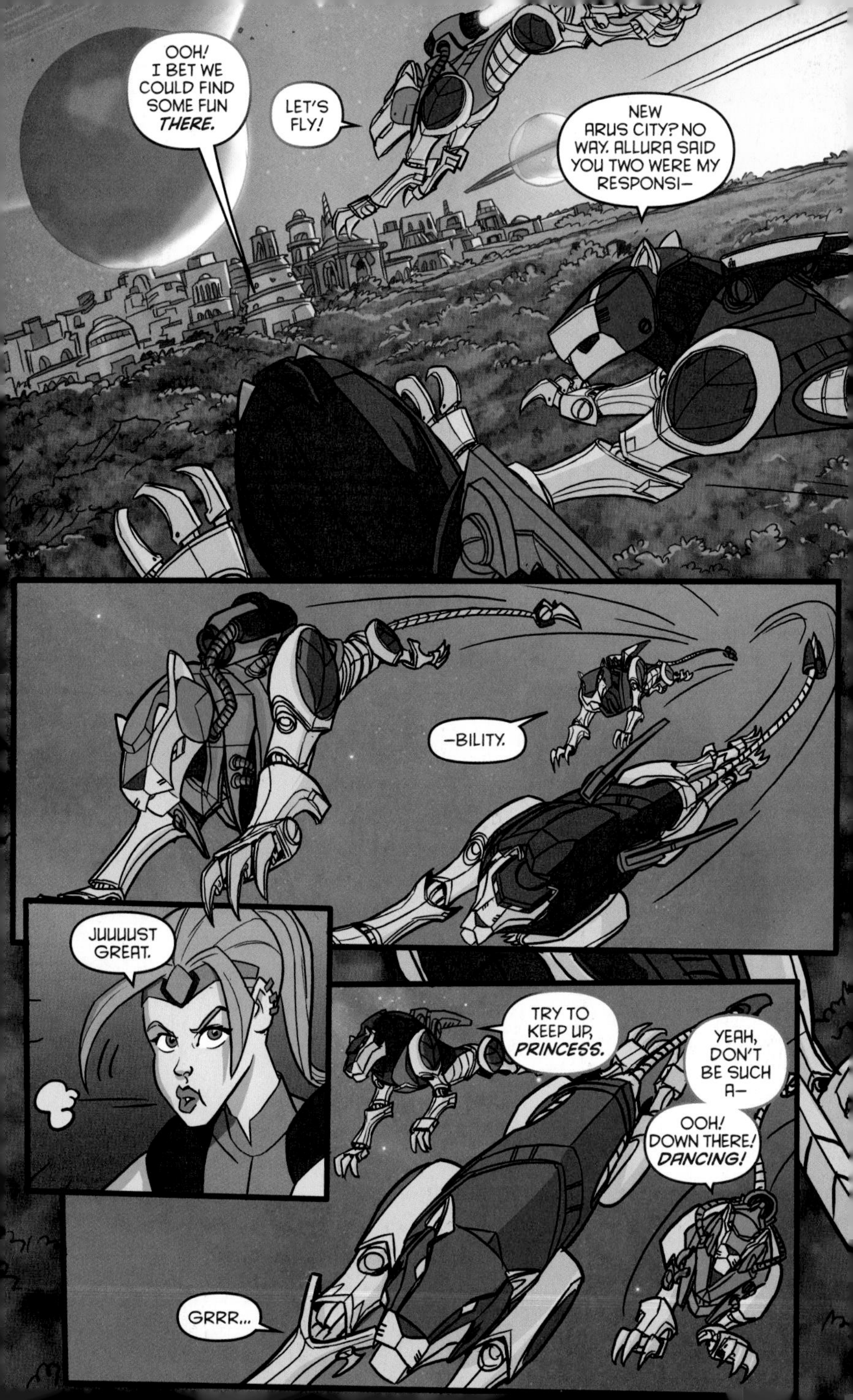
OOH! I BET WE COULD FIND SOME FUN *THERE.*
LET'S FLY!
NEW ARUS CITY? NO WAY. ALLURA SAID YOU TWO WERE MY RESPONSI—
—BILITY.
JUUUUST GREAT.
TRY TO KEEP UP, *PRINCESS.*
YEAH, DON'T BE SUCH A—
OOH! DOWN THERE! *DANCING!*
GRRR...

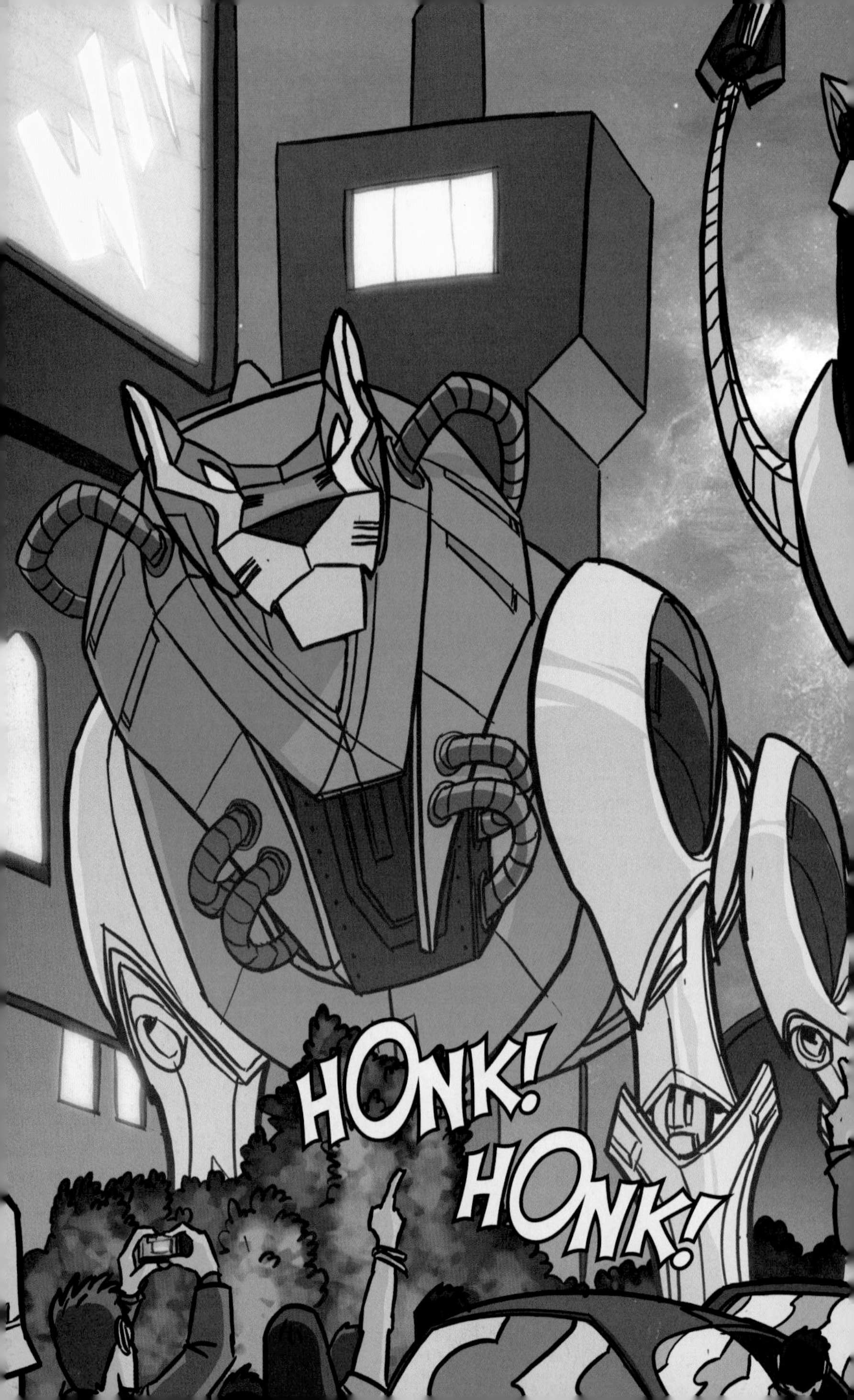
HONK!
HONK!

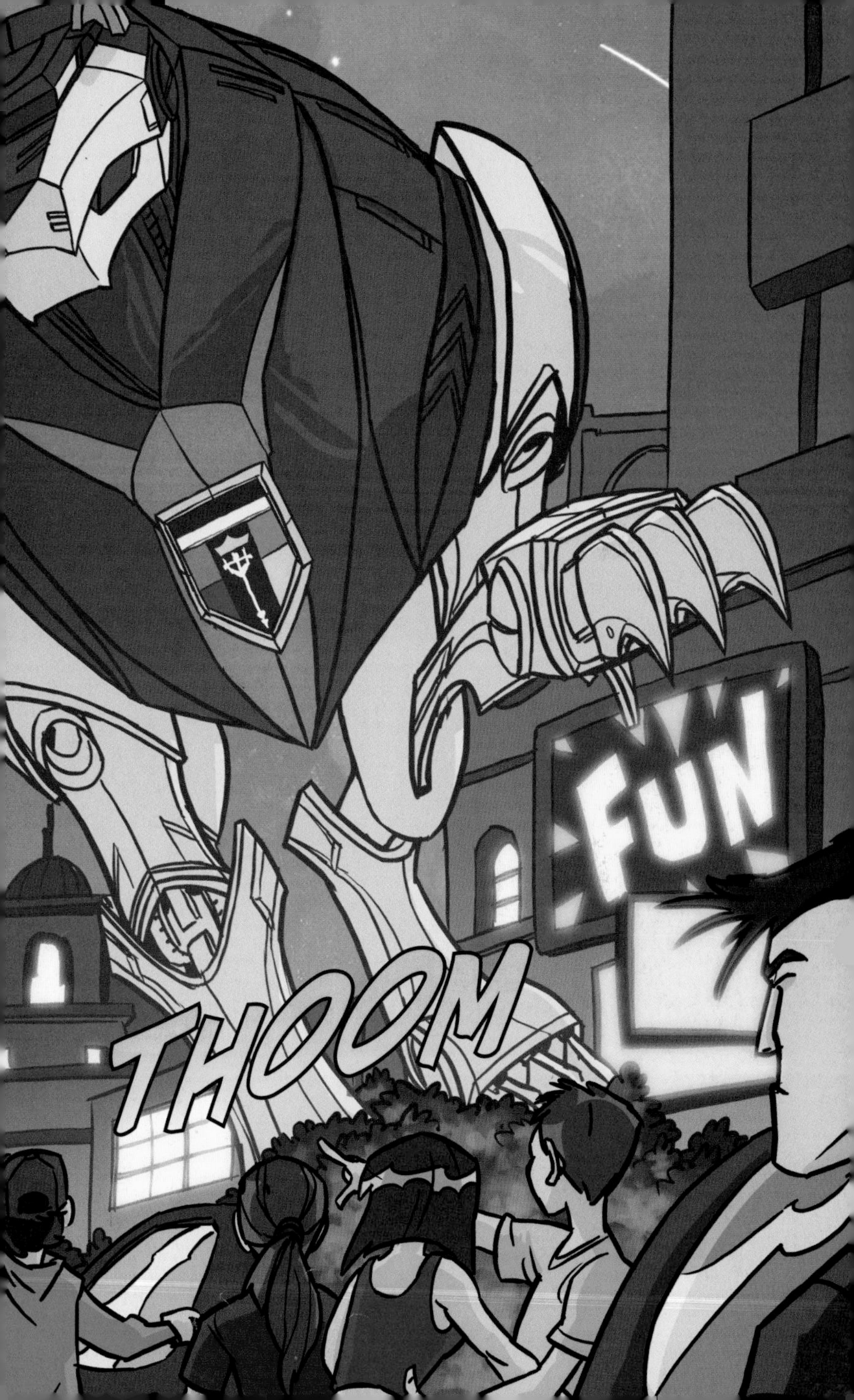
FUN
THOOM

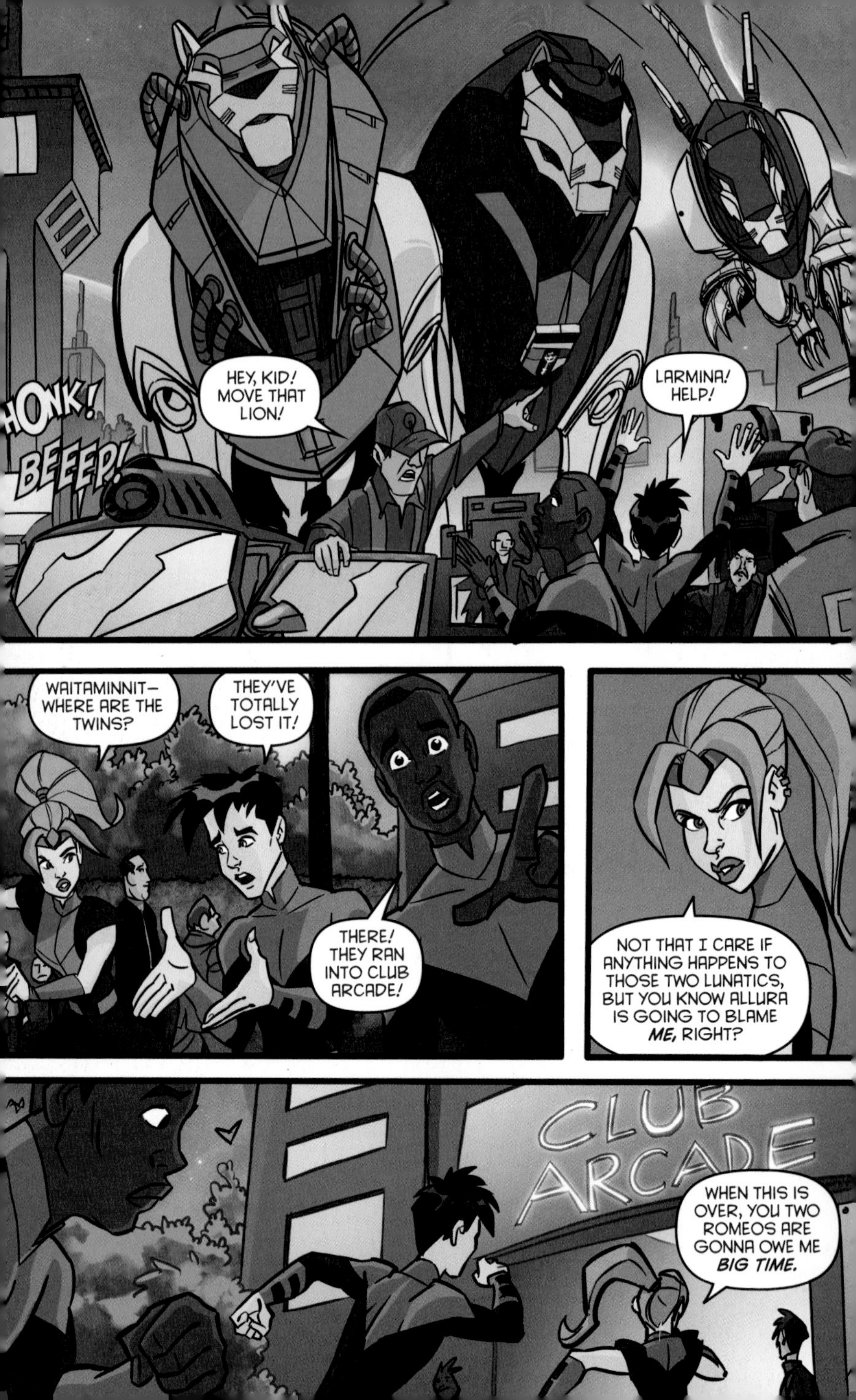
HONK!
BEEEP!
HEY, KID! MOVE THAT LION!
LARMINA! HELP!
WAITAMINNIT— WHERE ARE THE TWINS?
THEY'VE TOTALLY LOST IT!
THERE! THEY RAN INTO CLUB ARCADE!
NOT THAT I CARE IF ANYTHING HAPPENS TO THOSE TWO LUNATICS, BUT YOU KNOW ALLURA IS GOING TO BLAME *ME*, RIGHT?
CLUB ARCADE
WHEN THIS IS OVER, YOU TWO ROMEOS ARE GONNA OWE ME ***BIG TIME.***

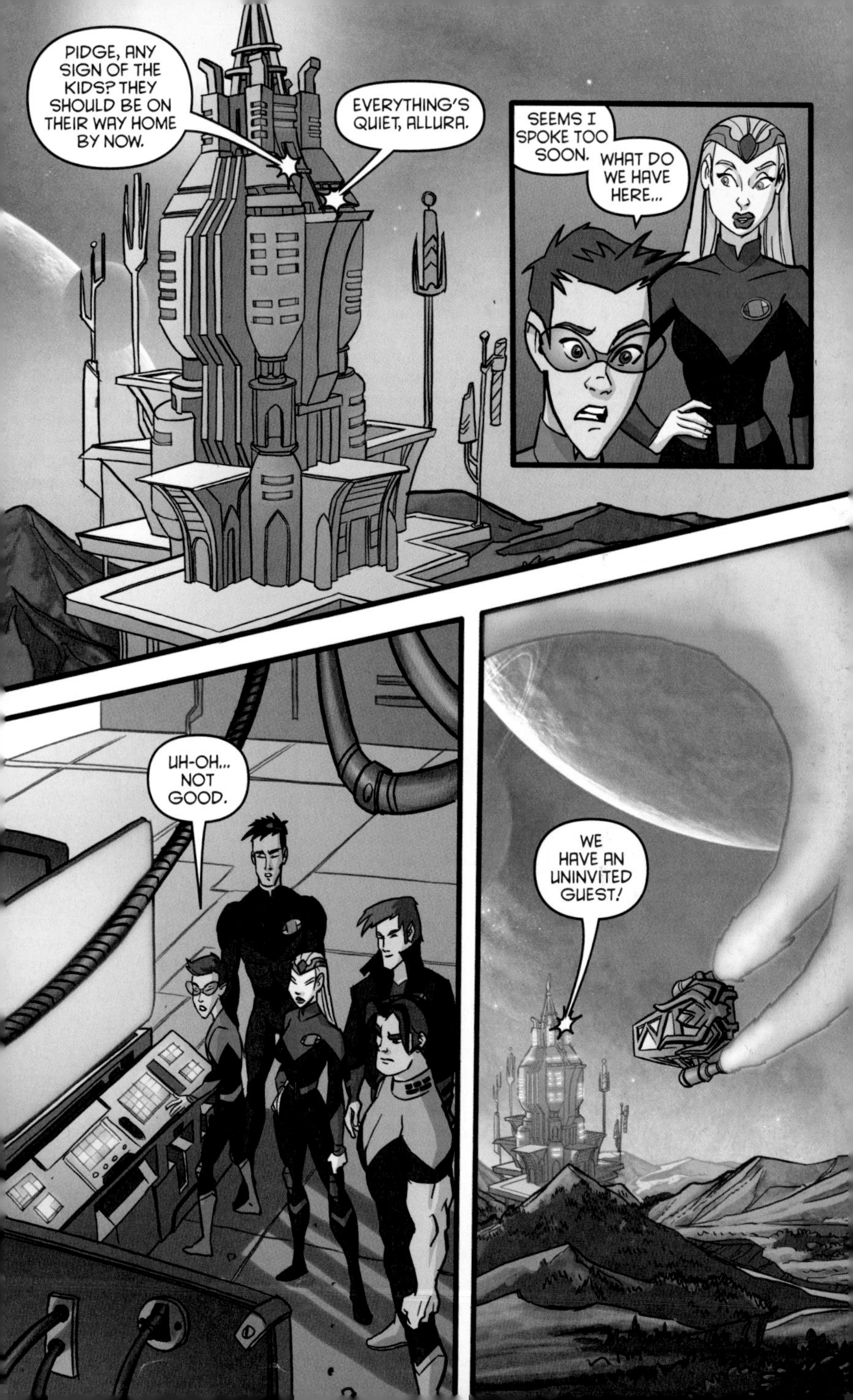
PIDGE, ANY SIGN OF THE KIDS? THEY SHOULD BE ON THEIR WAY HOME BY NOW.
EVERYTHING'S QUIET, ALLURA.
SEEMS I SPOKE TOO SOON.
WHAT DO WE HAVE HERE...
UH-OH... NOT GOOD.
WE HAVE AN UNINVITED GUEST!

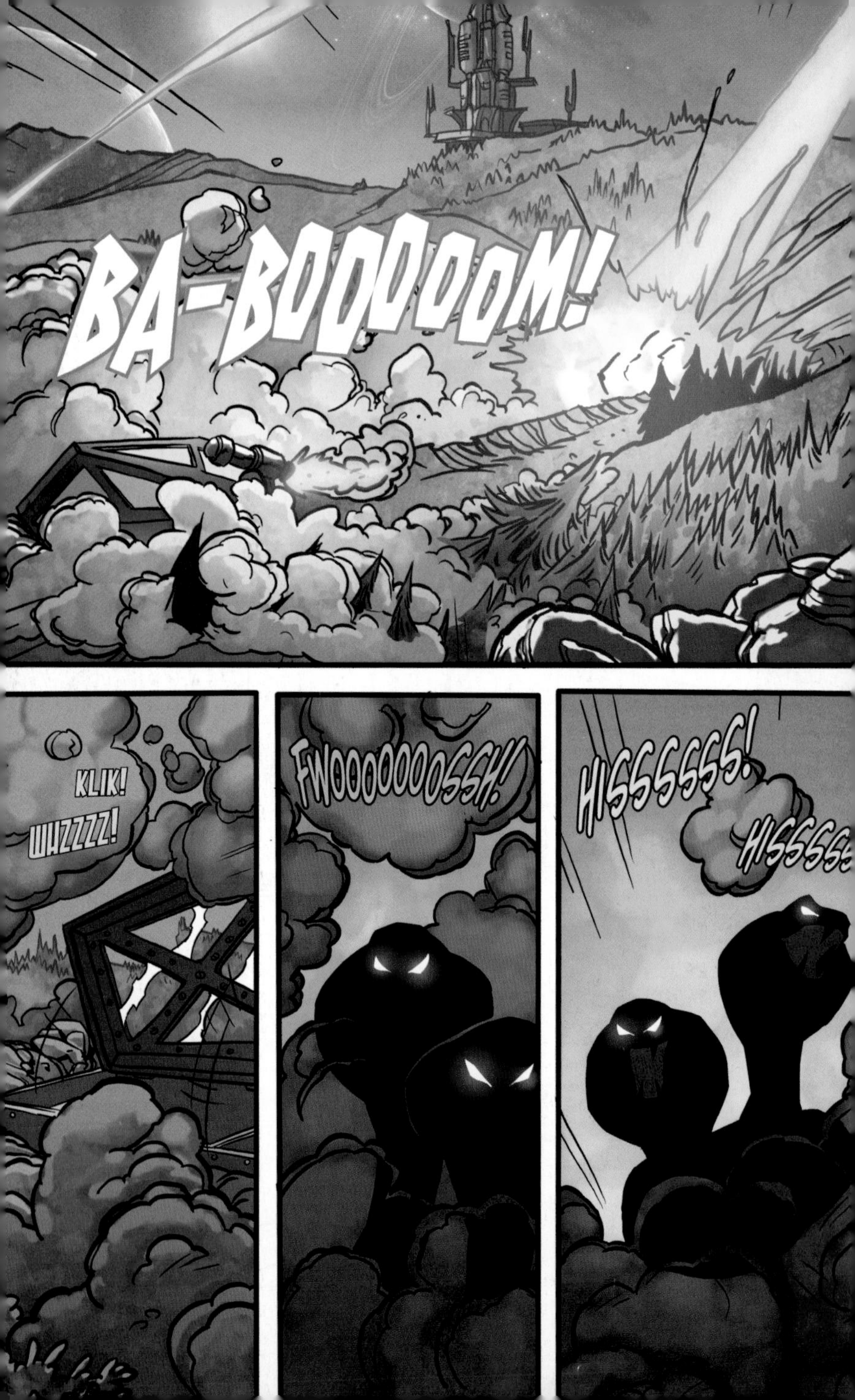
BA-BOOOOOM!
KLIK!
WHZZZZ!
FWOOOOOOOSSH!
HISSSSSS!
HISSSS

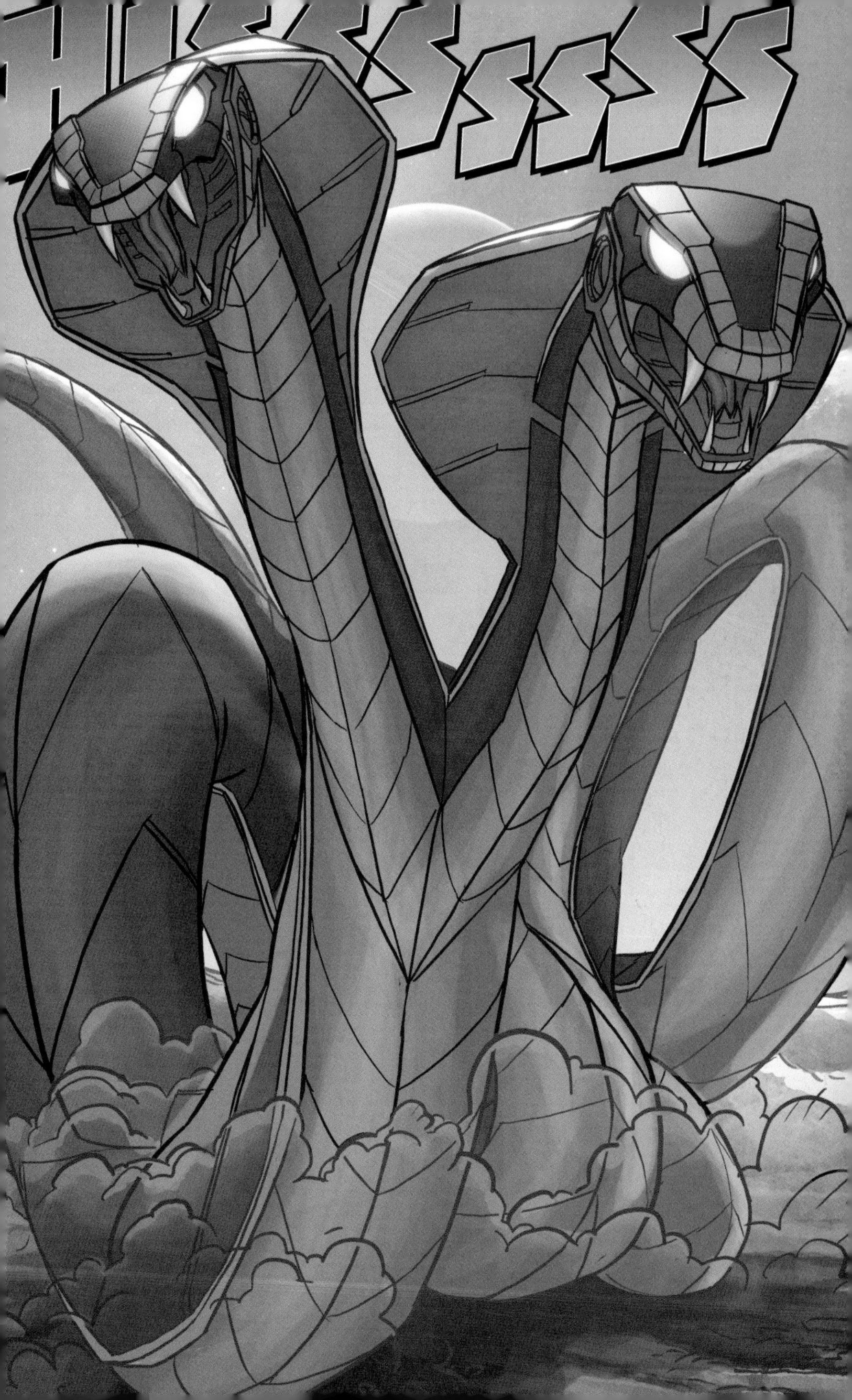
HISSSSSS

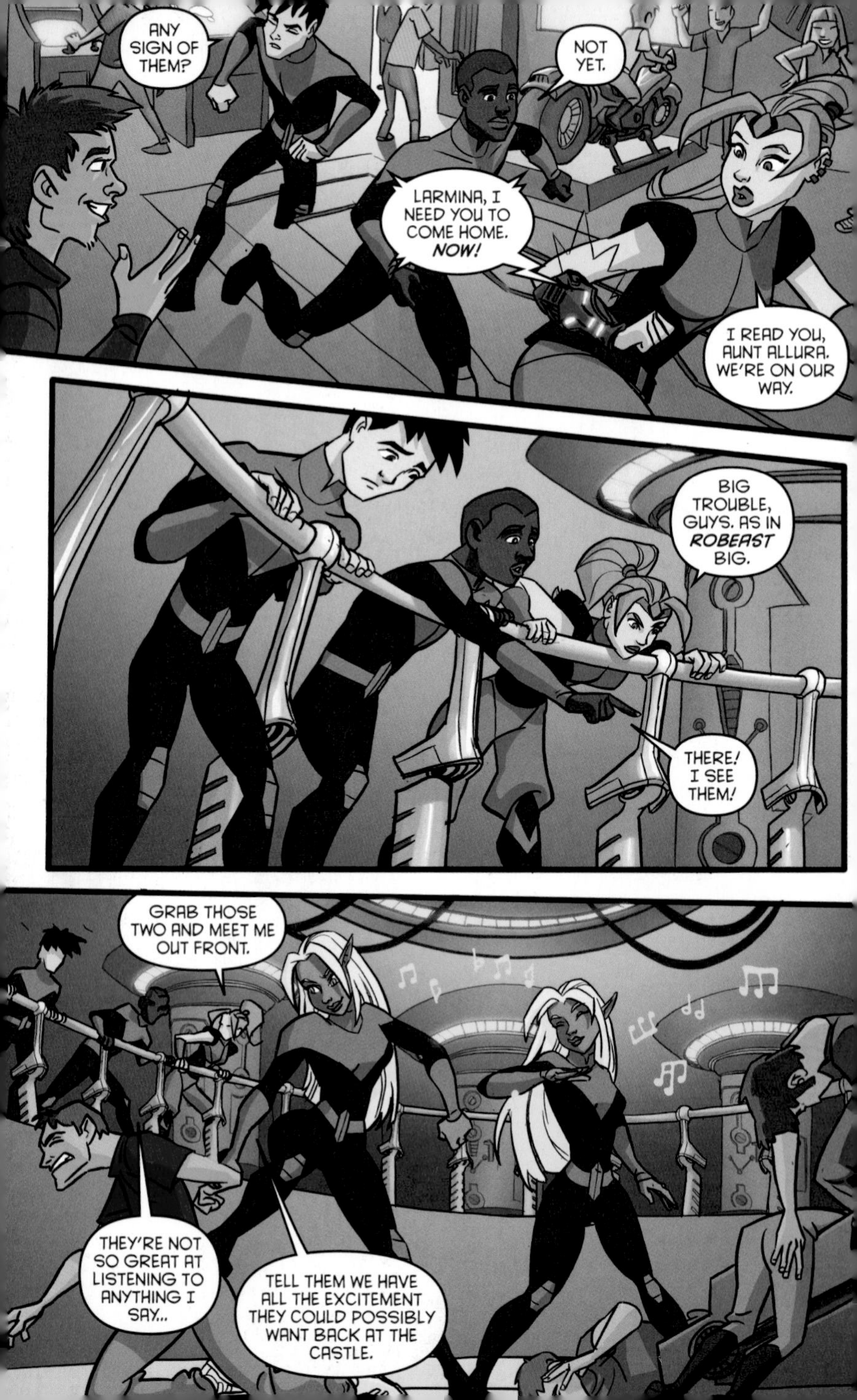
ANY SIGN OF THEM?
NOT YET.
LARMINA, I NEED YOU TO COME HOME. NOW!
I READ YOU, AUNT ALLURA. WE'RE ON OUR WAY.
BIG TROUBLE, GUYS. AS IN ROBEAST BIG.
THERE! I SEE THEM!
GRAB THOSE TWO AND MEET ME OUT FRONT.
THEY'RE NOT SO GREAT AT LISTENING TO ANYTHING I SAY...
TELL THEM WE HAVE ALL THE EXCITEMENT THEY COULD POSSIBLY WANT BACK AT THE CASTLE.

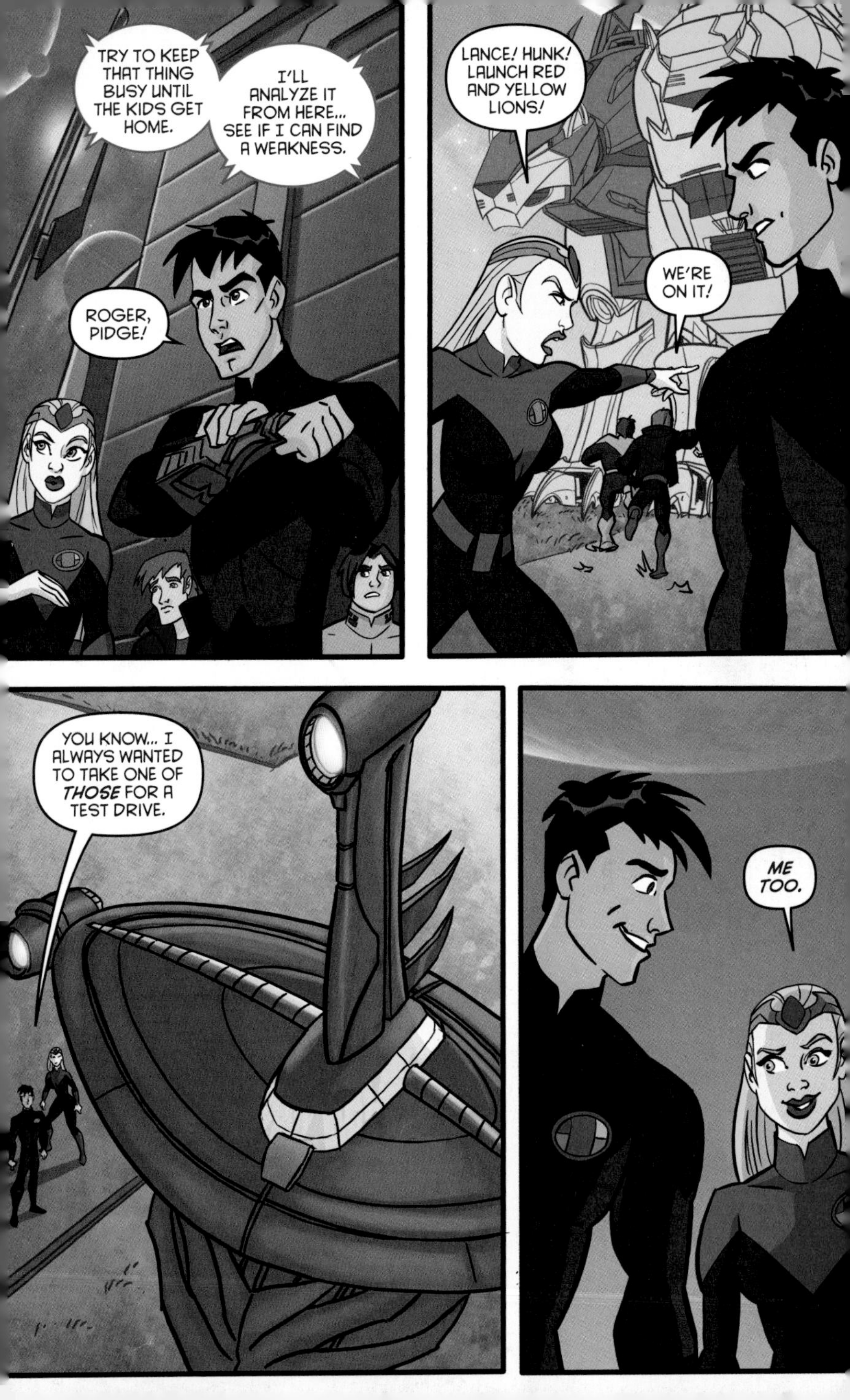
TRY TO KEEP THAT THING BUSY UNTIL THE KIDS GET HOME.
I'LL ANALYZE IT FROM HERE... SEE IF I CAN FIND A WEAKNESS.
ROGER, PIDGE!
LANCE! HUNK! LAUNCH RED AND YELLOW LIONS!
WE'RE ON IT!
YOU KNOW... I ALWAYS WANTED TO TAKE ONE OF *THOSE* FOR A TEST DRIVE.
ME TOO.

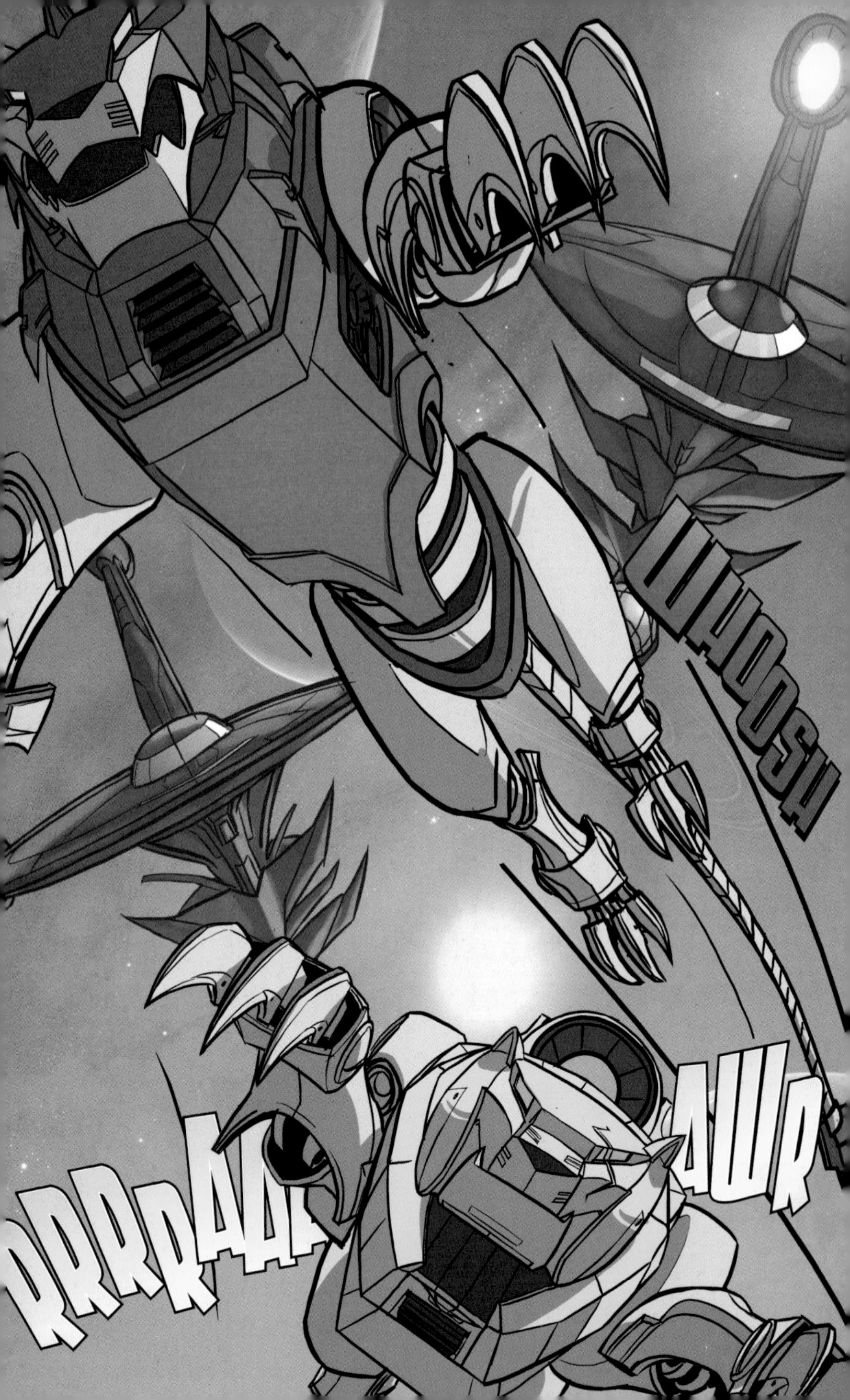
WHOOSH
RRRRAAA
AWR

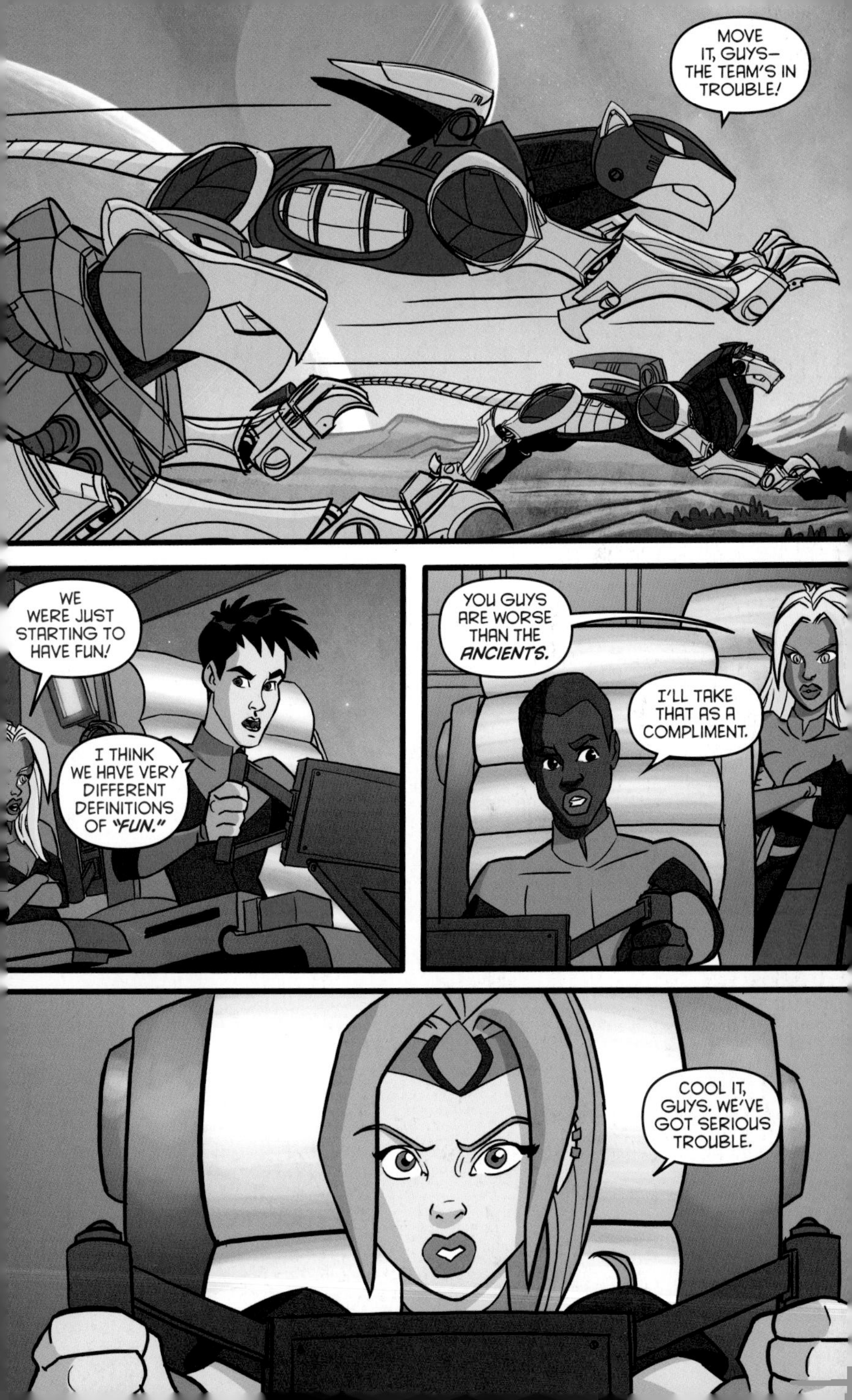
MOVE IT, GUYS— THE TEAM'S IN TROUBLE!
WE WERE JUST STARTING TO HAVE FUN!
I THINK WE HAVE VERY DIFFERENT DEFINITIONS OF "FUN."
YOU GUYS ARE WORSE THAN THE ANCIENTS.
I'LL TAKE THAT AS A COMPLIMENT.
COOL IT, GUYS. WE'VE GOT SERIOUS TROUBLE.

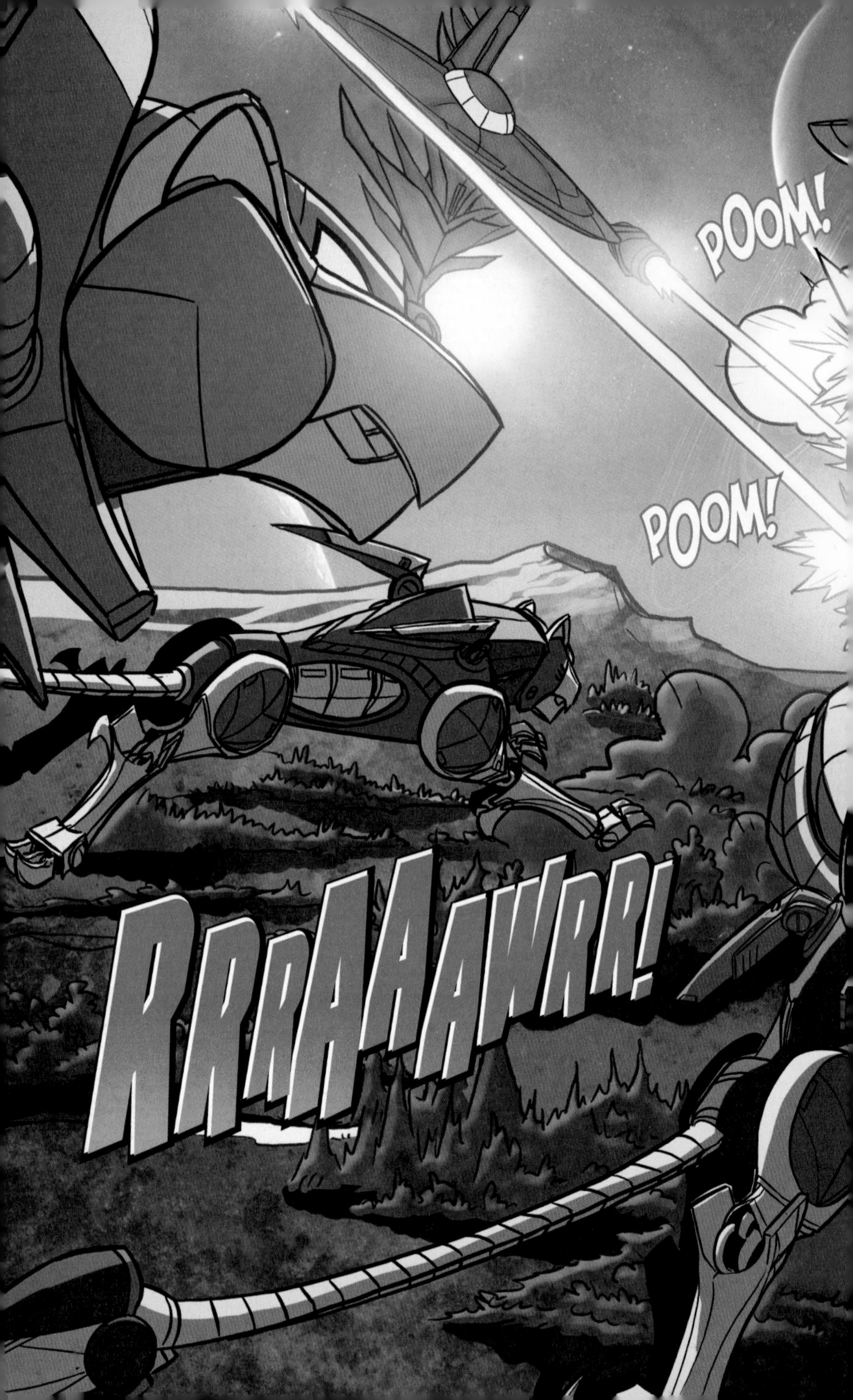
POOM!
POOM!
RRRAAAWRR!

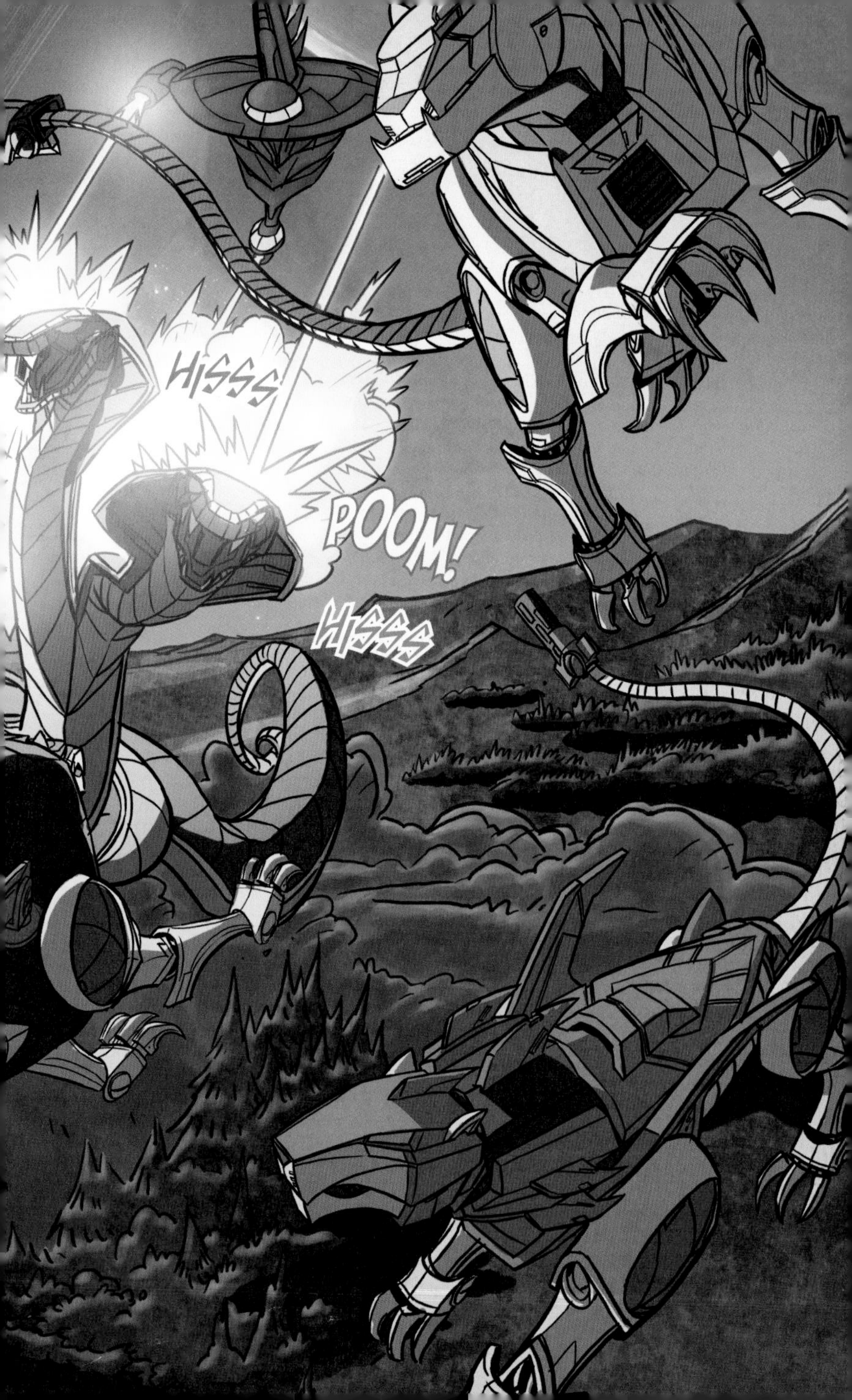
HISSS
POOM!
HISSS

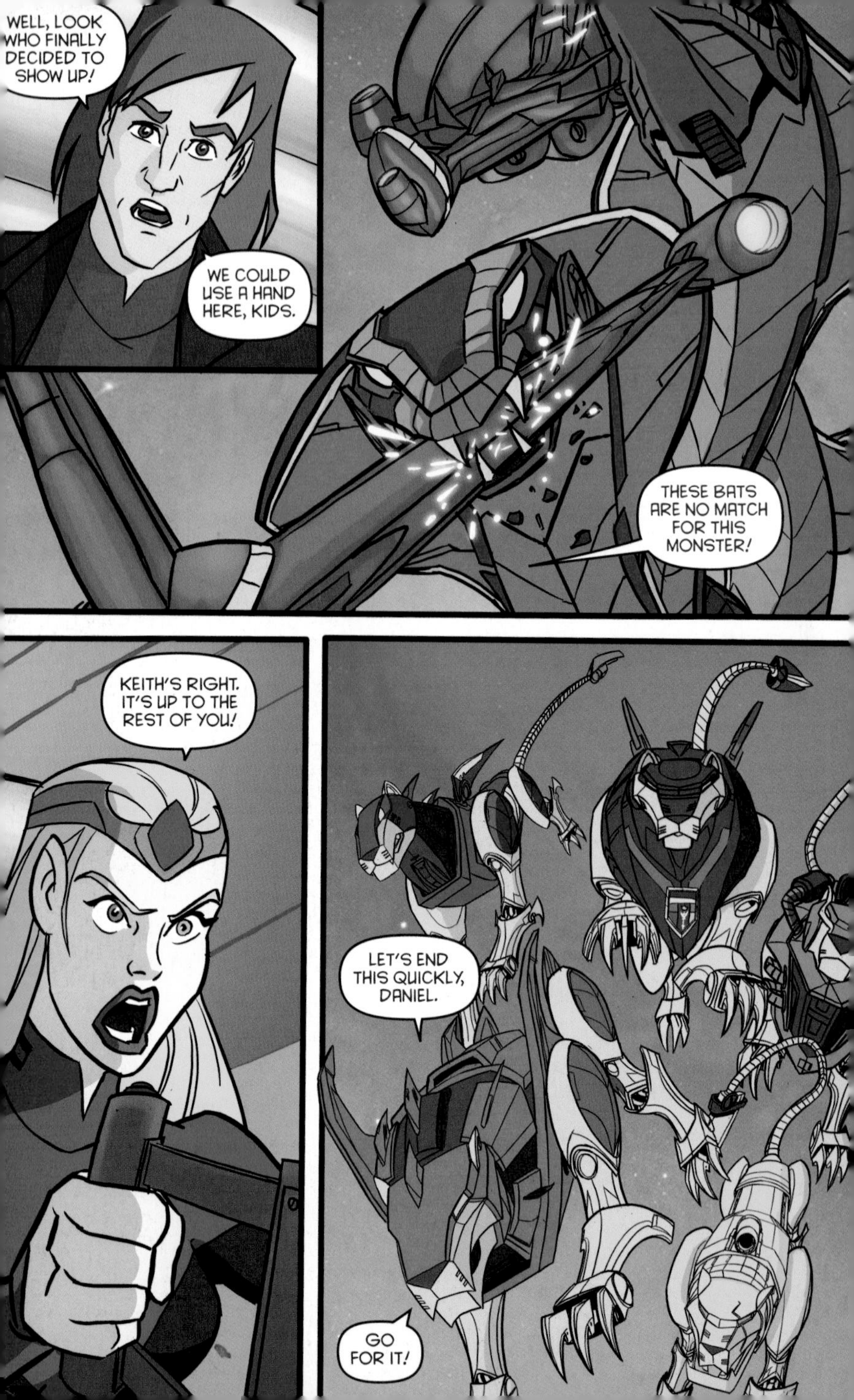
WELL, LOOK WHO FINALLY DECIDED TO SHOW UP!
WE COULD USE A HAND HERE, KIDS.
THESE BATS ARE NO MATCH FOR THIS MONSTER!
KEITH'S RIGHT. IT'S UP TO THE REST OF YOU!
LET'S END THIS QUICKLY, DANIEL.
GO FOR IT!

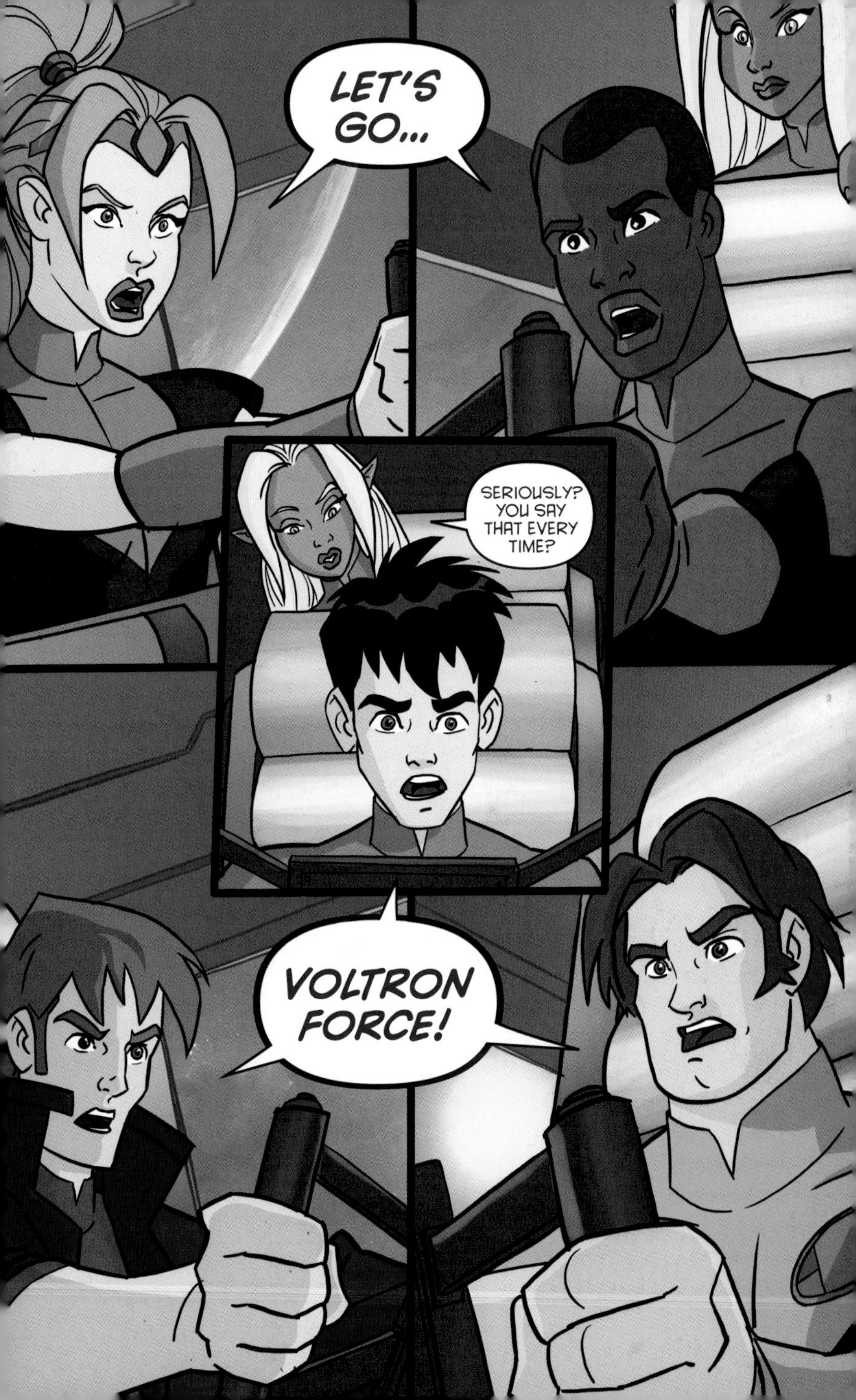
LET'S GO...
SERIOUSLY? YOU SAY THAT EVERY TIME?
VOLTRON FORCE!

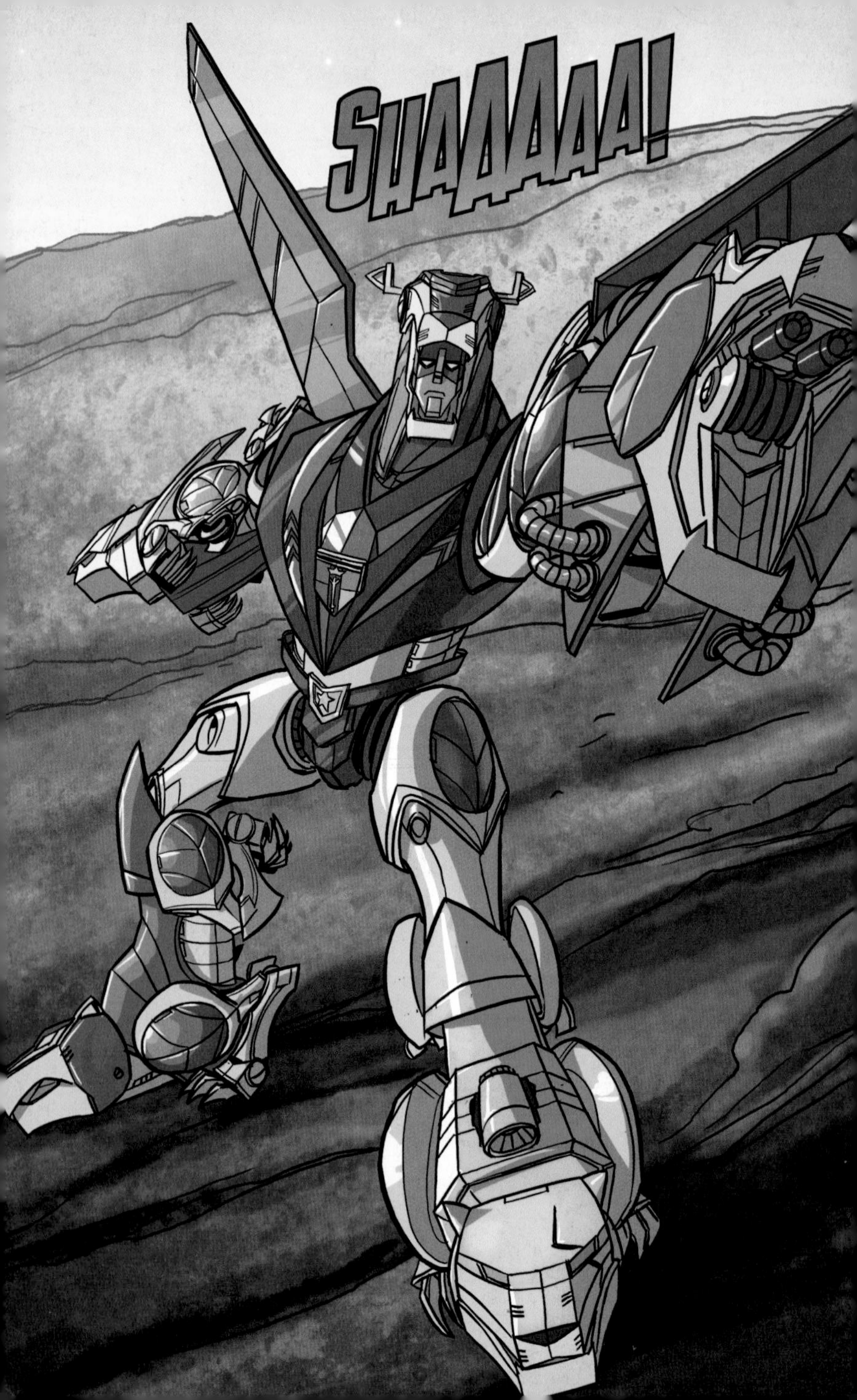
SHAAAAA!

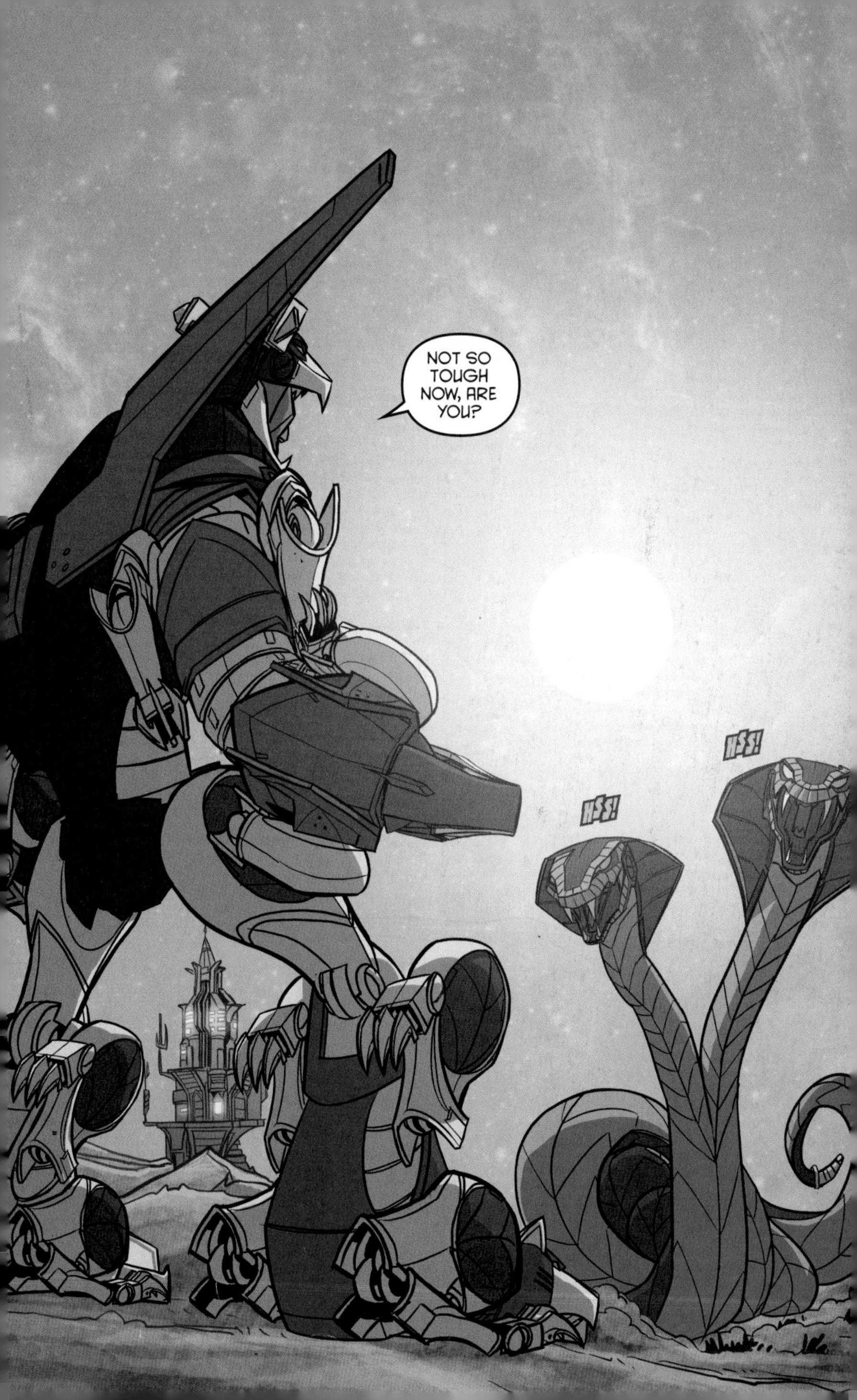
NOT SO TOUGH NOW, ARE YOU?
HSS!
HSS!

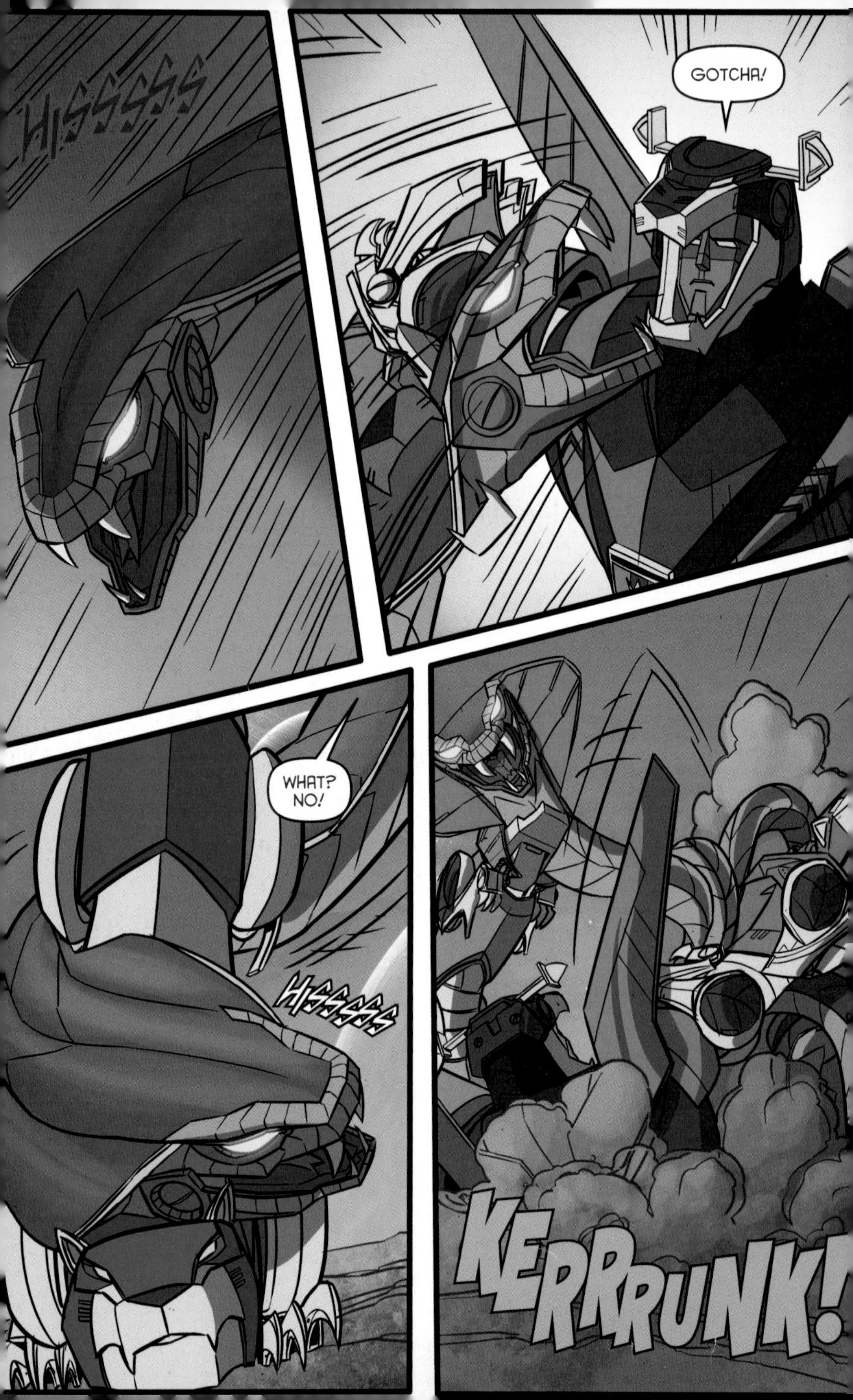
HISSSSS
GOTCHA!
WHAT? NO!
HISSSSS
KERRRRUNK!

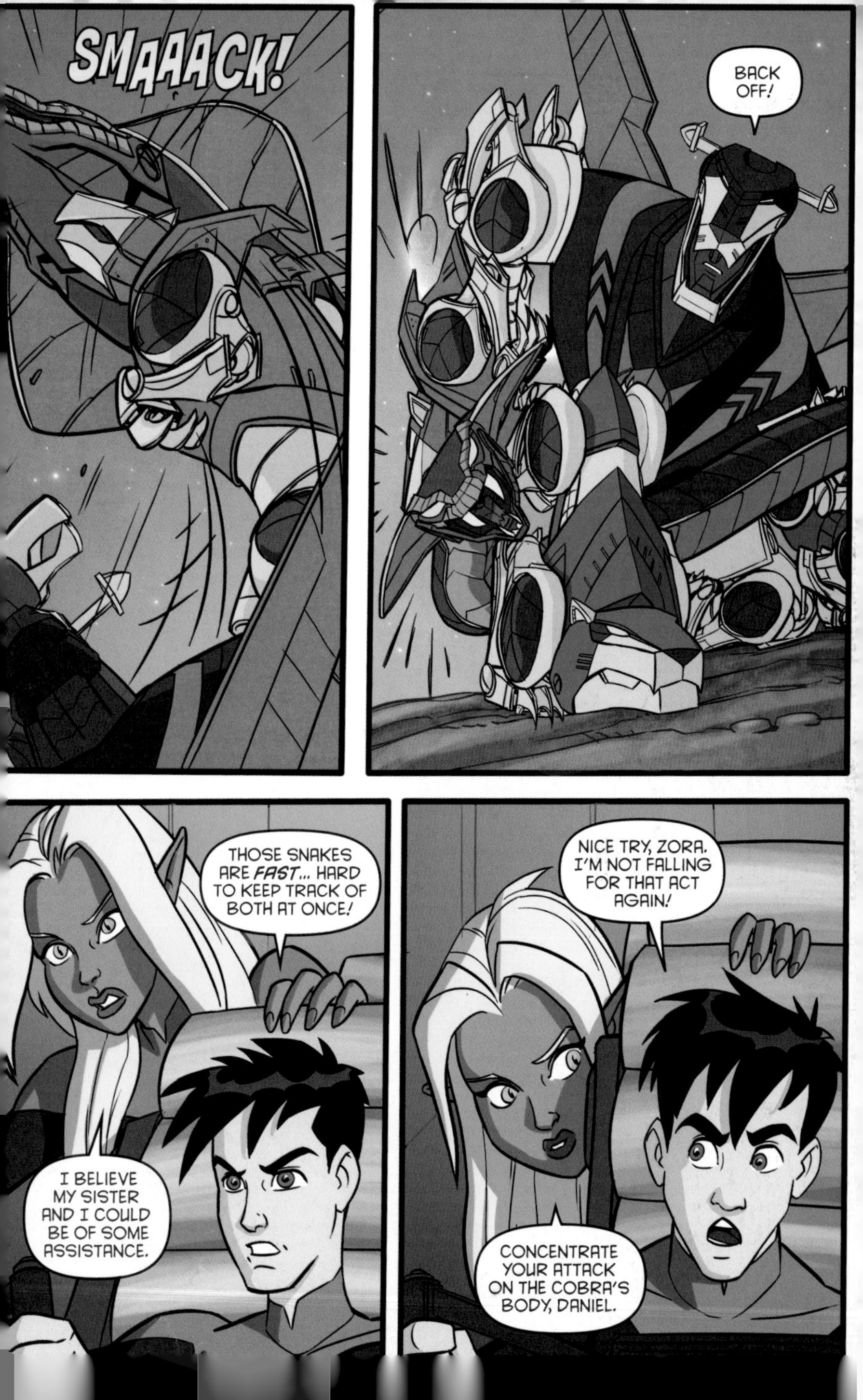
SMAAACK!
BACK OFF!
THOSE SNAKES ARE FAST... HARD TO KEEP TRACK OF BOTH AT ONCE!
I BELIEVE MY SISTER AND I COULD BE OF SOME ASSISTANCE.
NICE TRY, ZORA. I'M NOT FALLING FOR THAT ACT AGAIN!
CONCENTRATE YOUR ATTACK ON THE COBRA'S BODY, DANIEL.

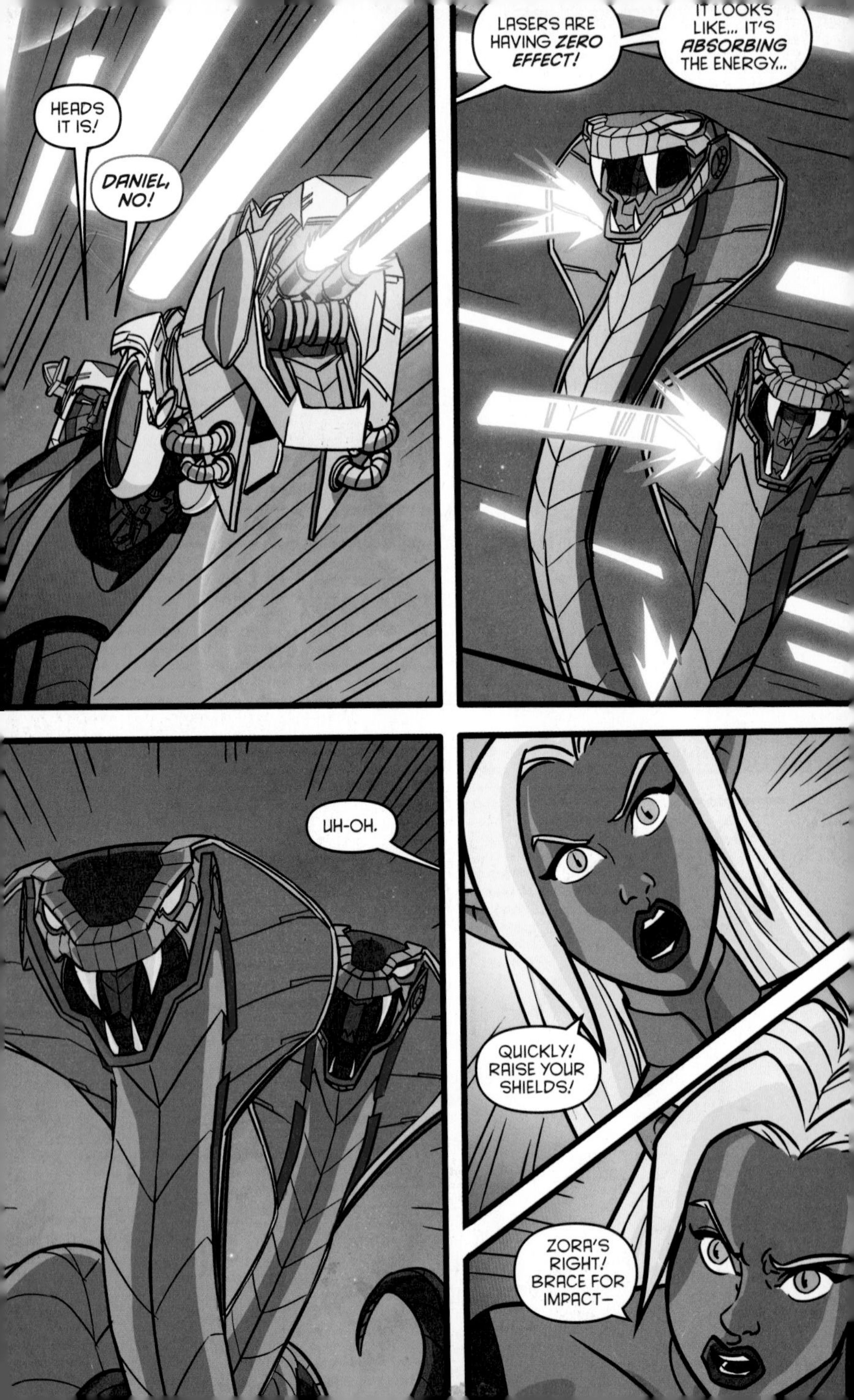
HEADS IT IS!
DANIEL, NO!
LASERS ARE HAVING ZERO EFFECT!
IT LOOKS LIKE... IT'S ABSORBING THE ENERGY...
UH-OH.
QUICKLY! RAISE YOUR SHIELDS!
ZORA'S RIGHT! BRACE FOR IMPACT—

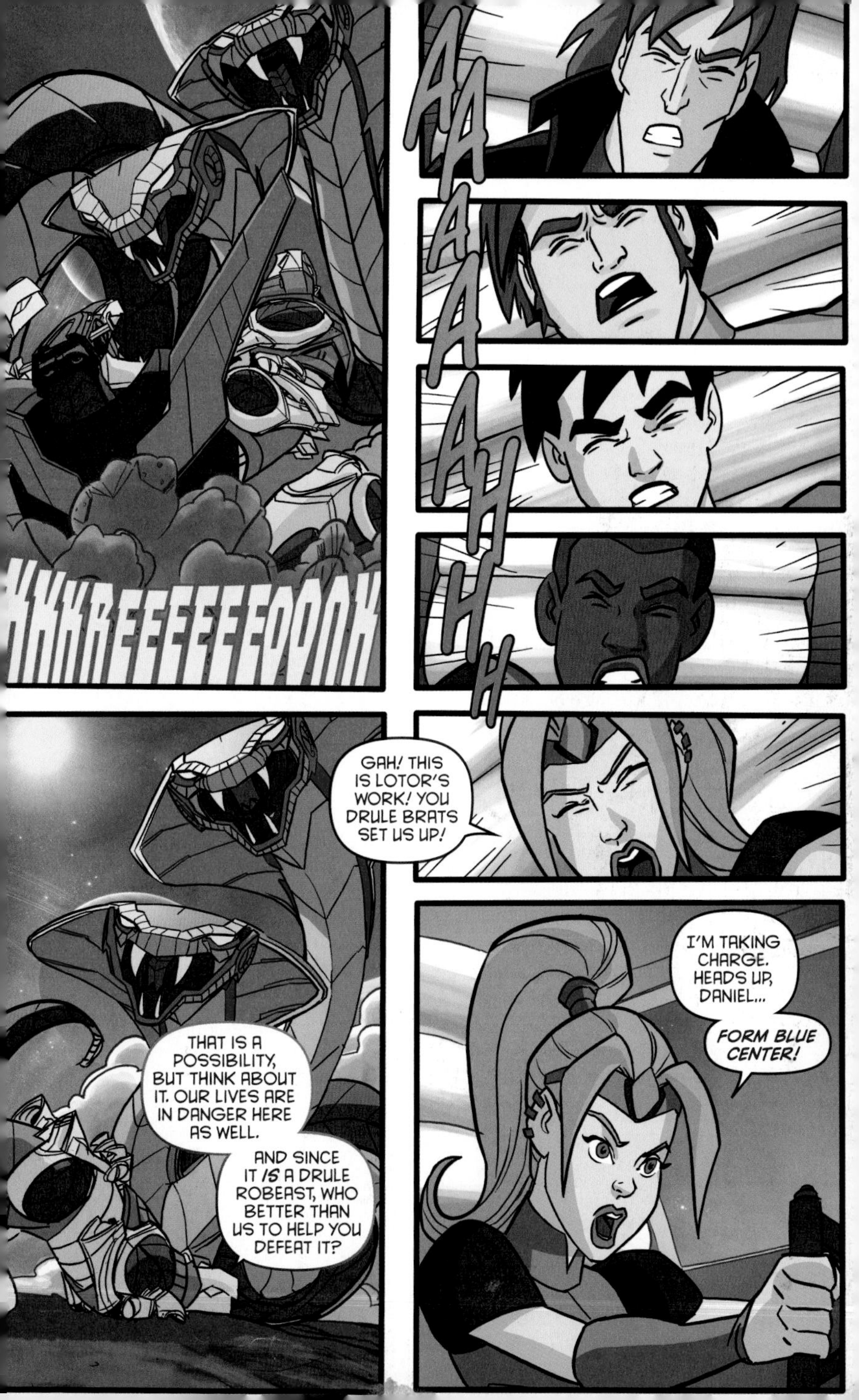
KKKREEEEEEOONK
AAAAAAAHHH
GAH! THIS IS LOTOR'S WORK! YOU DRULE BRATS SET US UP!
THAT IS A POSSIBILITY, BUT THINK ABOUT IT. OUR LIVES ARE IN DANGER HERE AS WELL.
AND SINCE IT *IS* A DRULE ROBEAST, WHO BETTER THAN US TO HELP YOU DEFEAT IT?
I'M TAKING CHARGE. HEADS UP, DANIEL...
FORM BLUE CENTER!

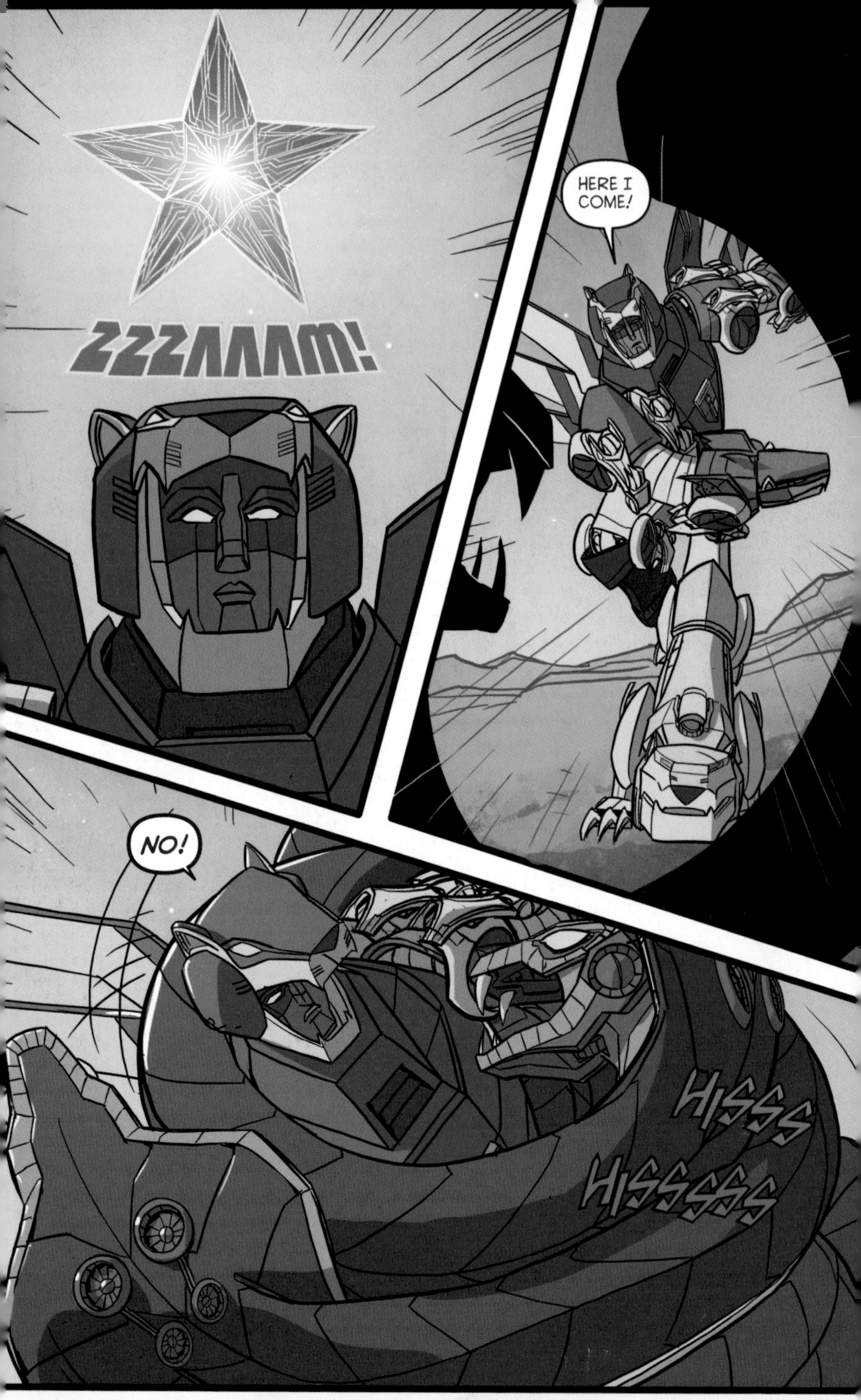
ZZZAAAM!
HERE I COME!
NO!
HISSS
HISSSSS

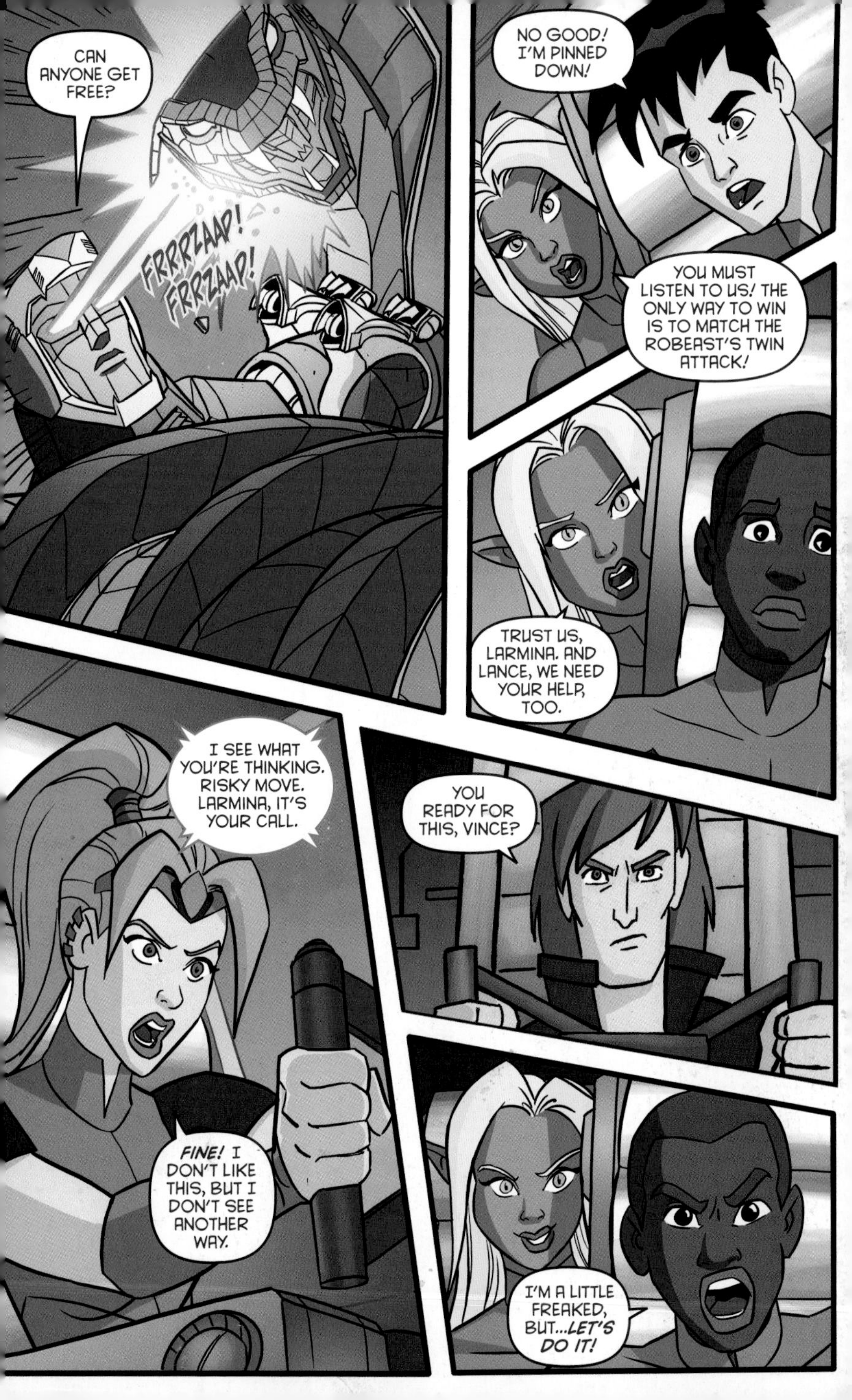
CAN ANYONE GET FREE?
FRRRZAAP!
FRRZAAP!
NO GOOD! I'M PINNED DOWN!
YOU MUST LISTEN TO US! THE ONLY WAY TO WIN IS TO MATCH THE ROBEAST'S TWIN ATTACK!
TRUST US, LARMINA. AND LANCE, WE NEED YOUR HELP, TOO.
I SEE WHAT YOU'RE THINKING. RISKY MOVE. LARMINA, IT'S YOUR CALL.
FINE! I DON'T LIKE THIS, BUT I DON'T SEE ANOTHER WAY.
YOU READY FOR THIS, VINCE?
I'M A LITTLE FREAKED, BUT...LET'S DO IT!

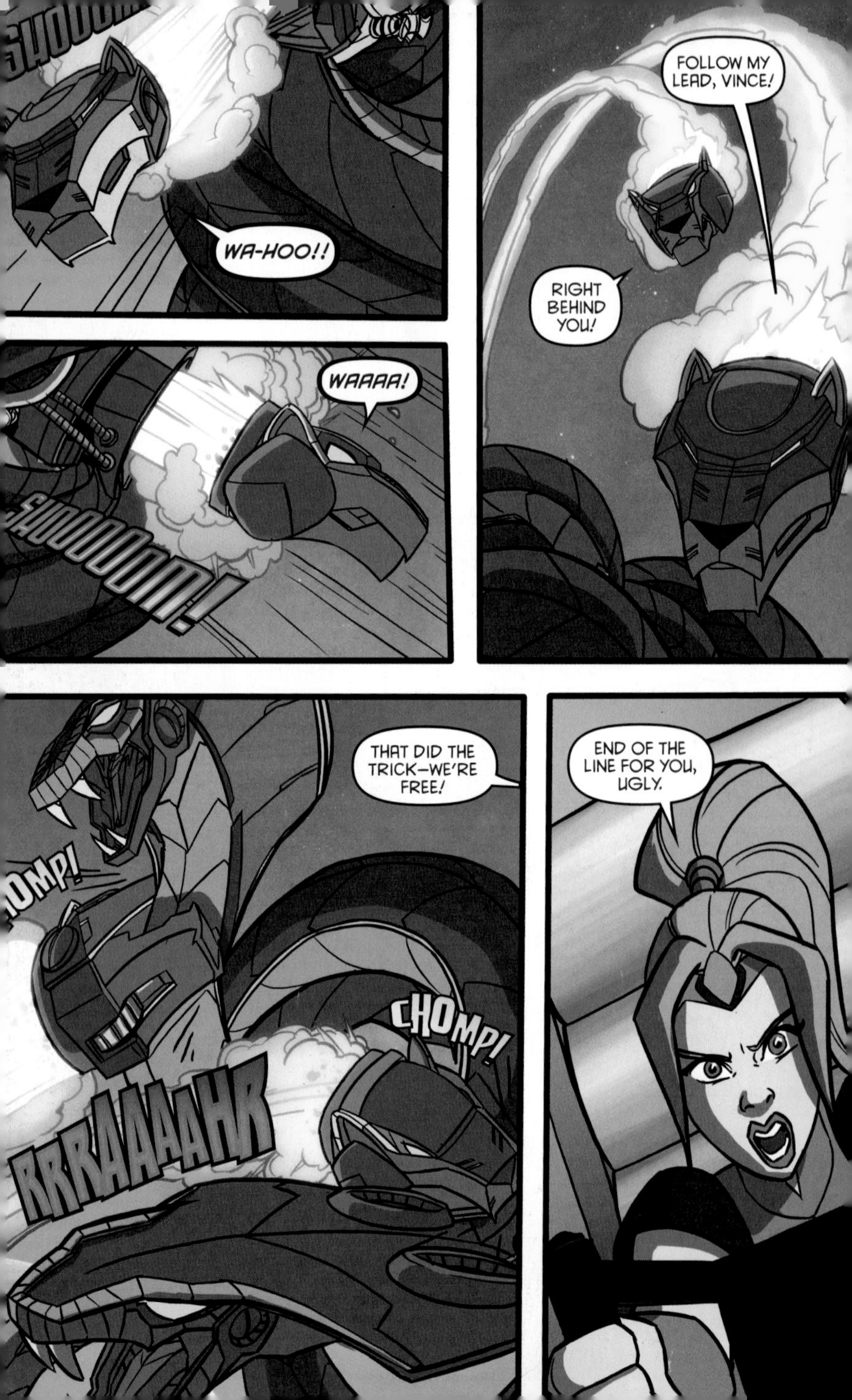
SHOOOM
WA-HOO!!
FOLLOW MY LEAD, VINCE!
RIGHT BEHIND YOU!
WAAAA!
SHOOOOOM!!
THAT DID THE TRICK—WE'RE FREE!
CHOMP!
CHOMP!
RRRAAAAHR
END OF THE LINE FOR YOU, UGLY.

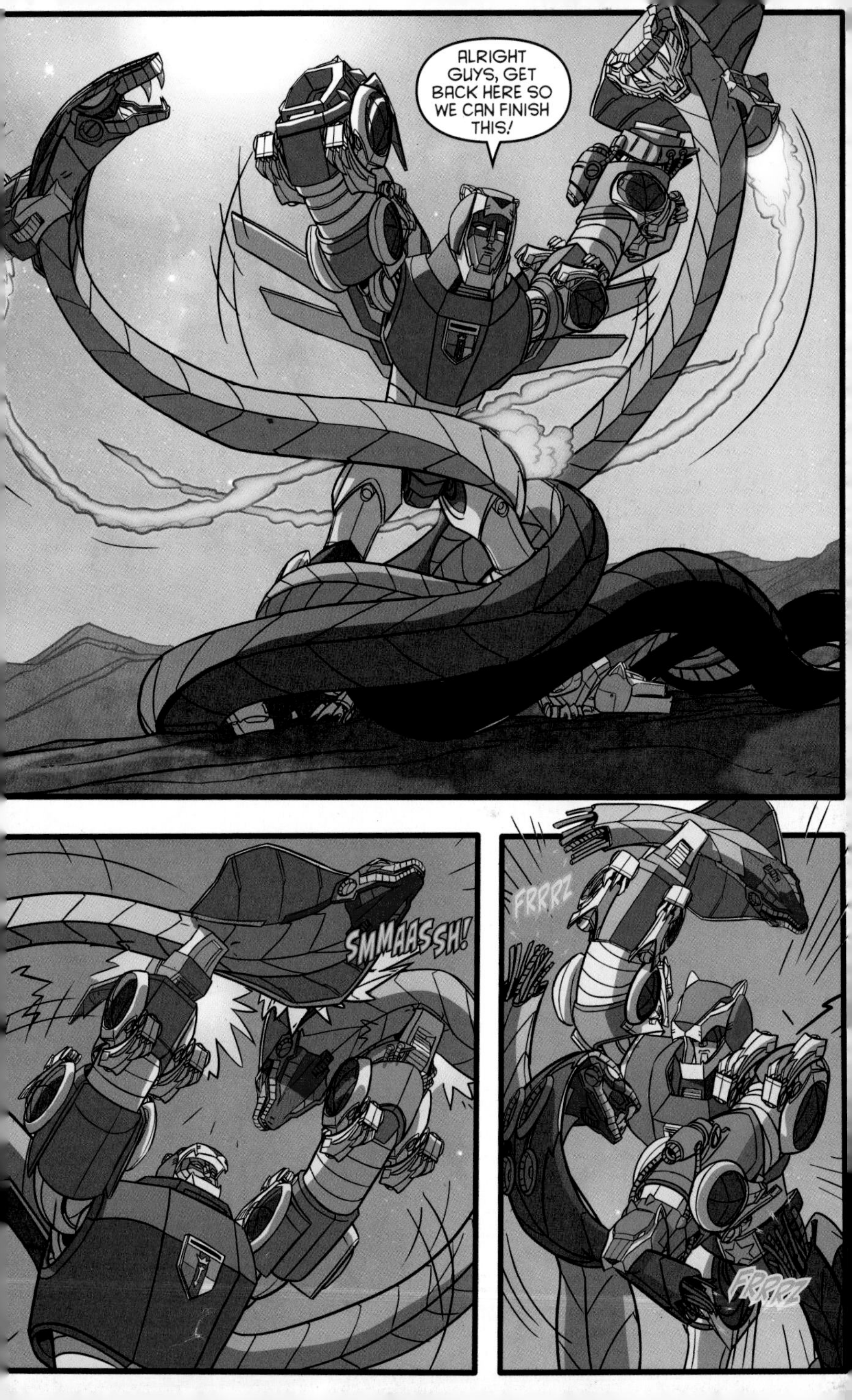
ALRIGHT GUYS, GET BACK HERE SO WE CAN FINISH THIS!
SMMAASSH!
FRRRZ
FRRRZ

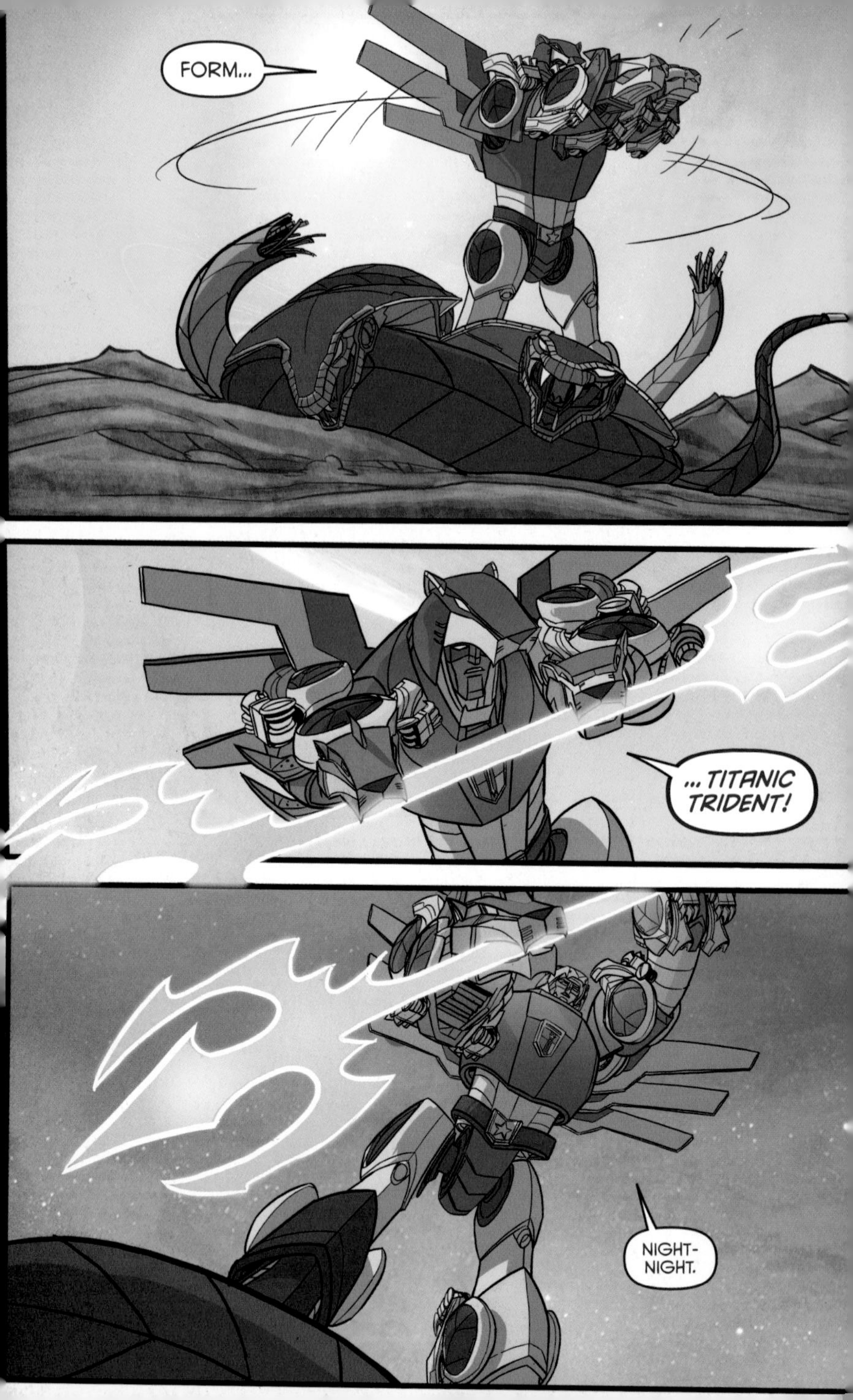
FORM...
...TITANIC TRIDENT!
NIGHT-NIGHT.

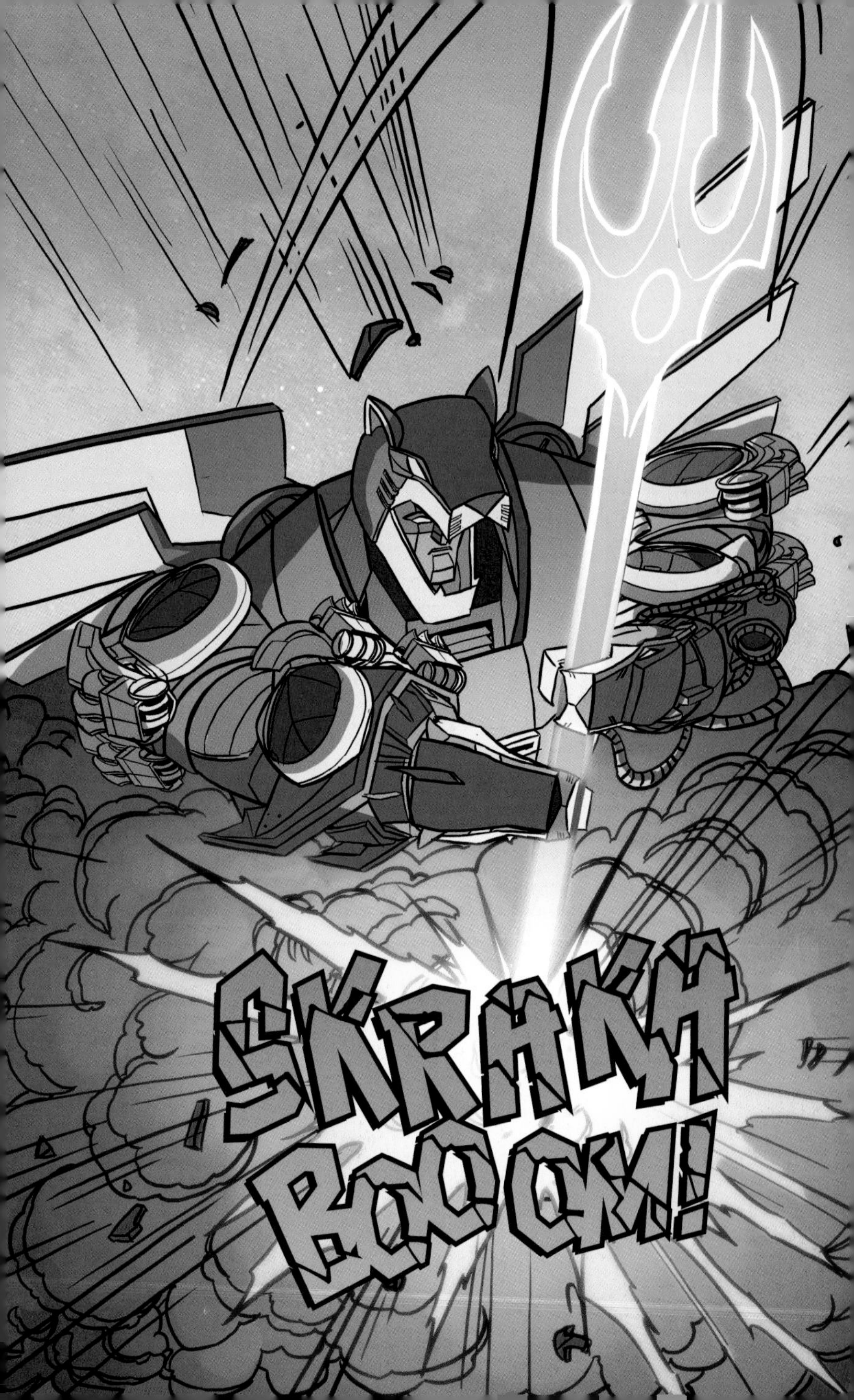
SKRAKH
BOOOM!

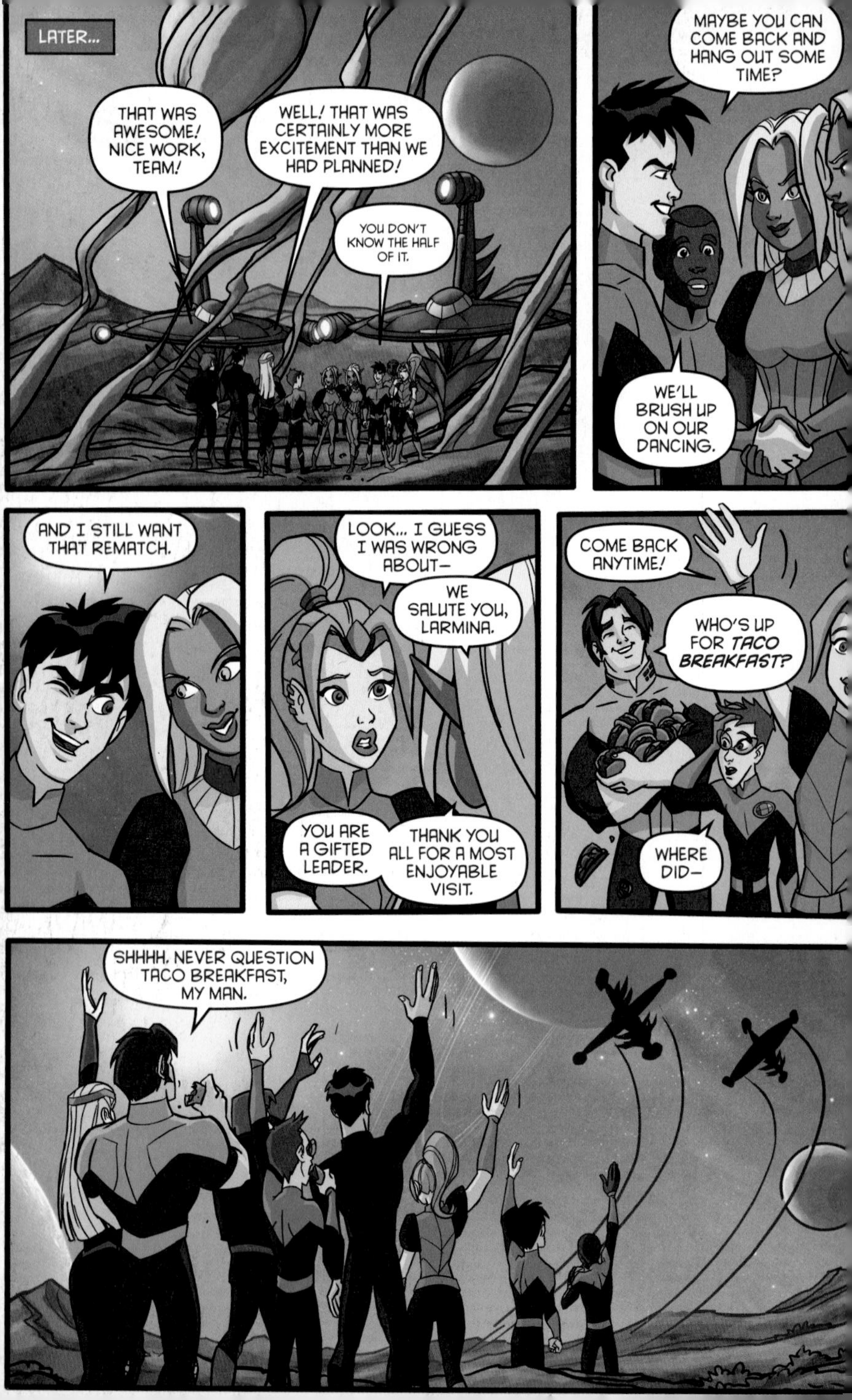
LATER...
THAT WAS AWESOME! NICE WORK, TEAM!
WELL! THAT WAS CERTAINLY MORE EXCITEMENT THAN WE HAD PLANNED!
YOU DON'T KNOW THE HALF OF IT.
MAYBE YOU CAN COME BACK AND HANG OUT SOME TIME?
WE'LL BRUSH UP ON OUR DANCING.
AND I STILL WANT THAT REMATCH.
LOOK... I GUESS I WAS WRONG ABOUT—
WE SALUTE YOU, LARMINA.
YOU ARE A GIFTED LEADER.
THANK YOU ALL FOR A MOST ENJOYABLE VISIT.
COME BACK ANYTIME!
WHO'S UP FOR *TACO BREAKFAST?*
WHERE DID—
SHHHH. NEVER QUESTION TACO BREAKFAST, MY MAN.

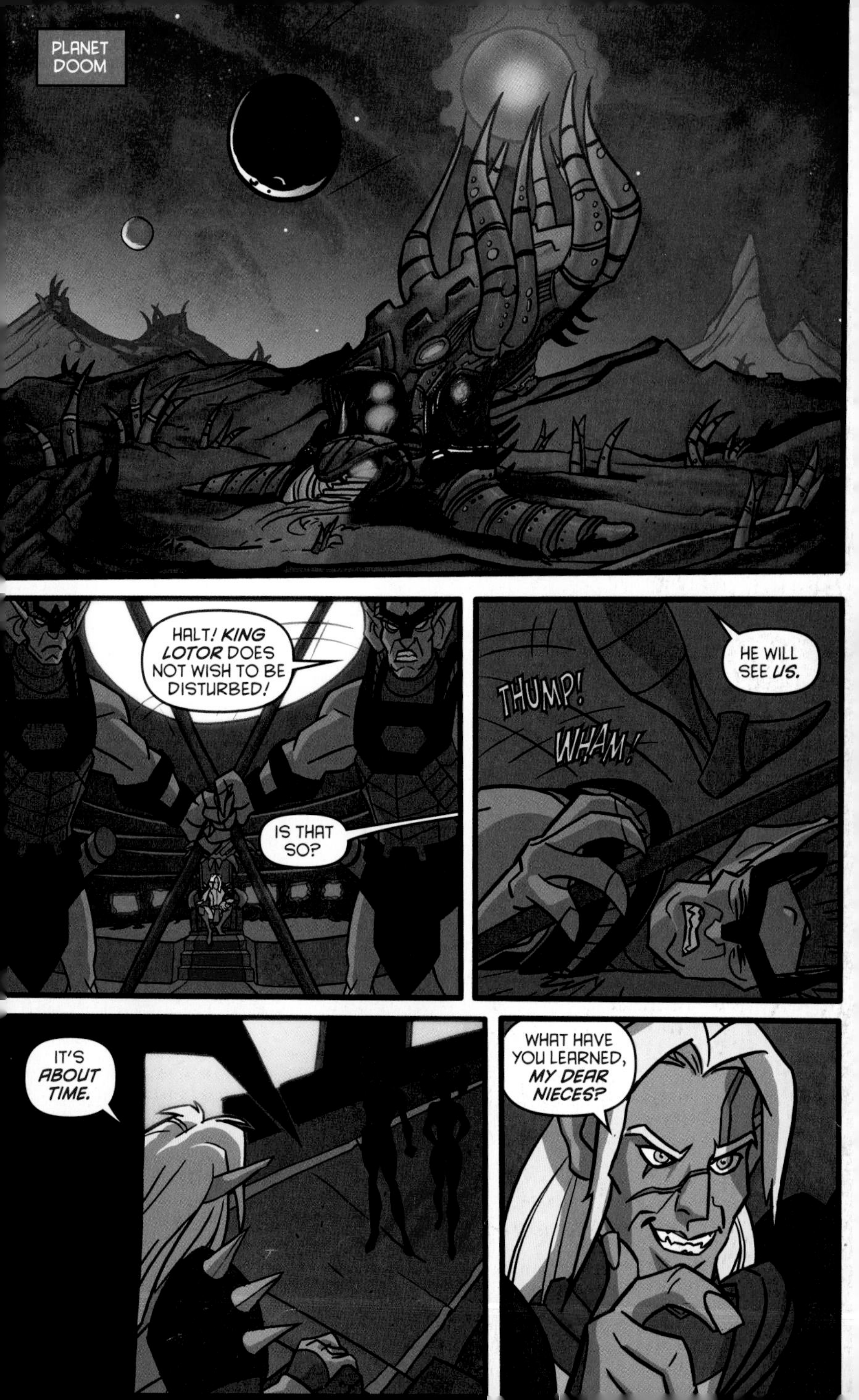

PLANET DOOM
HALT! KING LOTOR DOES NOT WISH TO BE DISTURBED!
IS THAT SO?
THUMP!
WHAM!
HE WILL SEE US.
IT'S ABOUT TIME.
WHAT HAVE YOU LEARNED, MY DEAR NIECES?

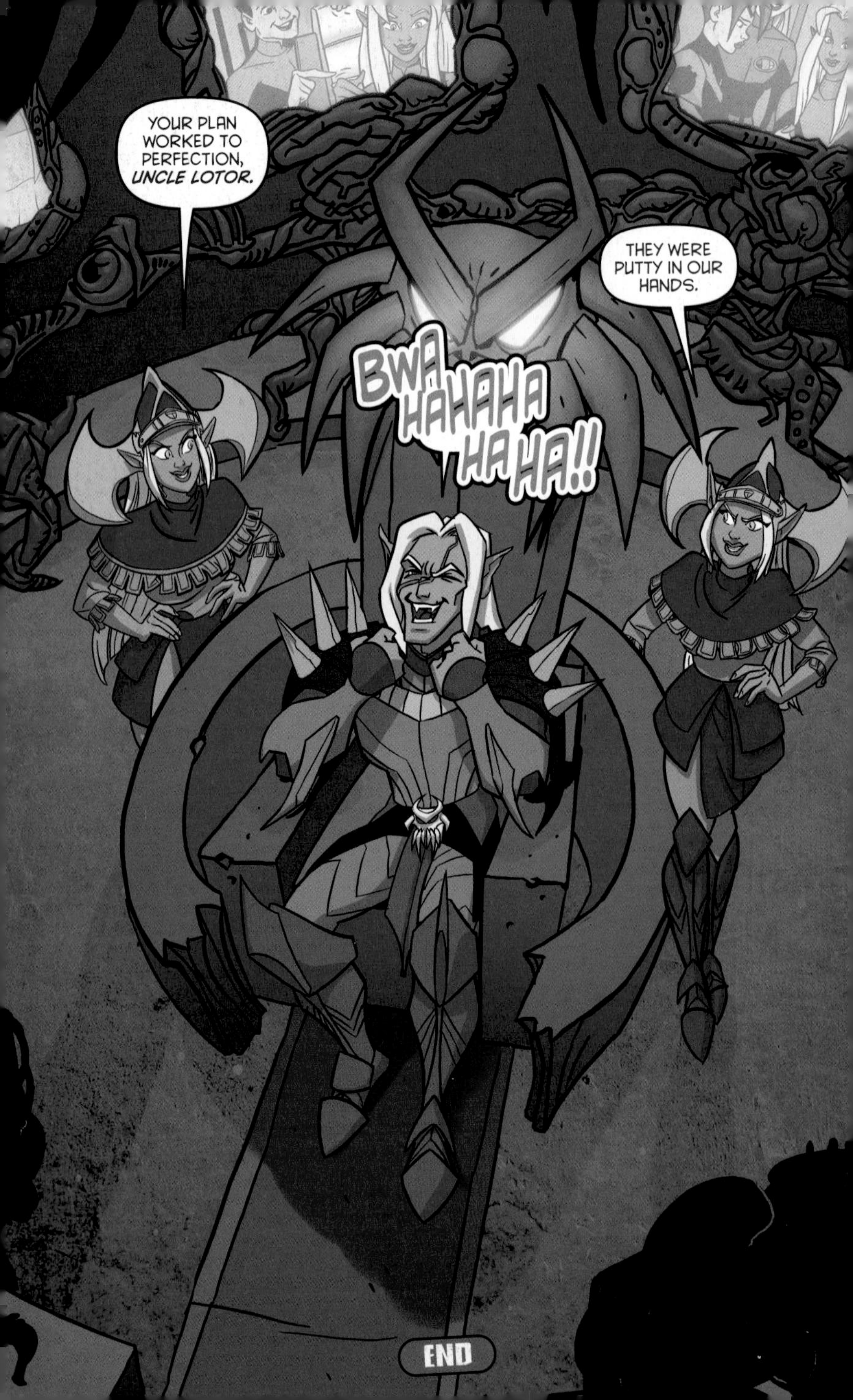
YOUR PLAN WORKED TO PERFECTION, *UNCLE LOTOR.*
THEY WERE PUTTY IN OUR HANDS.
BWA HAHAHA HA HA!!
END

BRIAN SMITH

Brian Smith is a former Marvel Comics editor. His credits include The *Ultimates*, *Ultimate Spider-Man*, *Iron Man*, *Captain America*, *The Incredible Hulk*, and dozens of other comics. Smith is the co-creator/writer behind the *New York Times* best-selling graphic novel *The Stuff of Legend*, and the writer/artist of the all-ages comic *The Intrepid EscapeGoat*. His writing credits include *Finding Nemo: Losing Dory* from BOOM! Studios and *SpongeBob Comics* from Bongo.

Smith is also the illustrator of *The Adventures of Daniel Boom AKA LOUDBOY!*, named one of The Top 10 Graphic Novels for Youths 2009 by Booklist Online. His illustration clients include *Time Out New York Magazine*, Nickelodeon, *MAD Kids Magazine*, Harper Collins, Bongo Comics, Grosset & Dunlap, and American Greetings.

HORACIO DOMINGUES

Horacio Domingues is a cartoonist and illustrator born in Argentina. He has worked as a cartoonist and children's book illustrator both at home and abroad for such publishers as Albin Michel and Glenat in France and Eura in Italy. In the United States he has worked for Dark Horse, D.C. Comics, Marvel, Boom Studios and IDW.

PEDRO PABLO PEREZ VALIENTE

Born in Madrid, Spain, Pedro Pablo Perez Valiente has devoted his life to drawing and animation. He created the storyboards for the animated film *Planet 51* and has contributed to Coca-Cola and Disney Channel advertising campaigns. His first comic book, *L'Amour Com* was published in 2010. *Los Tiburones de Rangiroa* is the first of Pedro's comic books to be released in Spain.

GUILLERMO PEREZ

Guillermo Perez has worked with many publishers including IDW, Lerner and VIZ Media. He currently lives near Madrid and works in his own studio, which is full of comics and arcade machines.

ALEJANDRO SANCHEZ

Alejandro Sanchez has worked for many publishers including Dynamite, IDW and DC Comics on such titles as *Zorro*, *Robocop*, *G.I. Joe: Cobra* and *Batman: Arkham Unhinged*.

COMING SOON!

4 STORY BY **BRIAN SMITH** | ART BY **ALFA ROBBI**

No one knows for certain where Voltron came from, but one ancient legend says the mighty robot had a sixth part: a terrible warrior called the Beast King. Asleep for many years, the Beast King has awakened and is determined to rejoin his destructive spirit with the Voltron Lions!